HOW TO SAVE AN UNDEAD LIFE

HAILEY EDWARDS

How to Save an Undead Life
Copyright © 2017 by Hailey Edwards

Edited by Sasha Knight
Proofread by Lillie's Literary Services
Cover by Gene Mollica
Tree of Life medallion drawn by Leah Farrow

ONE

I jolted awake sitting on the hardwood floor in my bedroom with my back wedged into a corner. Sheets tangled around my hips. Bruises purpled my shins. Blood crusted my fingertips under broken nails. Shallow pants fed my lungs and fueled my racing heart. I tasted copper in the back of my throat, and it hurt when I swallowed.

Starting my nights with a crick in my neck and a numb tailbone was getting old fast. I might live in a haunted house, but the only screams echoing through the halls belonged to me.

The bathroom door swung open under an invisible hand, and the light switched on.

"That bad?" While I plucked at the damp tank top plastered to my chest by fear-sweat, the faucets squeaked in protest. Water thundered into the shower basin, drowning out my grumbles. "Okay, I can take a hint."

Bracing one hand on the wall for support, I propped my feet under me and staggered to the bathroom, leaning a hip against the pedestal sink while I stripped. The clawfoot tub beckoned, and I climbed under the scalding water, let it pound the kinks from my aching muscles. All too soon the stream turned cold, and I hopped out with a squeak that made the hinges squeal in mocking laughter.

Curls of steam gamboled around my ankles, chasing me back into the bedroom, where I dried off and got dressed in jeans and a faded tee. I stomped on sneakers before combing the damp ropes of dark brown hair slicking my shirt against my spine.

A wobbly question mark cut through the condensation fogging the window above my desk.

"I'm fine," I assured the old house. "Just a bad dream."

The same one, night after night after night, since my release from the black stone prison called Atramentous.

Each dusk I expected to wake to iron bars, a grate in the concrete floor, the constant *drip-drip-drip* of water and other fluids as they fell from the ceiling into the drain. Enough to keep you alive if you worked at catching droplets on your tongue, but never enough to quench your thirst.

The glass turned opaque, as if someone had breathed warmth onto the chill pane, and the next drawing tugged on my heartstrings.

A frowny face.

"You've been working on your finger painting while I was away, I see." And her psychoanalyzing. "Okay, you win. I'm not fine." I rocked back on my heels. "I know you worry but..." I bit the inside of my cheek until I tasted iron. "I can't talk about it yet."

I might never be ready to discuss the events leading up to my incarceration.

The window cleared, the slate wiped clean.

Until tomorrow.

A blinking red light caught my eye in the window's reflection, and I skimmed my cluttered desk. "*Woolly.*" I pointed at the cheap digital clock with zeroes flashing on its face. "What time is it?" I lunged for the nightstand and woke my phone. "You let me oversleep."

The house let her unrepentant silence speak for itself.

Loudly.

"I have to work." I tromped down the stairs. "Otherwise the power goes off, and my belly goes empty. You don't want us to both starve, do you?"

One step creaked louder than the others in counterargument. She could go on like this for days...

I hit the foyer, slung my purse across my body, and palmed the last Honeycrisp apple from its porcelain cradle. Hand-painted blue roses climbed over the exterior of the elegant fruit bowl, the piece still one of my favorites despite the nocked rim on its everted lip. Or perhaps because of it. Each chip represented a memory, a good one, and I had few enough of those not to care if the reminders carried jagged edges.

The slight pressure of my fingertips against the basin sent the heavy antique console table beneath the bowl seesawing. The old house groaned around me, embarrassed about the uneven floorboards, and the hard point of my anger softened.

"I got this." I opened the table's single drawer, plucked the most recent bill off the top of a precarious stack, and wedged it under the short leg before hiding my unmet obligations from sight again with a satisfying bump from my hip. "There." I winked up at the chandelier that hung central in the foyer. "Good as new."

A gust of heated air swirled up my leg from a nearby floor register.

"You're welcome."

Thanks to my late start, my usual bowl of strawberry oatmeal was off the table. That left me with the apple to tide me over until the lunch break I took around midnight. Stomach tight with hunger, I brought the fruit to my lips. That moment when my teeth pierced the thin outer skin, the flesh firm beneath and juices flowing over my tongue, was perfection. Licking the sticky sweetness from my lips, I chased an errant trickle down my wrist with my tongue. I couldn't afford to waste even one drop. Not at these prices.

"See you later." I reached for the doorknob and found it locked. I jiggled it once more then sighed. "Woolly." The chandelier dimmed at the reprimand. "I promise I'll be home in a few hours."

A petulant *snick* announced I was free to go, not that the old house expected me to ever return.

What can I say? Woolworth House, Woolly to her friends, was a tad bit clingy. Though, if you asked me, she was entitled to her near-obsessive fear of abandonment after witnessing the brutal murder of her previous owner and the subsequent arrest of the Woolworth heir.

That would be me.

The door clicked shut on my heels as I stepped out onto the wraparound porch, and the locks engaged.

Click. Click. Click.

Can a haunted house pitch a hissy fit? Yes. Yes, it can. And, in my limited experience, the scope and duration of the tantrum was directly proportional to its square footage. Each time I left, no matter how valid my reason, she acted like I'd driven a rusty nail into her wooden heart. Or hearth. Whichever.

Woolly was all the family I had left. I wouldn't abandon her. Unless they dragged me away like last time.

Checking the wards protecting Woolworth House came second nature to me, and I spared half a thought for activating the complex spells. Or I did until the magic rebounded, delivering a slap to my skull that left my ears ringing and startled me into shifting a mental eye toward checking the perimeter. But whatever had left the wards singing near the garden hadn't breached them.

I was savoring my second bite of apple, pondering what the disturbance meant and why Woolly hadn't given me a heads up, when the hand cradling the half-eaten fruit ignited, and a whiff of charred skin stung my nostrils.

Swearing a blue streak, I flung my hand to soothe the burn and sent my snack rolling down the steps.

Dang it.

Uncurling my fingers, I spotted the blackened sigil I dreaded branding my palm.

Double dang it.

Bad enough I had wonky wards to contend with, but this? Keet really ought to stop dying on me. His timing couldn't be worse.

I was scheduled to lead a Boos and Brews tour through historic downtown Savannah, Georgia in two hours. I hadn't had my hair or makeup done yet, and Cricket Meacham, the owner of Haint Misbehavin' Ghost Tours—that's haint as in ghost and not hain't as in ain't—expected her crew in full Southern belle regalia prior to clock-in.

"Call Amelie," I ordered my phone in a loud, clear tone.

Hands-free voice commands were as close to practicing craft in public as it got.

"Why, I do declare," Amelie drawled in her thickest Southern accent, "if it's not my *Grierest* friend."

A snort escaped me at the play on words. "Your *dearest* friend Grier needs a favor."

"What? I can't hear you." A sigh blasted over the line. "Tell me I'm not in your back pocket."

"You're not in my back pocket." My phone was, though. "Hold on." I pinched it between my thumb and finger, tugging until my skinny jeans cried uncle, then pinned the cell between my cheek and shoulder like they did in ancient times. "There. Happy?"

"Yes, actually. You don't sound like you're talking through cotton gauze left over from a dental procedure."

Some people just don't appreciate the hands-free experience. "Can you cover my first tour?"

"*Woof. Woof.*" She paused for dramatic effect. "Hear that? That's the sound of my dogs barking."

Walking an average of ten miles on a good night was enough to make anyone's feet howl.

"How about this? Swing the tour by the house." I studied the sigil burnt into my skin, twitchy to get moving. "Do that, and I'll guarantee you get tipped like a cow tonight."

"Not sure what that means, but okay." Glee rang through the line. "I'm in."

Woolworth House wasn't part of any regular tour by design. Exclusivity increased the old house's cachet. Once or twice, when money got tighter than my loaner corset, I allowed the supernaturally devout to pay me obscene amounts of cash to sleep in one of my spare bedrooms. I did nothing to enhance the experience, but a lucky few had encountered Woolly's sense of humor, and that was enough to ignite fervor among the masses.

And more than enough to label me as a pariah among my own kind. Not that I hadn't already been branded.

Liar. Thief. Murderer.

"Grier?"

Closing my eyes, I sucked in a long breath that whistled past my front teeth, then I let it out slowly.

"Still here." I padded across the front yard barefoot, the plush lawn tickling the soles of my feet. The low wrought iron gate leading into the backyard opened under my hand, and I followed the flag-stone path under four connected archways dripping with fragrant jasmine blossoms and lush purple wisteria clusters. On the other end sat the carriage house, a scaled-down replica of the main house. "Buy me three hours, and I'll take your last tour."

"Done deal." A rowdy cheer rose in the background. "Oh. Gotta run. My victims have arrived."

Unlike the personable main house, the carriage house was simply an outbuilding that had once been responsible for storing horse-drawn carriages and tack. Maud had converted the wide-open space into a two-bedroom, two-bath guesthouse, but that had been a life-time ago.

Not once during the three weeks since my return had I stepped foot out there. Truth be told, I didn't want to be standing here right now. But I didn't have a choice. Not while my palm throbbed with the reminder of an old promise.

All the what-might-have-beens gathered on the fringes of my memory, tightening my throat until a ragged cough sounding too close to a sob broke free. I blamed the dust and choked down the burning ache before it consumed me, fisted my hand and let the burnt flesh sharpen my focus.

The overstuffed couches and reclaimed wood tables had been pushed against the walls to make room for thirteen oak and iron steamer trunks teeming with necromantic paraphernalia. Stacked in rows three high and four wide, they dominated the hand-braided rag rug in the center of the room. Each must have weighed a hundred pounds or more. Only lucky thirteen, the runt of the litter, sat all alone.

Boaz had done this for me, packed up all Maud's things and stashed them out here after...

After it all went so very wrong.

Once I could breathe again, I extended my burnt palm toward the stacks, and, like a dowser in search of precious water, followed the persistent tug of magic to its source, tensing when the faint energy ebbing above that final trunk nipped at my fingertips.

"Here goes nothing."

After crossing to the nearest window, I rose on my tiptoes and smoothed my fingers along the top of the frame until they brushed against lukewarm metal. I palmed the magicked skeleton key, right where Amelie had promised it would be, fit its teeth into the mouth of the lock, and twisted until the latch sprang free. I had to throw my shoulder into forcing up the cumbersome lid, and it yawned open on a breath perfumed with rosewater and thyme. Scents that still haunted Woolworth House.

Maud.

The trunk held one item that could be seen with the naked eye, an old-fashioned doctor's bag the color of midnight and filled with things even darker. Vials clinked within when I hauled it out onto the rug. That was the easy part. The trunk's lid refused to shut until I sat on it, and the lock fought me for possession of the key until I pricked my fingertip and let it taste me. Satisfied with a few drops, it twisted itself then fell out onto my palm. The bloodthirsty scrap of brass had been forged to obey Maud, but it tolerated me, so there was no point in hiding what no one else could use. But I did anyway. This time in a better place than above the window.

I doubted anyone could breach the wards surrounding Woolworth House, but the carriage house and the garage weren't as well fortified. Since I lacked the power for composing new sigils, the best I could do was direct the existing ones into a quicker tempo, more allegro than adagio.

The leather bag creaked when I gripped its carved-bone handle with bloodless fingers, its weight both a comfort and a painful reminder that Maud would never restock the depleted supplies within again. I exited the carriage house and gardens before the tears blurring my vision spilled over my cheeks. I hadn't cried since the night the door clanged shut on my cell, and I wasn't going to start now.

Retracing my steps up the stone path, I cut across the wide lawn in the opposite direction, powering down my phone so Amelie couldn't have second thoughts. I also didn't want the neighbors, her parents, to hear my ringtone and come investigate. The last thing I needed was to add more charges to an already robust arrest record.

Palm extended like a compass needle pointing true north, a pulse of magic guided me across the property line I shared with the Pritchard family. Elaborate flowerbeds created a maze behind their modest house, and I lost myself in its twists until my feet planted themselves at the edge of a bed teeming with drowsy-headed begonias. I knelt on the soft mulch, and dewdrops burst under my weight, soaking my jeans.

Spring had arrived a week ago, tossing clouds of yellow pollen like confetti at its own *welcome back* party, but the night air still held a bite even if the daytime temps caused me to break a sweat.

"I can do this," I murmured, placing the bag next to me. "Just like riding a bike."

Chunks of white gravel borrowed from the driveway formed a rectangular border the size of a shoebox on the mulch. I gathered each one and mounded them near my ankle. A fist-sized, black river rock crowned the design. Written in blue sidewalk chalk on the makeshift tombstone was the word *Twitter*. Cute name for a parakeet. Not terribly original, but not bad for the social-media-aware seven-year-old who had adopted Keet after my incarceration.

Back when the deceased had been mine, Maud had named him Keet Richards. I was five when she became my legal guardian, and I'm embarrassed to admit how long it took me to unravel the pun. I might still be clueless about Keith Richards of The Rolling Stones fame had I not stumbled across her vinyl collection while searching for monkey bones in the attic one summer.

Holding my breath, I plunged my hands into the rich soil. The soggy edges of a buried shoebox stood up to my fondling despite the dampness from this evening's thunderstorms. It helped that the deceased hadn't been buried long. A half hour at most. Longer than that and Mrs. Pritchard would have had a coronary by now considering how her youngest son had rezoned her bed full of prize-winning perennials as a pet cemetery.

I dug my toes into the lush grass and shivered as a garden spider bustled across my heel. I gave three good tugs, and the cardboard coffin pulled free. After dusting off the top, I traced the decorations scribbled in crayon down the sides then lifted the lid. Paper towels folded to resemble sheets on a bed rested high on the dead bird's chest where he had been tucked between them for one final snooze.

Keet's silver-white cheeks looked as plump and adorable as I remembered. His feathers as bright yellow as a fresh banana peel. His bill and legs held a reddish tint, and his eyes, when they opened again, would be deep crimson.

That was thanks to his Lutino coloring, not magic, but the effect was eerie all the same.

"Hey, little guy." I lifted him with care and set about tidying the area so no one would suspect precocious little Macon of playing mortician. "Long time, no see, huh?"

Having been dead for some time, the parakeet didn't answer.

That would have been creepy.

Fisting the bone handle on Maud's bag, I hauled it closer. The latches flipped with ease, and I cracked the top halves open, rooting around in the bag's cavernous belly until my fingers located my favorite round paintbrush in its case. I removed the brush and a jar of crimson ink that smelled of spiced pennies then set them at my knee.

Other necromancers-in-training in my age group had been raised with their familiars, but I had never stayed in one place long enough for a pet until I went to live with Maud. Things might have gone differently had she not sent a softhearted kid to pick up her order of feeder mice. After learning the writhing pinkies were snake chow, I bawled until the store owner, terrified of losing a lucrative contract, shoved a parakeet into my hands to shut me up as he nudged me out the door.

Keet was not the familiar Maud had in mind for her pupil, but she allowed the match to placate me. Sadly, the store owner had a reason for selecting that particular bird, and Keet kicked the bucket two days later. Cheered by the opportunity to use him as a teaching exercise, Maud coached me through inking my first sigils. But I must have smudged one, because bada-bing, bada-boom, I found myself the proud owner of a psychopomp.

I'll never forget how the blood drained from her face as his wisp of a soul reentered his rigid body, or how she made the goddess sign across her heart thrice with trembling fingers when his tiny lungs caught a second wind.

She enrolled me in public school the next day, where my peers consisted of plain-vanilla humans and the children of Low Society members. She claimed that in order to survive in our world, one had to understand theirs. But how I was meant to grasp the workings of the High Society while masquerading as a mortal, I had no idea. And after I met Amelie and her older brother, Boaz, I stopped caring how I was ever meant to fit into that world of castes, rules and blood magic.

Maud continued teaching me rudimentary herblore and basic warding magic on the weekends, always behind locked doors, and I excelled at both. But that one failure with Keet, who she refused to share air with, had cemented my fate.

Assistant.

The designation still smarted.

A quick dip of my brush, and I painted a modified sigil on my forehead that gave me the ability to perceive souls. Yep. Just as expected, the shimmery whorl of Keet's spirit drifted in a glittery cloud around him, bound to his corpse and the sigil burnt into my skin by a fine thread so that each of his deaths, and there had been many, summoned me. Using the end of my brush, I disturbed the halo of motes, scattering them into the night. Slowly, oh so slowly, they gravitated back to Keet and reformed as if I had never agitated them.

Here was proof positive that my magic had been wonky from the get-go.

Assistant indeed.

Sitting back on my heels, I rotated his small body in my palm until his belly faced the stars. I dipped my brush and swiped a few symbols on the smooth feathers covering his abdomen. The effect left him slashed with red, as gruesome as a disemboweled murder victim, but the sigils would wash off with soap and water later.

"What the hell do you think you're doing?"

"Boaz." The brush rolled from my fingers, and my heart clanged against my ribs. The urge to glance back at him twitched in my neck, but fear he might vanish like mist if I looked at him head-on kept me staring straight ahead. "Amelie said you got deployed."

"Yeah, well, I got undeployed." He nudged the tips of my toes with the blunt edge of his massive boot. "You'd know that if you hadn't been hiding from me."

"I haven't been hiding," I lied on reflex, shielding my own wounded pride.

"You don't call. You don't email. You don't snail mail." A growl laced his voice. "Sounds like hiding to me."

"At least I didn't run." I balled my empty fist in my lap. "How is what you did any better?"

"I *enlisted*."

"Maud was barely in the ground when you shipped out."

"You were already gone," he seethed. "What did you expect me to do? Stay in Savannah? Wake up every morning and see your house sitting empty? Torment myself with the knowledge you weren't there? That I would never see you again?"

"Stop," I whispered.

"They sentenced you to Atramentous without a fucking trial—"

"*Stop*."

Boaz was past listening. How his parents didn't hear us shouting, I had no idea. Then again, they ought to be used to yelling where he and I were concerned. After all, he was a firm believer that volume increased understanding.

"You kept in touch with Amelie." His hurt pulsed like a sore tooth he couldn't stop poking with his tongue. "Why not me?"

Telling him that facing his sister was easier wouldn't make the truth hurt any less.

"I'm standing right here, and you can't even look at me." He made a disgusted sound in the back of his throat, the kind the sentinels used to make before hocking a loogie in my face. "I might have lost a leg, but I can still kick your ass."

The world ground to a halt on its axis as his threat permeated my skull.

I whipped my head toward him, and my vision ran crimson with fury. "You *what*?"

"Landmine in Afghanistan." He bent over and knocked where his left femur should have been. It made a hollow sound that echoed in my chest. "Turns out they explode if you step on them. Who knew?"

One minute I was kneeling in the grass, the next I was climbing him like a tree.

Turned out I made for one pissed-off monkey.

"*Oof.*"

Impact knocked him to the grass, and I ended up straddling his hips with my right foot hooked over his shin, metallic and cold where he should be muscle and heat.

"When?" I fisted the front of his olive drab tee and thumped his head on the ground. "When did this happen? Why didn't anyone tell me? Amelie—"

"I told her to keep her yap shut." He glared up at me. "I told her if you wanted news about me, then you damn well came to the source or you'd go thirsty." He fit his hand around the base of my throat, stroking over my carotid with a calloused thumb. "You want to get a drink with me?"

"What? You're asking me out? Now?" I wriggled lower on his hips, trying to get off this crazy ride. His lips twisted in a grimace of pain. I scrambled off him so fast I fell on my butt in the cold grass. "I didn't hurt you, did I?"

"Naw, Grier. It feels good having my head bashed into the dirt. I worried I didn't have enough rocks rattling around in there already." He lifted his head and rubbed the base of his skull. "It happened two years ago. You're not going to hurt me. The new leg is titanium. It's tough, but don't tear it off and start whacking me with it, okay? TRICARE only covers so much."

Ducking my head, shame burning my cheeks, I murmured, "Can we start over?"

"Sure. Give me a second." Linking his hands behind his head, he crossed his legs at the ankles and wiggled his hips. "All right. You can straddle me again. I'm ready this time. I'll even keep my hands to myself." His mischievous wink made heat gather low in my stomach. "I like giving orders better anyway. I've learned I'm good at it."

"Pervert."

He rolled a shoulder, not disagreeing with me. "The offer stands."

I bet it did. "Nice try. I'm not checking out your crotch."

His husky chuckle was pure sin. "You never did say why you were skulking around in Mom's garden."

Glad for the safer conversational ground, I extended my hand so he could see. "I came to retrieve Keet."

His lip curled as he processed what I was holding. "Your zombie parakeet?"

A bird pecks at one brain and people start throwing around derogatory terms.

"He's not a zombie." Sure, his flight patterns were off, but he didn't shamble through the air or anything.

He nodded his chin to indicate the corpse. "Is resuscitating him kosher?"

"It's not a resuscitation. He was already dead, or undead. Whatever. All I did was bring him back from limbo and anchor him in his body." I showed him the blackened symbol charring my palm. "I was on my way to work when the locator sigil activated. I found him out here. Guess your little brother buried him rather than face the music with your parents."

"He was on restriction for not cleaning the water bowl before refilling it last time we talked." Boaz scratched his side, a grin tugging on his lips. "He must have figured hiding the body was better than another week of laundry detail."

"Poor kid." I combed through the blades of grass with my fingers until I found the discarded brush, its ends clotted with ink. "I'm guessing no one told him Keet can't starve to death?"

"Nope."

No doubt that was all his idea.

"Come on, Squirt." He leveraged into a seated position, his abs flexing beneath the thin fabric of his shirt—not that I noticed—then rolled to his feet in a motion so smooth he must have practiced it. "I'll walk you home so you don't get into more trouble."

At barely eight o'clock on a Friday night, with a full moon to boot, Boaz seriously underestimated my skills.

TWO

My feeble attempts at ignoring Boaz were about as successful as the time I tried resuscitating a T-rex skeleton at a natural history museum when I was eight. A security guard hauled me in front of Maud and explained how I had been caught painting the dinosaur bones red. She had laughed, brayed really, until tears streamed down her face and streaked her mascara. To prevent gums from bumping about the incident, she made a sizable donation to ensure the local media outlets wouldn't come sniffing around for coverage of the chubby-faced vandal with artistic aspirations.

The Society for Post-Life Management was about as forgiving of such indiscretions as an old-money wife spotting a nouveau-riche neighbor wearing white after Labor Day.

The third member of our trio that day had been Linus, Maud's nephew. He was five years older than me, so thirteen at the time, and he had spent that weekend with us. Call it a hunch, but I always suspected he was the one who'd tattled to the mortal authorities.

Even as a kid, he had been as stuffy as a taxidermied moose.

The short walk home thawed my limbs, and my unexpected

arrival so soon after departing meant Woolly didn't have time to mount an offensive. I strolled right in, Boaz on my heels, and headed straight for the kitchen. I set Maud's bag on the table in plain sight to remind me to wash out the brush before returning her supplies to storage then patted the squirmy lump nestled in the front pocket of my T-shirt.

"Look who's back," I called out to Woolly. "Our old pal Keet." I jerked my chin in Boaz's direction. "Oh yeah. This weirdo followed me home too."

The light cast from the overhead fixtures swelled with such bright joy I had to squint to bear the glare. Cupboard doors flapped open on their hinges, sounding like a round of applause as they bumped off the base cabinets, and he took a sweeping bow.

"Up high." His palm smacked an upper cabinet door that swung out to meet him. "Down low." He switched hands, and the lower cabinet bounced off his palm. Darting past me, he leapt up and tagged one of the smaller cabinets above the fridge before she guessed his next move. "Too slow."

"Okay, kids." I shoved him onto a barstool at the counter. "No running or jumping in the house."

The lights overhead dimmed to normal levels, minus the occasional surge as happiness shot through her wiring.

"You hungry, boy?" I gathered a wriggling Keet in my hand. "You're always peckish after rising."

A weak chirp melted me into a puddle of goo. I really had missed the little guy. My tiny family, such as we were, was now complete. Woolly, Keet, Amelie, Boaz and me. The gang was back together again.

"What are your plans for the night?" I wedged a stopper in the deep farmhouse sink then shredded a few paper towels to make a comfortable nest. Keet's poor little stick legs proved too wobbly to support him just yet, so I placed him on his side and went to make good on my offer. "Anything interesting?"

"My next stop is home. I've had all the interesting I can handle for one night."

"Home?" I glanced up at him. "Your parents don't know you're back yet?"

"Figured I'd surprise them." He shrugged. "I wasn't sure the commander would let me go." His gaze flicked up to mine. "This wasn't my first attempt. More like my third." He rubbed the base of his neck. "I was pissed at you, yeah, but I filed paperwork the day Amelie told me you got out. I wasn't staying away to punish you. Or me. Or hell, both of us. I came as soon as I could without having desertion charges brought up against me."

"You're here now." In my house. In my kitchen. In my life. "That's all that matters."

"It's really not, Squirt." His arms fell to his side. "How are you here? Why did they let you go?"

"I don't know." I shook my head. "No one told me. Even if they did..."

A sentinel had written my home address on a sticky note and pinned the yellow square to my shirt like I was a kid about to ride a school bus for the first time instead of an inmate with the mental capacity of a kindergartener. He escorted me onto the plane, and I flashed the note at the first taxi driver to approach me after I landed, just as I had been instructed. The nice old man with his crooked smile had taken me to Woolly, hooked his arm in mine, walked me up to the door, and said in a crackling voice, "You're home."

That girl? The one who stumbled reading that sequence of numbers and letters, who wondered why the combination sounded so familiar? She had asked no questions. Not a single one. And I didn't blame her.

"Grier..." The way he rumbled my name was better than being wrapped in a warm blanket. "If you ever need to talk about what happened..."

"Thanks." My throat worked over a hard lump. "But I can't."

"I get that." He kicked out his amputated leg. "I understand witnessing horrors you can't put into words. I'm just saying I'm here. You need to talk, you come to me. Understand?"

I cocked an eyebrow at him. "What about Amelie?"

"I don't care who you talk to as long as you open up to someone when the time comes." He flashed me a crooked grin. "But I'm willing to make out with you to help take your mind off things after. Amelie won't go the distance like I will."

I almost swallowed my tongue.

To give my cheeks time to cool, I turned my back on him. I kept a basket of fresh veggies from the greenhouse on the counter near the fridge. I grabbed a box grater from a drawer then selected a carrot and started shredding Keet a snack. I would have to buy him fresh seed and a cuttlebone tomorrow. I could afford those if I skimped on dinner this week. I'd also have to hike the stairs leading up into the attic and find his old cage and floor stand. Unless I could con Boaz into doing the work for me.

The blare of Boaz's cellphone ringing made me jump on my way back to the sink, and a few veggie shreds spilled from my fingers before I could catch them and mound them with the rest in Keet's temporary nest.

"Hey, sis," Boaz answered, still laughing. "How did you know—?" His gaze bored a hole through my spine. "Figures." He grunted. "I'm still not convinced Mom didn't have us microchipped." A pause. "Yeah, I'll remind her."

"Well?" I prompted, joining him at the bar after he ended the call.

"Mom overheard our *conversation*. She called Amelie to scream at her for not telling her I was home, so she called to yell at me for not telling anyone I was home, and then she put two and two together and got five."

"I asked her to cover my first tour so I could recover Keet while he was still fresh." A groan left me slumped over the counter. "She must think that I... That we..."

"There's still time." His eyes twinkled. "She said you've got forty-five minutes left. I can get you there in ten."

Crossing my arms over my chest, I tapped my fingertips on my elbows. "Are you offering me a ride to work or an orgasm?"

"Both? Either?"

"You should go." I planted my palm in the center of his rock-hard chest and shoved. He swayed a centimeter. Maybe. "Your mommy is waiting to smother you with kisses."

If he heard the faint undercurrent of jealousy, that he still had someone to fret over his boo-boos, real and imagined, he ignored it. "I'd rather *you* smother me with kisses."

I flashed him a saccharine smile. "I'd rather just smother you."

"Kinky."

"I have to run." I ushered him toward the door. "That means you have to go too."

Boaz shuffled along until we reached the foyer, but when I tried opening the door, Woolly fought me. Big surprise. While I was busy jiggling the knob, Boaz slipped behind me. He wrapped his thick arms around my middle, twisting me until my head spun, and I found myself sandwiched between a hardwood door and an even harder man.

I hadn't let myself look at him, not really, but I had no choice now.

Boaz was taller than me by a few inches, so I had to tip my head back to hold his gaze. Milk-chocolate irises striated with lighter bands, like swirled caramel, stared back at me. White scars stood in stark contrast against his tanned skin. His platinum hair, baby fine and impossible to style, was shaved on the sides and longer on the top. Grudgingly, I admitted the blunt cut suited his square jaw and harsh features. Boaz was not a handsome man, but his charm made him irresistible. Sometimes I had trouble seeing past his personality to all the rest. At least when all the rest wasn't pressed hip to hip with me.

"I missed you," he rasped softly. "So damn much it hurt to breathe."

I melted against him, allowing him to hold me, and rested my forehead on his chest. "Me too."

"I want to kiss you."

Lungs tight, I snapped my head up to find his mouth hovering inches from mine.

"But I'm scared you'll hide from me again if I do."

A thousand denials sprang to my lips, and they each died a thousand deaths.

"Woolly, you mind?" He flicked a glance up at the foyer chandelier. "Don't want to keep Mom waiting."

The door *snicked* open under his hand. The traitor.

I scurried out on his heels before she could slam it shut in my face.

"Night, Grier."

"Night, Boaz."

The boy next door left me standing on my front porch, unkissed and unsure where this left us.

"This has been a night full of surprises," I told the old house, and the porch light hummed agreement.

I left Woolly with the usual instructions on how to behave once Amelie and her guests arrived. A flickering light, a couple of curtains blown by the floor registers, that kind of thing. Simple stuff that wouldn't get me in trouble. The architectural spotlights had to go. Nothing killed ambiance like floodlights. Plus, darkness facilitated better shots. The odds were in the tour's favor of snapping pictures of orb lights or other traceries indicative of a true haunting since Woolworth House was steeped in old magic from the not-so-secret lab in the basement to the junktique paradise under the rafters.

Despite the boost to my morale—and libido—Boaz had gifted me, resorting to whoring Woolly out to human gawkers left me feeling dirty.

"Make no apologies for surviving."

One of Maud's favorite sayings, and my personal talisman against the tough choices I made daily.

The garage door whined in protest when I mashed the button on my fob, and I couldn't suppress an eager grin. Boaz would kill me when he noticed I'd helped myself to Jolene. Not waiting on the mechanism to grind all the way up, I ducked under the door and crossed to the coat rack holding my riding leathers and helmet. Both were from *before* and a smidge tight, but I made them work. Replacing them was light-years outside my budget.

I zipped up the plated jacket, plopped down on an overturned plastic bucket, then pulled on thick socks and boots. Done with that, I wiggled on flexible gloves. I waited until after I'd straddled the motorcycle, a crimson Yamaha V Star 250, to slide on my helmet. Dark, tight places made me nauseous, but I gritted my teeth and rolled us down the driveway. I wanted as little distance between me and the road as possible just in case Mrs. Pritchard wasn't holding on to Boaz when he heard Jolene's familiar growl.

Twist, flip, press. The engine caught, and her rhythmic purr blocked out the garage door closing behind me. The steady rumble vibrated through my body, soothing my frazzled nerves, and I fought a grin imagining his expression when he realized his mistake in storing Jolene in my garage. I blazed a trail into town as though the hounds of hell—or one really pissed-off necromancer—were chasing me.

A large crowd milled in front of the bar where Cricket asked our victims to meet and mingle while waiting for their tours to begin. I pulled into the employee parking lot in back and did my best shadow impersonation before the boss caught me showing up late *and* out of costume.

"Cricket is looking for you." Neely hooked his arm through mine as I walked in the door and whirled me in the opposite direction from the downstairs salon, guiding me up a flight of stairs to the cramped room where the guys changed. "Smoke is pouring out of her ears."

"Family emergency." The reminder that my next of kin was a newly resurrected parakeet put my whole life into perspective. "Amelie is covering my tour, right?"

"Yes." He rolled his eyes. "That doesn't mean Cricket won't chirp at you about responsibility and accountability and all her other favorite *ilities* until either she's blue in the face or you are."

"Ugh." I was not in the mood for a lecture tonight. "Blue is so not my color."

"Tell me something I don't know. Why Cricket assigned you as Blue Belle, I'll never understand," he lamented. "I moved your costume into booth two." He hauled me onto the landing then shoved me toward a curtained-off corner. "Go on. Shoo."

Sidestepping the puff of azure fabric that was my dress, I skimmed over the costume accoutrements, checking that all the thingamajiggers and doohickeys were present. Afraid of being caught with my pants down, I stripped to my bra and panties then fitted the corset in place.

Fiddlesticks.

This next part wasn't happening without divine intervention or a glob of Crisco to lube up my torso. Squishing into the silky torture device left me winded from sucking in my belly to fasten the bottom hooks at my spine. The laces... Yeah. Not happening. Not without the aforementioned shortening so I could twist it to the front, lace it, and then spin it around back.

Usually Amelie and I changed together for this very reason. Except she was at my house right about now. Poor Ame. Being that close to her annoying oaf of a big brother without being able to pop in for a hug must be torture. Much like this corset.

While I wriggled in my best worm-on-a-hook impersonation, the stairs groaned loud enough for me to hear over my frustrated panting. I held my breath, afraid to give myself away. Excuses tripped over my tongue as I armed myself to face the Wrath of Cricket about the time a husky, masculine groan preceded ardent smacking noises.

"Um, Neely?" I called, crossing my arms over my chest to pin the corset in place. "Little help here?"

A handsome man with tanned skin, black hair and dark eyes yanked back the curtain, wearing a stern expression. "Should I be concerned about Neely hiding a half-naked woman in his dressing room?"

"Guess it depends." Blushing under his frank scrutiny, glad I'd worn my good underwear, I curled my toes in my stockings. "How do you feel about half-naked women?"

"They're like avocados. I can appreciate they exist, but I wouldn't want to eat one."

Hooting laughter exploded through the room. "Dang, baby." Neely hooked his arm around Cruz's wide shoulders. "You didn't have to be so mean. We like Grier, remember?"

"We do like Grier," he agreed. "We just prefer she wear more clothes around happily married men in the future."

"You're so cute when you get jealous." Neely planted a loud kiss on Cruz's cheek then shoved him aside. "Now scoot back so I can get her tied up." A wicked grin lit his face. "Behave, and I'll let you tie me up later."

Cruz's molten gaze skimmed the length of Neely's body. "Deal."

"Do you mind if he stays?" Neely waded through a parade of half-naked women in various stages of undress nightly. He was blind to girl bits. Cruz, however, was not. Boobs clearly intimidated him. "I can blindfold him if you'd like." He wet his bottom lip. "I know I would."

"Neely." I snapped my fingers at the end of his nose. "Focus."

"Sorry." He jolted to attention. "It's just he's been working a case in Atlanta all week."

"The quicker you finish with her," Cruz said, retreating to a chair he angled to face the wall, "the faster you can get back to me."

Neely sighed dreamily at his gallant husband then whirled his finger for me. I did as he instructed, planted my palms against the wall, and sucked in my stomach until my navel touched my spine the way Cricket had taught me. He laced me up in record time then helped get the rest of the outfit straight before hauling me into the well-lit bathroom suite and starting to work on my hair and makeup.

"How did you get so good at this?" I gazed at the sagging ceiling while he applied my eyeliner.

Neely was about three years older than me, so I remembered him from high school, but I hadn't gotten to know him until I worked my first summer as a Haint when I was fifteen. Things went south for me soon after, but Neely hadn't changed a bit, and I could almost pretend no time had passed instead of facing the gap that yawned in our friendship.

"Are you asking because he's a guy?" Chair legs scraped in the corner. Cruz twisted his chair and sat down facing my back, all the better to glare at me in the mirror. "Or because he's gay?"

Mostly I was asking out of desperation. That almost-kiss with Boaz was occupying too much of my headspace for comfort.

Tension thrummed in the warm hand Neely rested on my cheek, and the eyeliner pencil wobbled.

I touched his wrist to let him know I was all right. "Are you asking because you're insecure or paranoid?"

Cruz growled low in his throat, but very little scared me these days. When the worst had already happened, there wasn't much left to dread.

"Grier is good people," Neely said softly. "She's not like..." He mashed his lips into a hard line. "Just dial it down, okay?"

A quiet breath hissed from between Cruz's teeth as he stood. He left without saying another word.

Neely swayed toward the empty doorway like the bond between them was tugging him after Cruz.

"Do you need a minute?" I rested my hand on his forearm. "This can keep."

"Cruz runs hot." He shook his head and got back to applying the finishing touches. "Cooling off before we talk about this will help us both."

Sensing Neely craved a distraction as much as I did, I picked up where Cruz had cut us off earlier.

"I don't know the business end of a sponge applicator from one of those eyelash crimpy things." Maud had been a fan of the natural look, but one glance in her bathroom proved how many cosmetics were required to achieve that bare-skin glow. "How did you learn?"

"Trial and error. Mostly error." He clicked his tongue, going to work on braiding my unruly hair into an artful crown that circled my head. "It's a miracle my sisters didn't murder me for stealing their makeup. Erin, the second youngest, was the one who noticed I had a good eye and a steady hand. She started asking me to doll her up before dates. Later, Regan, the eldest, let me do her makeup for graduation."

"How many sisters do you have?"

"Four. Two older and two younger. I'm the middlest."

A twinge drew my chest tight as I imagined his big heart and wide smile multiplied by four. "That must be nice."

"*Nice* is a strong word for growing up in a two-bedroom, one-bathroom house with four siblings." He scooted back, giving me a clear view of my reflection for the first time since Cruz left. "Well, what do you think?"

The bags under my eyes had vanished beneath a layer of concealer, and the ragged skin on my chapped lips was hidden by the careful application of tinted gloss. Rather than appearing washed out from my confinement, he somehow smoothed my flaws into a porcelain glow. Even my frizzy hair behaved itself, sleeked back and coiled into demureness upon my head.

I flicked my gaze up to his. "Explain to me why you don't do this professionally again?"

"There's a reason so many people hang up on their calling. Dreams don't always pay the bills." He tapped the end of my nose with his fingertip. "Mom raised us on her own, and she was always worried about paying the bills. She figured the best way to have money was to work for people who had plenty. That's why she nudged me into corporate accounting."

"And that's how you met Cruz." That much of their story I had heard.

"He gave me the last bear claw during the longest, most boring meeting of our lives when the sugar might have given him the will to live through closing arguments. That's when I started believing in love at first bite." He flicked his wrist. "Now scoot. You've got victims waiting."

I rose, straightening my skirt, then balanced on the edge of the top step. "Good luck with the kissing and making up."

"Thanks." He swiped a coat of clear gloss over his bottom lip with his pinky then pressed them together. "But I got this in the bag."

Leaving Neely to hunt down his man, careful not to comment on the length of untied cravat in his hand that would do as a blindfold in a pinch, I braved the narrow staircase. Fabric rustled against the walls on both sides, and the ribs of the hoop skirt groaned as they were compressed. I counted the steps to make sure I didn't fall flat on my face and breathed a sigh of relief when I hit bottom.

Thankfully, we were allowed to wear color-coordinated sneakers. Otherwise, I would have broken my neck in period-appropriate shoes on the way down. Not to mention grown a blister the size of some small children after a few hours.

The bulletin board where Cricket pinned our nightly assignments stood empty. I almost panicked before smacking my forehead with my palm. *Duh.* Of course my packet was gone. Leaving it up there for all to see would have shined a spotlight on my absence. Refusing to let panic wrestle me into a chokehold, I patted down my skirt in search of its hidden pockets. The crisp edge of stiff paper under my fingertips reassured me, and I pulled out an assignment sheet Amelie must have stuffed in there before enlisting Neely to the cause.

The note pinned to the top said the waiting group was twenty-nine strong. Considering the cutoff was thirty, it was a healthy size. My night was looking up already.

Stepping out into the cool air, I popped open my parasol, set it on my shoulder and twirled it all the way to The Point of No Return, which was a neon yellow line we used to cue up the next tour for departure.

My victims waited inside the red square, my favorite color. Another good omen. The blue and yellow squares stood empty, so those tours had already left. Most of the people in the green square had staggered outside of it, which was not a good sign. Drunk folks didn't tip well. Except themselves. It was a miracle none of them had kissed asphalt yet.

"Evening, y'all." I poured on the Southern charm. "I'll be your guide through haunted downtown Savannah. Feel free to ask any questions you might have, but do please stay with our group. Trespassers will be shot on sight." The crowd gasped on cue, and I tittered like a kitten on helium. "I'm kidding." My face went stone-cold serious. "Or am I?"

While inviting them to join me at the starting line, I finished my spiel and reminded the crowd of the local liquor laws. Grateful for the routine, my nerves calmed for the first time since the sigil charred my skin. I had the local history memorized, and I knew how to pull a laugh out of the crowd, how to gauge what kind of guide my group required.

All was well until we reached the house often billed as the most-haunted location in the city.

I stepped off the sidewalk, urged them into a huddle, and grasped the wrought-iron railing that surrounded the mansion, the metal chilly in my hand.

"This is Volkov House. Back in 1765, Anatoly Volkov passed away, leaving his estate to his son and daughter. Now, Nestor and Dina Volkov had both survived ugly divorces. Neither had much money, even with their inheritances, so the pair returned to their ancestral home to make ends meet." The crowd shifted, studying the home and trying to picture the downtrodden siblings returning with their tails tucked between their legs. "Nestor was a bit of a bookworm —both the siblings were—and one night he came home from work, pulled an old favorite from the house library, and settled into his favorite chair while Dina started supper.

"*Bang.*" I clapped my hands, and the folks in the front row jumped. "A single gunshot blasted through the library. Dina was so shocked that she tipped the pan on the stove, and the oil she was using to fry pork chops spilled on her. Dripping grease, she ran into the living room and found her brother sitting in his chair with a book spread over his lap, a shotgun in his hands, and the back of his skull decorating the living room wall." Shocked gasps rose, and I suppressed a chuckle, because that never got old. "Earlier that day, he had received a letter from his ex-wife, alerting him of her impending nuptials. Still in love with her, he took his own life rather than live without hope of ever winning her back."

Searching window after window, their gazes touched each frame in search of the library.

"Two weeks later, Dina was home alone reading in her bed, recovering from her burns." I clapped my hands again. "*Bang.*" I was rewarded by a young woman's shriek. "Dina heard the sound again, coming from downstairs. Figuring it must be a heartless prank by some of the neighborhood kids, she jumped out of bed, ready to set them straight. Except nightgowns in those days were long, frilly affairs, and she tripped over her hem and fell against her nightstand. She knocked over the kerosene lantern by her bed, and her gown caught fire. She burned to death alone in the house. By the time the neighbors saw the flames, it was too late. Volkov House was nothing but ashes."

A heavy silence blanketed the crowd, and I thrived on the high of knowing I had shaken them.

"If the house burned down, then what are we looking at?" my first skeptic of the night asked.

"Well, the thing is, Volkov House was a local institution. It was the most beautiful, most luxurious and most extravagant home in town, and the mayor had had his eye on it for a long while, hoping the destitute heirs would consent to sell it." I painted on a frown. "When he heard about the tragic deaths of the Volkovs, he set about convincing prospective buyers the property was haunted by Nester and Dina's ghosts. The property went to auction, and with no one to bid against him, the lot and the charred skeleton of the house went for five hundred dollars."

Someone whistled. "That was a steal."

"Yes, it was." I tapped the bronzed plaque marking the place as a historical landmark, one best known for the mayor who went on to be governor and pitched a hissy to have his home declared the state manse. He failed, by the way. "Mayor Rouillard, for he was at the time, rebuilt the home from partial plans found in the builder's records and redecorated it down to the gold-tasseled couch cushions from memory."

"Creepy."

"Very," I agreed with absolute conviction.

"Is this the part where you claim the locals report hearing a gunshot every night at midnight?" a thickly accented voice sliced through the crowd. "Or where you tell us passersby have seen a flaming woman pounding on the windows, trying to escape the fire?"

The gathering parted to reveal a man who wore his charcoal suit with the ease of a businessman, but violence beat beneath his skin, the same as mine. A knowing passed between us, and I felt his awareness of me as *other* to the tips of my toes.

The expensive threads matched his thundercloud eyes, and his wavy hair was so black the moon lent him blue highlights. He strode forward, and I leaned in, two opposite sides of a magnet caught in helpless attraction. His eyes, predator-sharp, searched my face for some unknown revelation. He invaded my personal space, crowding me against the fence. The fragrance of his skin reminded me of old coins and crushed rosemary.

"Have you been on this tour before?" The words tore from me on a ragged whisper.

Had he been in my group earlier, I would have noticed. My knees would have liquefied sooner.

"No." His tumultuous silver gaze swept over me, lingering on my throat. "I overheard you last night."

I palmed the side of my neck to get his eyes off my pulse. "Come again?"

"I'm Danill Volkov." His cocky smile bared straight white teeth. No fangs in sight. "This is my home."

Had his family name meant nothing to me, I would have recognized his breed.

Vampire.

The intoxicating pheromones he was tossing my way, his lure, had me ready to mewl for his kiss.

"I apologize." I flattened my spine against the warming metal. "I didn't realize you were in town." I peered around him, aiming my parasol at a stop sign marking our next turn. "Why don't you guys hang out over there and give me a moment alone with Mr. Volkov?"

The name raised more than a few eyebrows. Afraid they might be trespassing, or perhaps taking me too seriously about the shotgun warning, they scurried off to give us privacy.

Cricket orchestrated our tours to cause as little disruption to the locations and owners as possible, since pissing off fourth-generation locals meant stern calls from the chamber of commerce. She would not be thrilled to hear about the disruption Mr. Volkov's appearance caused in tonight's haunted history lesson or the fact she would lose the crowning gem of her downtown tour in the interim.

"I arrived three days ago." A smile tugged at the corner of his mouth, and his canines sharpened before my eyes. "Perhaps I will see you here. Tomorrow night. Around the same time."

"That's not a great idea." For too many reasons to count. "I'm not what you think I am."

"Oh yes, you are." He lowered his head, the tip of his nose trailing along my jaw. His lips moved against my skin, the warmth of his exhale puffing in my ear. "You call to me, necromancer."

Breath hitching, I swore I felt the rasp of teeth against my skin. "I don't practice."

"Liar," he breathed. "I smell the grave on your skin."

"I should go." Volkov might as well have been carved from stone for all the give when I pushed him. "I have a tour to, uh, guide."

A cool smile bent his mouth as he let me escape. "I will see you again."

"I'll talk to my boss about removing your house from the tour." I stumbled toward the scattered group waiting on the corner, impatience and curiosity mingling on their faces. "I don't want to disturb you."

"You do not disturb me." His nostrils flared one last time. "Good night..."

The single, damning word tumbled past my lips without consulting my brain. "Grier."

"Grier," he repeated, possessing my name as if I had given it to him for safekeeping.

Sneakers glued to the sidewalk, I stood there while he let himself through the gate then disappeared inside his house. Only when the front door closed did the others rejoin me.

Smoothing my skirts, I faced them with a pasted-on smile meant to reassure. "Now if you'll all follow me..."

I set off at breakneck speed to the next destination, desperate to put distance between Volkov and me.

The rest of the night passed in a different kind of blur. When I reached The Point of Hey You Made It Back, I collected my tips, waved off my group, and made a beeline for HQ. I was counting on Amelie's teensy obsession with the new guide, who was about as theatrical as a moth-eaten curtain, to delay her.

Sure enough, I found her all but swooning over his historically inaccurate retelling of one of my favorite ghost stories.

"Come on." I hooked my arm through hers on my way past and hauled her into the parlor where the female Haints changed. "We need to talk."

She stumbled after me. "Boaz made me promise—"

"This is not about that." Though that talk was coming. "I saw something tonight."

"Based on your reviews on Yelp, I'd say you make sure you see something every night." She disentangled from me and started unpinning her hair from its elaborate twist. "Not that I'm jealous or anything. Except I am. Totally. My skin is green under this dress."

Envy was a sore topic between Amelie and me, always had been, so I pretended not to hear. "I'm serious."

"Okay." Her fingers hesitated before she unspooled her first curl. "What happened?"

"I met Danill Volkov."

She barked out an incredulous laugh. "Wait. You're serious?" She bared her teeth and tapped her canines. "Like an honest-to-God Volkov? A descendant of the guy who built the crazypants murder house?"

I bobbed my head like a juicy apple floating in a water-filled barrel.

"Wow." She leaned her hip against the sink. "Did he speak? Or did he just glare from the porch and shake his cane at the kids on his lawn?"

"Oh yeah. He spoke all right." Recalling all the things he'd said, the heat of his breath on my skin, raised gooseflesh. "He's not grandpa material either. He's mid-twenties or early thirties. At least that's how he appears."

Clapping her hands together, she squealed, "Tell me *everything*."

I repeated him word for word and watched her eyebrows ratchet higher and higher toward her hairline.

"You didn't give him your last name?" She smacked her forehead with the heel of her palm, illustrating where I had picked up the habit. "Or your phone number?" She bit her bottom lip. "Maybe you should have given him your number if he's that hot."

"Best-case scenario is he's a *vampire*. Necromancers are like catnip to them." And Volkov had already pawed me once tonight. "The options get worse from there."

The undead came in several flavors, and I wasn't about to taste Volkov to determine his. He struck me as the kind of guy who bit back. Hard. Vamps were common in necromantic society. Not unexpected since they were our creations. Not to mention our bread-and-butter. But there were vampires, and then there were *vampires*. I got the feeling he fell into the latter category.

Your basic undead are created when a necromancer tethers a human soul with very, *very* deep pockets to its body after death. Those vampires are classified as resurrections, humans resuscitated by necromantic magic, and they rise as the undead with a thirst for human blood. They come equipped with a lure, a sensuous magnetism, that helps them ensnare prey. But only the oldest among them are a threat to necromancers. We have a natural immunity to them. So, pretty classic by horror-movie standards.

Those don't last forever, and most go insane and have to be put down before the half-century mark.

Then you've got the Last Seeds. Turns out sperm can stay alive inside a dead man's body for up to thirty-six hours. Freezing the swimmers doesn't work. Magic and medicine don't always see eye to eye on such matters. But that still gives resurrected vamps plenty of time to knock up willing surrogates (or human partners) for the purpose of creating offspring. For a fee, of course. A steep one. Last Seeds are just that—a male vampire's last drops of humanity preserved for all eternity in his child. They're also so rare and so cosseted by their vampire clans as to be fabled.

Last Seeds are immortal from birth and stop aging in their thirties. The Society allows them to live because in addition to being rare, they're also sterile, making their population even easier to control. Otherwise, there's no way those High Society stuffed-shirts would allow the Last Seeds and their irresistible lures to traipse around ensnaring necros willy-nilly, as I suspected Volkov had done to me.

Stashed in the bottom drawer are ghosts, ghouls and wraiths, byproducts of violent deaths, resuscitations gone wrong, and dark magic used to take lives.

The creation of psychopomps were a specialization as well. I won't even lie. Necros who focus on pets make all the money. We've all seen people carrying teeny-tiny toy dogs around in designer purses. Offer a rich owner the chance to give Mr. Fluffy Lumpkins a second leash on life and *cha*-ching.

Even the fae deigned to bargain with us for the lives of their most beloved companions.

I got hot flashes just thinking about all that cold, hard cash.

Despite all appearances to the contrary, necromancy was a lucrative field, regardless of your specialty. Practitioners made bank, but skilled assistants, those without criminal records, earned more than I would see in a human lifetime.

How the mighty have fallen.

"I'm kidding, Grier. Sheesh. Give me some credit. I might be Low Society, but I'm not *human*." Her sobering words brought my attention swinging back to her. "Volkov would have recognized your last name."

Maud had been famous in her own right. Me? I was more infamous. Not quite the same thing.

"You were smart to protect yourself. We have no idea how the Society as a whole, let alone the Undead Coalition, will react to the news of your release once it trickles down." She worked three more bobby pins loose from her hair. "Boaz will start knocking heads together if any of the factions take exception to your pardon, and that will get messy fast." She winked. "And that's not counting what I'll do."

The cold fingers of dread traced a line down my spine. "Amelie, you can't—"

"I'm not afraid of the Society, and they don't even know I exist. I'm too far below their notice." Bitterness tinged her voice. The title of assistant might have stung my pride, but she burned for even that much respect among our peers. "Can you imagine if they did try to silence me?"

Actually, I could. Easily. After all, they'd done a bang-up job of muzzling me.

"Rumor has it that poor Amelie Pritchard took on a ruthless secret society and was silenced for her daring." She strode toward one of the dressing booths and pushed aside the curtain as though she were opening a door. "Amelie was shoved down three flights of stairs by Matilda Bolivar at Sorrel-Weed House while leading a tour, and now she haunts this very house. It's said that only people she once guided can see her, and that she awaits them to join her as she tours the afterlife."

I cracked up at her ridiculousness. "You're horrible."

"I think the word you're looking for is *hilarious*. You're not the only one with Yelp reviews, you know."

I pinched my lips closed to prevent more snark from slipping free.

"So, what are you going to do about the vamp?"

"Tell Cricket to remove his house from the tour routes and avoid his street like the plague."

"I approve of this plan." She cleared her throat delicately. "Speaking of avoidance..."

"Yes, yes. I saw your brother tonight." The skin of my throat tingled in memory of his wide palm wrapping the delicate column like a necklace. "Most of him anyway."

Blood rushed from her cheeks, and she leaned against the nearest wall for support. "He made me promise."

"Did he honestly believe it would make any difference to me?" I picked at the worn lace on the front of my dress. "I never thought I'd see him—or you—again. Does he think I'm that shallow?"

"He's a man, and men are ninety percent pride." She chewed on her thumbnail. "And I think, even if he doesn't want to admit it, he was punishing you. He had no idea what was happening to you inside..." She let the sentence fade. "He must have figured it was only fair you had no idea how bad things had gotten out here for him either."

"He tried to kiss me," I blurted.

"This is Boaz we're talking about." Amelie didn't blink. "What did you expect?"

"For him to ignore the fact I'm a grown woman until the day he died? Probably from having sex with a set of triplets half his age?"

She didn't disagree. "Do you remember how you two met?"

I narrowed my gaze. "You're not helping his case here."

"Picture it." Her tour guide voice came back in full force. "The playground. Kindergarten. Me and you. Sitting on the swings at recess, eating apple slices instead of sour candy straws, because even then Mom didn't want me to live my best life. Boaz steps out the double doors, hops down the steps and walks right up to you. He stuck out his hand and—"

"He basically karate-chopped me in the chest," I protested. "I wasn't holding on to the chains. I was eating my apple. I *fell*."

"The facts are these: he walked up to you, and you hit the dirt on your back with your legs sticking straight up in the air." She snickered. "He's been trying to get you back there ever since."

"He got plenty of other girls in the dead-bug position." So many I'd lost count of how my heart broke each time he brought a new girl home on his arm. "He just wanted another specimen to add to his collection."

Having nursed me through many of those late-night crying jags, I recognized her world-class diversion techniques. All he'd had to do was crook his finger, and I would have been his for the asking. We both knew that. Heck, all three of us did, and that made the shame of my open secret so much worse.

Amelie flounced over, bumped hoop skirts with me in solidarity, and I started pulling on her laces.

"You were fifteen when he noticed you were a girl and not just his kid sister's best friend." She clicked her tongue. "He was eighteen. You weren't ready for sex, and he'd just figured out he could sweet-talk his way into girls' panties and what to do when he got there." She shuddered at the thought. "He was a decent guy, but he was still a hormonal teenager. He wasn't ready to give up his new favorite hobby while he waited for you to mature."

"But *has* he matured?" The searing intensity in him when he ticked off his reasons for leaving still smoldered in my memory. But Boaz was blessed with a silver tongue, and he had slipped it down way too many throats for me to believe mine was anything special.

"Boaz doesn't come home often, and he never stays long." Her casual shrug didn't fool me for a minute. She was close to her brother, and she must miss him something fierce. "Part of me hopes having you back home will anchor him." She rubbed the spot over her breastbone. "The other part knows in order for you to heal, you need to figure yourself out first." She dipped her chin to hide the moisture pooling in her eyes. "But I know how determined he can be. He won't stop until he gets what he wants. And it terrifies me that it's you. I'm worried if he cuts and runs again, if he breaks your heart for real this time, that I'll lose you both."

I crossed to her and gathered her in my arms, ignoring the dampness spreading across my shoulder. "I don't know what I want for breakfast most mornings, let alone who I want to share it with."

No matter how solid Boaz had felt trapped between my thighs, Amelie was right. I might hide from my problems, but he had a bad habit of running from his, and I was tired of being the reason he avoided his home and family. Maybe it was time both our inner teenagers grew up before we ruined a good thing.

"The late-late tour leaves in a few. I need to get out there and twirl my parasol before Cricket has a coronary." I waited until Amelie peeled out of her corset before I turned. "See you tomorrow?"

"Call if anything else creepy happens." She pointed a warning finger at me. "I mean it."

"I will." I curtsied and unlocked the door on my way out. "Promise."

On my way downstairs, I ducked into Cricket's empty office and left a note on her desk about the Volkov heir's mysterious return then slipped back into the parking lot with a sigh as cool air teased my skirt. Sunlight bathing my face was nice, but give me the kiss of the moon, the call of night birds, the smells of light extinguished, of the darker world rousing to wakefulness, any day.

The ardent cry of a mockingbird caught my attention, and I glanced up at the lightning-struck Bradford pear tree leaning over the entryway. The pale gray bird perched on a charred limb, deep in shadow that ought to have concealed him, chest fluffed out as it completed a pitch-perfect impersonation of Cricket's car alarm. But I saw him, and when he noticed that, he took personal offense and flew away.

Enhanced night vision came with the necromantic package. We had evolved alongside the vampires we created, both of us embracing nocturnal lifestyles. Us through choice, them through necessity. Vamps wouldn't go up in flames if exposed to sunlight, but the effects weren't pretty. Made vamps rose with solar urticaria, an allergy to UV radiation, while born vamps developed a less severe form of photosensitivity similar to polymorphous light eruption, another form of sun allergy.

Theories abounded as to why the vampire population was afflicted. The most prevalent theory, the one printed in our textbooks, was that because Hecate was a goddess associated with the moon, and necromancers were her children, that our magic bound them to the dark, to her whims.

As I hadn't believed in gods of any kind for a long time now, I had no opinion on the topic.

Careful to avoid the street where the Volkov House sat, I guided fourteen brave souls down a secondary route where I whiled away the early-morning hours. Once the last slightly wobbly patron had pressed damp bills into my palm, I headed inside to change. I met another guide in the dressing room, and we stripped each other with the eagerness of two virgins under the bleachers at homecoming.

Amelie's warning about keeping her posted about creepy goings on rang in my ears when I arrived home and found an unexpected guest waiting in my driveway on the wrong side of the fence. I parked Jolene, palmed an ash stake from a hidden compartment under the seat, then closed the garage and joined him. "Can I help you?"

"Grier Woolworth?" The stranger eased into a sliver of moonlight, his skin flawless, his gaze fathomless. His presence weighted me in place, and for the second time in one night, I felt myself being measured by predatory eyes. Though these held none of Volkov's primal attraction. A made vampire then. "Can we talk?"

"It's late, and I'm tired." And I had a healthy sense of self-preservation these days. "We'll have to do this some other time."

Point to him, he stepped aside and allowed me to reach the porch. "I represent someone eager to make your acquaintance."

A foreboding chill rippled down my arms, and I clenched the stake tighter. "I have enough friends, thanks."

"Aren't you curious why you were released from Atramentous?" He strolled forward with a spring in his step. "Only the worst of our criminals are sentenced to that pit and only after lengthy deliberation. You were a child when they closed the grate behind you. Sixteen. The youngest inmate in its long and miserable history. And, rumor has it, you had no trial at all."

The moisture wicked from my tongue. *Shut it down. Shut. It. Down.*

"You are the sole exception any Grande Dame has ever made, a singular pardon. Why?" He tapped the side of his nose. "That debt would make me nervous if I were you."

The ground trembled beneath me as the bomb he'd dropped detonated.

I should have probed the ragged edges of my personal miracle before now, but I had been all too happy to slap a bandage over the wound and pretend I wasn't slowly bleeding to death from a thousand cuts. I had been living a small life, a quiet life, a *safe* life, since my release. But safety was an illusion, wasn't it?

The hand that had guided me into the light could just as easily shove me tumbling back into the dark.

The Grande Dame had spared me. I ought to feel grateful. Instead a feverish heat swept chills over me.

"I'm going to bed now." Turning my back on him gave me the willies as I gripped the front doorknob.

I was still holding the brass sphere when his hand landed on my shoulder in a touch meant to ask for my attention. I barely had time to register the potential threat before Woolly used me as a conduit, zinging an electrical charge through me and into him. I whirled around as the vampire was blasted clear off the porch and tumbled across the lawn, landing in a tight crouch that spoke of feline reflexes.

"Night, Grier," he said, a chuckle in his voice as though the volts had tickled his funny bone.

I slipped inside and locked the door behind me.

Two vampire sightings in one night. What were the odds this was a coincidence?

Slim to none. Emphasis on the *none*.

Say he was right about the Grande Dame pardoning me, what did she want in return? And could I afford to give it to her?

THREE

I woke at dusk curled in a ball in my usual corner with salt drying in itchy tracks on my cheeks. A horrible weight in my gut kept me from dry heaving, and I started regretting my policy of not talking about what had happened to me. Even one person could help me sort through what was real and what was imagined, what had been forgotten. So many years spent reliving the seconds that had cost me my freedom had both burned those moments into my mind's eye and faded them after so many viewings. What I remembered, I didn't trust, and what I had been told in Atramentous I believed even less.

Talking probably wasn't the worst idea I'd ever had, but who did I wreck with the burden of those memories? The man who had offered me his unconditional support or the woman who would never refuse me if I asked her to prop me up? The man who had suffered his own horrors or the woman left behind to imagine them? Boaz or Amelie? And could I ever look either of them in the eyes again after?

I didn't know, and until I did, they were both safe from me calling in any favors.

Determined to check at least one item off my to-do list before work, I hauled myself up the narrow stairs into the stuffy attic and rummaged through lifetimes' worth of accumulation until I located the antique cage Keet once called home and its matching base. That segued into me dusting the chandeliers, and ended with me falling down in sweaty exhaustion onto my bed, thus dooming me to laundry detail.

Hours later, still dressed in cut-off shorts, a tank top with a hole exposing my navel and half my right side, I plucked at the itchy yellow dish gloves encasing my hands. Suds climbed up my elbows, because I failed at mixing the proper water-to-mopping-solution ratio, and I worried more than once I might be making a bigger mess than I was cleaning. Factor in my frizzy ponytail, the bangs plastered to my forehead and the allergies causing my eyes to redden and itch, and I had reached the mecca of sexiness that promises you'll run into your smokin'-hot ex if you leave the house.

I didn't have an ex. I guess that's why I didn't even have to leave the house to get run into.

The doorbell rang out in a clear, strong note, one of Woolly's all-clear chimes. Secure in the knowledge whoever awaited me wasn't the kidnappy vampire from last night, I tossed my sponge in the bucket to go investigate. Palms braced on the door, I stuck my eye to the peephole and sucked in a sharp breath. The man standing on my porch, hands folded in front of him, had me fighting back a panic attack, because he wasn't a man at all really.

"Are you insane?" I glared up at the foyer chandelier. "You let him on the porch?"

The light brightened then dimmed, the Woolly equivalent of a shrug.

After ripping off the gloves, I tossed them near the other supplies then smoothed a sweaty hand over my hair before opening the door. "Mr. Volkov."

An unassuming male dressed in a dark suit stood behind him and to his left. He closed the large, black umbrella he must have used to escort Volkov onto my porch then made himself scarce. I hadn't even noticed it was raining again, but that explained why my hair was crackling like I'd stuck my finger in a light socket. This was Georgia humidity at its finest.

Volkov stared at the crown of my frizzy head, sweeping his gaze down my frayed outfit. He lingered over my legs for what felt like hours, a mathematician going for the mental recitation of pi. "Ms. Woolworth."

Fiddlesticks.

"Eyes are up here, bud." Walking between five and fifteen miles five nights a week kept my calves and thighs toned, but not many people got the chance to admire them thanks to my voluminous skirts. Uneasy with his gaze on my bare skin, I snapped my fingers to snag his attention. "How did you find me?"

"I followed your scent," he said, as if tracking me like a bloodhound was a totally reasonable answer.

"Oookay." Shifting to my left, I blocked the entrance to the house. "And you're here why?"

"What are your plans for lunch?" His attention lingered on my throat.

Lunch for necros tended to occur around midnight with dinner being served around six in the morning. Breakfast, for those who indulged, was usually a sunset affair. Though it was hours too early for lunch, I had abstained from breakfast due to my upset stomach, so brunch was sounding good right about now.

"I'll probably make a sandwich." I had one scoop of peanut butter in the jar, two squirts of jelly in a bottle, one square of processed cheese, and a few slices of bread. I had done a little of my own math and decided one PB&J and one grilled cheese would hit the spot until I went shopping.

Volkov stood there, an air of expectation suspending a single moment into many.

"Would you like to join me?" To my knowledge, no vampire had stepped foot inside Woolworth House during my stay with Maud. I wondered if today would prove the exception. What about this one had piqued Woolly's curiosity? Especially considering her violent reaction to the one from last night.

His regal nod indicated a certain expectation I had to nip in the bud. And soon. He attempted to cross the threshold with his confident strides, but a burst of ward magic from Woolly suspended him in the doorway while she conducted a thorough evaluation. I didn't rush her decision. I was interested in her assessment as well. He took a fumbled half-step back—the house trying to gently shove him out? But he pressed forward with a determined scowl, swinging his narrowed gaze toward me, and shut the door behind him as if that might prevent his premature eviction.

"Don't look at me. She's the boss." I gestured to the house around us. "I just live here."

"The rumors are true then?" He examined the entryway as though expecting a ghost to walk through the walls and boop him on the nose for being a bad vampire. "The house is haunted?"

"Yep." That was mostly the truth. Close enough for my conscience anyway.

"Do you know the identity of your ghost?" Genuine curiosity guided his perusal. "Is there more than one?"

"Maud isn't here if that's what you're asking." Had he known who I was last night? All signs pointed to *yes*. That would explain his interest in me. "Still want that sandwich?"

"Of course."

Pivoting on my heel, I led him toward the kitchen. On my way past the bucket, I stepped in a patch of fizzing suds, and my foot shot out from under me. I flung out my arms and braced for an impact that never came.

"I have you." Warm breath fanned my throat as his arms cinched around my middle. "You should be more careful."

"I was..." I breathed in the scent of his skin and lost my train of thought as that same magnetism from last night flipped switches in my brain. The tension thrumming in me uncoiled until I melted against him. Giddiness frothed in my mouth, and I had to swallow giggles. "Cleaning. The floor. It was dirty."

"I see." He swiped a dollop of bubbles off my thigh, rubbing the film between his fingers while I prayed to every god I had ever read about that I'd shaved the night before...or even the previous week. Work was my one social outlet, and hoop skirts hid a multitude of sins. "The kitchen is this way?"

"Hmm?" I would have said most anything to keep him talking. His accent was kind of sexy.

"You did not hit your head." His accent thickened as though he had plucked the thought right out of my mind. "I caught you."

"The kitchen is this way." There. I sounded perfectly normal. "Hey, whoa." I flailed in his grip as he lifted me against his chest and started walking. "You can put me down now."

"And risk you slipping again?" He strode through the wetness and bubbles without sliding an inch. His shoes were quality leather, expensive, and murky suds were bursting on them.

Once in the kitchen, I put up a token struggle that caused the corners of his eyes to crinkle. I wasn't going anywhere until he released me, and we both knew it. "Put me down," I said again, hating the breathless catch to my voice. "Please."

"As you wish." He set me on my feet and began a slow examination of the kitchen. "You have a lovely home."

"Thanks." My dreamy tone evaporated once he crossed the room. As my head cleared, blood rushed into my cheeks over the damsel routine I'd pulled. His lips curved at the sight, and my stomach quivered. Touch must be the key to his lure. Good to know. "How do you feel about grilled cheese?"

"I haven't had grilled cheese since I was a boy." He studied the ingredients as I placed them on the counter as though each were a foreign object. The processed cheese in particular seemed to fascinate him.

"Then consider me your walk down memory lane." I patted the

island, and he took the hint and sat on one of the barstools. "Can I get you something to drink?"

Almost on reflex, he flicked a glance at my throat, and I swallowed. Audibly. But he just chuckled.

"I do not take what is not freely given." He stacked his forearms on the marble countertop. "Do not fear me."

"Can I get back to you on that?" I started preheating my pan. "You're the first Last Seed I've met."

Volkov canted his head to one side. "How can you tell?"

"Twice now you've made my brain melt at a touch. Made vamps can't hook me with their lures."

A fact he ought to know, unless it was me he was testing. Yeah. That seemed more likely.

While he mulled over his response, I poured him a glass of lemonade. Our fingers brushed when I passed it to him, and a flash of heat swept through my limbs too fast for me to do more than gasp before he ensnared me. Sweat beaded on my forehead and rolled stinging tracks into my eyes. The cord powering my brain disconnected with a *pop*, and I twirled down the path to La-La land.

I was hot. Burning up. Ready to peel off my clothes and dance in the sprinklers. Summer in the south was killer. I really ought to crank up the AC or crack a window or stick a palm frond in his hand.

A palm frond? the distant voice of reason echoed. *Do you hear yourself? It's not even summer.*

"Apologies." As he withdrew, so did the urge to strip naked and jiggle on the front lawn for his entertainment. "I had to be certain you understood how fast a touch from one such as me can ruin you."

"Where I come from, it's considered bad manners to brainwash your host." I scrambled backward until my butt hit the fridge, wondering what the heck Woolly had gotten me into with him. "Explain yourself, or get out. I'm good with either."

"I have a gift for you." He produced a powder-blue jewelry box from his suit jacket and slid it across the counter to me so I wouldn't have to risk an accidental touch. "Open it, please."

"Woolly?" I asked for her opinion. "This was your bright idea."

The lights flared in response, and the fridge hummed soothingly behind me.

Trusting she wouldn't steer me wrong, I palmed the box and lifted the lid. "You shouldn't have." A ruby-red bangle rested on a bed of white velvet. I tilted it to inspect the intricate metal clasp, and an air bubble disrupted the solid color of what I realized was a clear tube filled with tinted fluid. "Is that...blood?"

"Yes." The tips of his fangs showed as he spoke. "Mine to be precise."

"You *really* shouldn't have," I repeated.

"Try it on," he urged.

"I can't possible accept this—" *highly disturbing and inappropriate bangle* "—but I appreciate the sentiment. I know what the gift of blood means to your people. This is too generous."

"This is not an act of sentimentality." He gestured toward the box again. "Please, try it on. There's something I wish to show you."

The lights overhead burned brighter in encouragement.

Here goes nothing.

I pinched the bangle between my fingers and examined its curve. Glass doesn't bend without breaking, so what I'd first assumed was a hinged clasp must be merely decorative. At Volkov's urging, I slid the bangle over my hand and yelped as it pinched my wrist. No, not pinched. *Pierced.*

"I'm trying very hard not to stake first and ask questions later." Too bad I had returned the ash stake to Jolene. I would have to knife him and run if things got ugly. The sharp pain receded, and the bangle slid higher on my arm. "What just happened?"

"Take my hand." He splayed his fingers, waiting. "What's an ounce more faith?"

The door to the fridge opened, nudging me forward.

Our palms slid against each other and... The urge to naked polka never emerged. His skin was warm, smooth. His fingers meshed with mine, his thundercloud eyes intent on me. A line appeared between his brows as though he were deep in thought, but that was the only outward sign of his concentration.

"This gives me immunity to your kind." I dropped his hand and twirled it aside to check the puncture marks on my wrist. Gone. Healed in a blink. "Why would you surrender the greatest weapon in your arsenal?"

The real question was why did he think I was deserving of his gift? I was no one. Nothing. The ashes of a once-bright future. Where was the benefit for him?

"I'm offering you an alliance with Clan Volkov."

I shook my head to clear the ringing in my ears. "Why would you possibly want an alliance with me?"

Stripped of my title as the Woolworth heir, I had no position, no money, and no worth as a bargaining chip in any alliance. Factor in the years spent with magical restraints grounding my powers in Atramentous, and I was little more than human to boot.

"Trust me." His mouth crooked to one side. "Soon you'll be drowning in such offers. I mean for mine to be the first and the most generous."

"I don't understand."

Genuine pity darkened his eyes. "I'm not at liberty to explain."

"I can't accept an offer without knowing the consequences." I started to remove his gift, but his hand stilled me. "I can't accept this either."

"I'm not asking for an answer now, only that you consider me." He tapped the bangle. "This is all the protection I can offer until you decide. Please, wear it. It will keep you safe."

From him went unsaid. The odds of another Last Seed wanting a piece of me were...incalculable.

"I can't make any promises." I would need a second opinion before I removed the darn bangle, let alone promoted it to daily accessory status. Once bitten, twice shy and all that. "But I will consider your request."

"That's all I can ask." His quick smile was nice, tinged with triumph I didn't understand, but not bone-meltingly irresistible. "Except... Might I still trouble you for that sandwich?"

"That I can do." I set about preparing our meal, falling into the comfortable routine while my mind whirred. This gift must have been the reason Woolly allowed him entrance in the first place. Did that mean she wanted me to accept his alliance or take the gift and run? Times like these, I really wish she had writing skills above kindergartener level. "Was this the only reason you came to town?"

"No, I have other business matters to attend while I'm here." He traced a vein in the granite countertop with his finger, and it wasn't a stretch to imagine that same touch on my throat. "Perhaps I could engage your services for the night."

I burned my palm on the pan I was heating. "Come again?"

"You are a guide, yes?" He quirked an eyebrow. "I am not familiar with the area. I would appreciate someone with your qualifications to show me around town."

"You're a long way from home, huh?" At his puzzled expression, I elaborated. "Your accent."

"Ah. Yes." A grin told me he was well aware of how it affected the ladies. "I was born in Nizhny." He corrected himself, "Nizhny Novgorod, Russia."

I sliced a tablespoon of butter and let it hit the pan with a sizzle. "How did you end up all the way in Savannah, Georgia?"

"My mother passed away recently."

"I'm sorry to hear that." His father was a made vampire, his mother human, for him to be an LS. Meaning that Volkov's twenty-something appearance might be an accurate indication of his true age.

"We weren't close." He shifted in his seat to study the photos on the wall—all pictures of me and Maud, some including a somber Linus, and our escapades. "Not like it appears you were with your family."

Family was a complicated subject for me, and not one I was eager to discuss. "Was Volkov House part of your inheritance?"

"Yes." He returned his attention to me. "I'd heard stories of my mad relative and seen pictures of his home. When it passed into my hands, I was tempted to donate it to the town to be used for recreational purposes."

"What changed your mind?" I finished browning the grilled cheese to perfection, plated it, sliced it horizontally and shoved the dish toward Volkov.

"A...situation arose. My mother was a woman of many secrets, and some were revealed after her death. Much like the house, I inherited other responsibilities as well." A grim line flattened his lips. "I hoped that coming here might give me insight into what my obligations truly are."

A small part of me wondered if that situation was *me*.

"I get that." I pulled my bread from the toaster and slathered on the PB&J then cut off the crust. "Some responsibilities our loved ones leave behind are too large for us to shoulder alone."

Surprise lit his features. "Just so."

"About tonight—" If I had a lick of sense, I would tell him to buzz off and find another flower "—I have two late-late tours scheduled. I can't break those engagements."

Plus, I had to get Keet back in his cage and out of my bathroom, where I'd stashed him before bed. At least now he could hang in the living room near the windows overlooking the garden instead of being stuffed up in my room all the time.

"Are you available tomorrow?"

The way he said *available* made me think he meant something different than what rested on the surface. "Sundays aren't usually as hectic, but I'm covering two tours for a friend."

His chin dipped, as if he had expected the brushoff he apparently thought I had given him.

"What about Monday?" That gave me a small window to find answers about the bangle and arm myself with questions to ask about this proposed alliance of his. "We can do an early lunch in town."

A smile overtook his face that caused my pulse to leap, bangle or no bangle. "Are you asking me out?"

I choked on my sandwich and stole his lemonade to wash it down. Pretty sure my response still came out as a gurgle.

"Your blush intoxicates, *solnishko*." He lifted half his sandwich, bit into it, and let his eyes roll closed. A pleased rumble issued from his chest. "I want to repay your hospitality. We will meet Monday, and I will take you out for lunch." He cut his eyes my way. "As you requested."

"Okay." I didn't dare risk a longer response until I had drained his glass to the bottom. Thankfully, eternal life came with one heck of a boost to the old immune system, and I couldn't catch anything from sharing. "I'll pencil you in."

"I make you nervous," he observed.

Around him, I felt like a long-tailed cat in a room full of rocking chairs. "You're a stranger." A *vampire*. "In my home." Even if said home had invited him in.

"After Monday, we will have spoken three times. We will be strangers no longer. We will be..." his lips pursed, "...friends."

A laugh welled up in me. "Sure."

Once I showed him the sights and he realized I had zero powers or influence, he would lose interest and our friendship would crash and burn alongside his offer of alliance. I just hoped he let me keep the bangle as a consolation prize. Having experienced the helplessness of confinement behind iron bars, the misery of having my will suppressed, the horror of doubting my own sanity, I could appreciate an accessory that protected me from a fraction of the population at least. Volkov, whether he knew it or not, had given me a gift potent with symbolism as well as being practical for our future dealings.

"I hear your doubt." He finished his sandwich with equal rapture. "I will prove to you I am a constant man."

I schooled my features into a bland mask. Seeing him as a man was not part of the plan. Even his use of the word rang hollow. Made vampires often referred to themselves as men or women, a habit some of them never broke, but born vampires had been taught the trick as camouflage to make them harder to distinguish from their brethren.

Volkov was a vampire, and vampires—born or made—meant trouble for me. No matter how sincere those thunderous eyes blazed, I couldn't afford to let biology lead me around by the nose.

The doorbell chose that moment to ring, a pealing sound as joyful as laughter, and I had a good idea who to expect. So it was no surprise, three minutes later, to find myself squaring off with Boaz over the threshold.

"I wasn't sure you'd be awake yet."

"I'm not a total laze about."

"No, but you worked late." He inhaled, and the groan he released made my stomach tighten. "Is that a grilled cheese sandwich with extra butter I smell?"

"Yes, but I'm out of cheese. And bread." And I really didn't want him to discover I was harboring a vampire.

"Don't hide from me."

"Hello? I answered the door. I'm standing here, talking to you." My guest? Yes, well, okay. Him, I was hiding. "I haven't been grocery shopping because of those late nights you mentioned."

"Is there a problem?" Volkov purred over my shoulder.

I closed my eyes on a groan then squinted up at Boaz. "This is not what it looks like."

"It looks like you're cavorting with a vampire." His gaze sharpened. "Are you out of cheese? Or is it O positive you're low on?"

"Is this your boyfriend?" Volkov asked conversationally.

"No. He's my—" I stalled out. "Neighbor?"

"Friend," Boaz corrected through a flash of teeth. "Her very close friend."

"Danill Volkov, meet Boaz Pritchard." I gestured between them. "Boaz is my best friend's big brother. His parents live next door."

"You still live at home?" Volkov stood so close his heat caressed my spine. "I suppose in this economy..."

"I'm on leave." Each word sliced through the air. "I haven't been home in thirteen months, so yes. I will be staying with my family." His gaze shifted to me. "Besides, my old room has the benefit of giving me a view of Grier's bedroom window each morning. What more can a man ask for?"

"Boaz, did you need something?" I restrained the urge to throttle him. "Or are you only here to validate my decision to invest in blackout curtains?"

"I can't find the key to Jolene." He indicated a toolbox and a bulging plastic bag he'd left on the top step. "Figured the old girl was due for a tune-up."

"Oh." I deflated. "Guess I should have seen this coming." I palmed the keychain off the console table where I'd dropped it last night. "Here you go."

"Tuck in your bottom lip." He tapped my chin up with his fingertip. "Amelie told me you've been using her to get to work. I'm not here to steal your transportation."

Volkov uttered a growl that dared Boaz to try, but we both ignored him.

"She's yours. You can take her any time you want." Generous of me to give him back his own bike. "I'll figure something out. Really, it's okay."

He shook his head at my stubbornness. "Do you have a dollar?"

"Yeah." I pulled a wrinkled bill from my pocket and offered it to him. "What do I owe you for the oil and the filter I see in that bag? A dollar won't cover those."

"Congratulations. You just bought yourself a bike." He turned on his heel. "I'll draw up the papers. You can sign them later."

"You can't sell me Jolene." I chased him across the porch. "You love that bike."

"I bought a new one this morning."

My jaw dropped. "Why would you—?"

"Don't pester me, Squirt, or I might change my mind." He raised his hand as he set off toward the garage. "Later."

"Later," I murmured.

"I should go."

A flush warmed my cheeks. I'd forgotten Volkov was still here. "Sorry about that."

"You have nothing to apologize for, and certainly not to me." He took my hand and brushed his lips across my knuckles. "I look forward to seeing you again soon. I will call to make arrangements."

"You have my number." It came out as an accusation. "Why does that not surprise me?"

The sharp edge of his grin made zero apologies for him getting what he wanted.

"Thanks for the gift." I trailed him down the steps onto the lawn where his driver waited. "I'll think on what you said." And the implications of all he *hadn't* said.

"Good." He inclined his head. "Good night, Grier."

"Night, Mr. Volkov."

"Danill," he corrected. "We're friends, remember?"

"Danill," I agreed, willing to play nice until I got my answers. "Enjoy the rest of your night."

The bangle caught the light as I jogged back up on the porch, and I whirled it around my wrist. I had to admit it was as pretty as it was creepy. Since I had yet to go out tonight, I curled my toes against the cool planks, shut my eyes and brushed my thoughts against the wards encircling Woolworth House.

A percussive blast radiated through my skull as a warning chimed in my head. A new quadrant had been weakened within feet of the last assault. Almost as though someone were systematically checking Woolly's defenses.

That...was not good.

Hard to know who presented the more tempting target. Me or Woolly. Neither of us were inviolable.

Woolly should have reached out to me when she was in danger, not let it pass. Unless the reason she no longer mentally pinged me when the wards got buzzed was because I was too weak to hear her sound the alarm. That weakness might also explain why she'd rolled out the red carpet for our fangy guest.

After spending time with Volkov, I had no doubt he'd orchestrated our first meeting to occur at a time when I was professionally obligated not to turn tail and run. But he'd also chosen an environment where I would be surrounded by witnesses despite the late hour, humans, who he couldn't reveal himself to on that scale without dire consequences, Last Seed or not, so there was that. He had wanted me comfortable and relaxed, not intimidated.

That left me with the second vampire as a possible suspect, the one with a master eager to make my acquaintance. Or, even worse, another necromancer.

Rivals might have been attempting to crack Woolly like the safe she was all along. Her treasure trove of necromantic knowledge and artifacts were priceless to the Society. Desperation could be making them reckless now that I was home to defend her. Of course my being home might also be the issue.

Maud had been ruthless in her pursuit of knowledge, and she had earned her fair share of enemies. Now I had to wonder if I might have inherited them along with everything else.

FOUR

Dawn warmed my shoulders as I drove Jolene out to Tybee Island. Her sultry purr after having Boaz's hands on her kept my thoughts cycling back to him. A dollar. He'd sold me his bike, the one that cost him three summers' worth of grass-cutting money, for a freaking dollar. And he hadn't stopped there, either. He had more than changed her oil.

Golden light from the streetlamps caressed the fuel tank, her crimson and black paint glossy under the layers of wax he had lovingly applied after washing off the grime caked on her from months of hard use. It hadn't slipped my notice that my gas tank was now sitting on full too.

He had laughed himself silly when he realized I still wore the jacket I had inherited from one of his exes. *Jerk.* Let him laugh. It's not like I could afford to buy a new one, and it fit. Okay, fine. It zipped.

I wore a corset five nights a week. Breathing was overrated.

Ahead the road thinned to a single lane, and that was a generous assessment. I bumped along, avoiding potholes, until I reached a bungalow with mint-green siding and peppermint-pink shutters.

White trim accented the eaves, and clear plastic sealed the windows to keep in the cool like the house was hard candy still in the wrapper.

I parked in the sandy driveway, shucked my gear and approached the front door. It swung open before I got there, and a tiny woman with dark brown skin and long white braids squinted at me through Coke-bottle glasses from the threshold.

"*Ma coccinelle.*" She removed her glasses and wiped the thick lenses on the hem of her faded tank top. "Tell me, *bébé*, this is today and not tomorrow?"

"Tomorrow is still a day away, Odette." I embraced her frail shoulders to anchor her in the present. "Sorry it took me so long to visit."

Odette Lecomte was a seer, and she tended to get her yesterdays, todays and tomorrows scrambled.

People came from all over the world to invite her to sift their futures through her gnarled fingers. But her value, at least to me, wasn't in her guidance, but in what treasures she had unearthed while divining possible eventualities. Her vast network of clients made her a veritable encyclopedia of knowledge both common and forbidden.

"Bah." She held me at arm's length and grinned through black-ened teeth. "Wounded animals heal best in their dens. You owe no one an apology for doing whatever it takes to survive."

The sentiment, so similar to Maud's credo, left my eyes burning raw.

"Come inside." She hauled me into her living room and shoved me down onto a plush sofa the off-white color of bones. "Tell Odette what you need, and you shall have it."

"I made a new friend." I held up my wrist and shook the bangle. "He gave me this. Any idea how to get it off?"

"*Ma déesse.*" She made the sign of the goddess. "Why would you want to do a crazy thing like that?"

Not the reaction I'd expected. "Are you saying I *should* wear it?"

"Evie and Maud didn't agree on much where you were

concerned, but neither wanted me to hold the power of your future in my hands. Both wanted you to forge your own path, make your own mistakes."

The casual mention of my mother knocked the wind out of me, and Odette noticed my breathlessness.

"You look so much like your momma, the goddess weeps." She cupped my cheeks between her palms. "What would she say if she could see us now?" She laughed softly. "Other than for me to keep my nose in my own business."

"I don't know," I answered honestly. "I don't remember much about her."

Evangeline Marchand died when I was five. I can't recall her face from memory, but I studied Maud's albums often enough to know I saw a younger version of her each time I looked in the mirror. Thin lips, high cheekbones, sharp chin. I inherited those from Mom. The dark tangle of my hair belonged to her too. Whoever my father was, he hadn't contributed much. Not to my DNA and not to my life. But I got his amber eyes.

"More's the pity," Odette sympathized. "Maybe if she had been allowed to choose..." She flexed her fingers as though recalling how she had once held Mom's hand, guided her. "Evie walked her path with her eyes wide open. There was only ever one outcome available to her once she knew the end I foresaw."

That end came in the form of a car wreck the morning after we arrived in Savannah.

Maud admitted once, on a night when guilt had tipped back more than one wine bottle, that she had been the one who begged Mom to stop zigzagging across the country. The best thing, in her opinion, was for us both to put down roots. But the second Mom stopped being a moving target, death had struck her down.

Maud never forgave herself for her advice, yet another reason she wanted Odette blind to my future.

The lovingly renovated carriage house Maud had intended to be our home never received its promised family. Instead, a kind man dressed in black sat me down in Woolly's parlor the morning after the funeral to explain that Maud had been named my legal guardian.

She formally adopted me when I turned thirteen. Though she could have passed for a woman in her midfifties, she was four hundred and twenty-five the summer we met, well on her way to the maximum life expectancy of a necromancer. Any hope for biological children had died centuries earlier. That didn't mean having an heir of her own shaping didn't appeal to her. Up until that point, her nephew, Linus Andreas Lawson III, had served as both Woolworth and Lawson heir. But in order for my claim to be recognized by the Society, I had to first take her last name so that her line might be continued.

Considering all she had given me, how much I had desperately wanted to belong to her—to anyone—I decided the cost of my last name was a fair price for that acceptance.

"The bangle," I said, dragging Odette's eyes back into focus and my thoughts from the past. "What can you tell me about it?"

"They're called avowals. They're symbolic of a blood oath given between two consenting parties." Her lips compressed. "Gifts of this caliber are rarer than the Last Seeds themselves. Pins, broaches, bangles, rings. Each carries a significance. Such baubles are reserved for clan heritors and persons of great import the vampires want protected from tampering by enemy clans. And also for lovers, wives, children."

Throat dry, I asked, "What is the symbolism of a bangle?"

"The tube is seamless. There is no end or beginning." She worried the piece of metal affixed in the center. "This is a promise that your union will be the same."

I almost swallowed my tongue. "Our *what*?"

"The metal is the curious part," she prattled on. "What is its purpose?"

"When I put it on, these needlelike things stabbed me in the wrist. Are they not supposed to do that?"

"The band should be unadorned, a statement in its own right, but this one is not. That it wanted to taste your blood... Hmm." She tapped a finger against her bottom lip. "Can you remove it? Have you tried?"

"I wanted a second opinion first." I offered a weak smile.

"Well, go on then." She folded her hands in her lap. "Let's see what it does."

"That's not as comforting as I'd hoped." I slid the bangle off my hand as easy as pie. "Huh. Guess it comes off easier than it goes on." She gestured for me to go ahead, and I put it back on. "Well, that went—" I hissed as its prongs stabbed me. "*Dang it.*"

"Tell me what the vampire said when he offered this to you."

"He offered me an alliance with Clan Volkov." I scrunched up my nose. "He said I would be drowning in such offers soon, and he wanted his to be the first and the most generous."

"An alliance?" She chortled. "What did you say?"

"That I couldn't imagine why he would want to align with me, and that I couldn't possibly accept this—or him—until I had answers. He convinced me to keep the bangle, but as to the rest... What does this mean?"

Her eyes drifted closed for a moment before a frustrated growl parted her lips. "I thought perhaps I could divine the future for Monsieur Volkov and seek your answers there, but he flew too close to your sun and has been burned from my psychic eye." She tapped the side of her head. "Sometimes I glimpse your future from the corner of another's destiny."

"It's all right." I took her papery hands in mine. "Don't strain yourself trying."

"I have a theory, if it helps." Her fingers tightened around mine. "Until and unless you accept his proposal, the bangle will remain unmastered. He's released it into your care for now, but it must verify your identity prior to each wearing. Should you accept, I imagine it will be attuned to you and the metal removed."

"That makes sense." I spun it around my wrist. "As long as I keep it on, I can avoid the bite."

Her eyes glittered. "Avoiding the bite seems unlikely if you continue your dalliance with Volkov."

"Hold up. There is no dalliance." I clamped a hand on the side of my throat in reflex. "No one is getting dallied."

Her tone gentled. "You do understand what an offer of alliance means, don't you, *bébé*?"

"He wants to unite Clan Volkov and the Woolworth bloodline..." Dread ballooned in my chest. "Oh."

"Yes. *Oh.*" Odette patted my cheek. "You are the Woolworth heir for all that they stripped you of your title and fortune. The match is a good one, if unorthodox. To offer up what must be their heritor instead of a clan noble speaks to their hunger for your acceptance."

"Plus, I'll be dead in four hundred or so years, and he can move on to a wife of his choosing. What's a half millennium in the grand scheme of his immortality? A drop in the bucket."

"Men like Volkov are not for keeping, not for loving," she agreed sadly. "They are for savoring during the time we possess them and then releasing them when we can no longer hold them."

Nice of her to gloss over the bits where he would remain forever young while I aged. Slowly, yes, but no less surely. What woman's pride could survive waking one day and realizing your husband could pass for your son? Your grandson? Not that children would be an option for us.

Maud had never hinted at planning an arranged marriage for me, but such mutually beneficial unions were the threads that bound High Society families. You couldn't walk through an assemblage without rubbing elbows with the victim of a marriage of convenience.

"There's more I haven't told you." I started with the hinky wards, segued into vampire stalking me for his friend-deficient master, and ended with his implication the Grande Dame had a vested interest in me. "None of this makes sense."

The old seer inclined her head, eyes distant. "We are limited to what the goddess reveals to us."

"What the vampire said..." I linked my fingers in my lap. "I didn't know if the Grande Dame signed my pardon." Talking to Odette, with her hazy eyes and dreamy voice, helped loosen the words that wouldn't come when I was around Amelie and Boaz. "The drugs used to subdue the inmates, to keep us quiet and content to lie in our own filth, drove us quietly insane." Bile splashed the back of my throat, but I forced myself to keep going. "When the sentinels came for me, I didn't believe they were real. What they promised sounded too much like a fever dream. One I'd had a million times since I was assigned a cell."

"Oh, Grier."

"I signed whatever they put in front of me without reading it. I tried, but my brain wasn't working right. When they tossed me into detox, the clock on the wall in the clinic gave me some sense of time. I was confined to a bed for a month while they flushed the drugs from my system. I wasn't allowed to leave until the withdrawals stopped, and for a while they weren't sure they would." A bitter smile curled my lips. "I wasn't meant to leave. They weren't as careful with my doses as they should have been."

Odette wept beside me, her thin shoulders hunched with sobs. I should have gathered her in my arms, comforted her. But Atramentous loomed too dark in the shadows gathered in this room for me to do more than fight the instinctive scrabble of my lizard brain to lock down those memories, tuck them in a corner of my mind where no one would stumble across them again, least of all me.

Weak. I was so weak. Worthless. I couldn't face the memory of the punishment, let alone the crime.

"I have to go." I shot to my feet. "It's late. I should be getting home before Woolly worries."

"You don't have to rush off." She wiped her cheeks dry. "You could stay the day in the guestroom."

"I appreciate the offer, but I can't." As much as confiding those memories of Atramentous hurt her, enduring my night terrors might break her. "I'll come back soon. I promise."

"All right." She followed me to the door in a whirl of sandalwood and opened her arms. Despite the fact she stood inches away, the distance was too great for me to close. "Oh, *bébé*, what they have done to you."

This frail woman with one foot in this world and one in the next was the last remaining bridge between the two most influential figures in my life. But instead of her embrace recalling happier times —walking the beach, the gulls crying overhead, the surf nursing my toes—her pity burned hotter than those extinguished summer suns. Touching her would have burned me and my fragile pride to ashes, so I fled to Woolly, where I could hide behind my tattered wards in the comfort of my own home.

MUCH TO MY RELIEF, no vampires lurked on my property when I arrived. The visit with Odette had stretched into early morning, and sunlight had burned the shadows from the porch. That didn't stop me from carrying the stake, which I noticed Boaz had sharpened after meeting Volkov, at my side while I walked from the garage to the front door.

The locks snapped open for me in quick succession.

"Sorry I'm late." I patted the doorframe on my way in. "I drove out to Tybee and visited Odette. I figured she might be able to shed some light on the Volkov situation."

Somewhere a floorboard groaned with apprehension.

"You're the one who let him in," I reminded her. "Now it's up to me to figure out what to do about him."

Boaz swung around the corner with a half-eaten sandwich in his hand. "Who are we doing what about?"

The door slammed shut behind me or else I might have stumbled right back out onto the porch in my shock.

Drawing myself up taller, I squared my shoulders. "What the heck are you doing in my house?"

"Figured turnabout was fair play." Boaz took another bite. "Why should you have all the fun? I didn't even break in. I asked Woolly if I could wait until you got back, and she opened the door."

The chandelier dimmed, its crystals tinkling.

"Didn't mean to throw you under the bus, girl." He placed the hand holding his sandwich over his heart, as true a vow as any man had ever made. "Grier, this is all my fault. I acted alone. Woolly tried to stop me, but I forced my way in."

The lights warmed to normal levels, and all was forgiven.

I rolled my eyes at their antics. "Mmm-hmm."

"That reminds me." He extended an envelope stained with a giant, muddy boot print to me. "It must have been pushed through the mail slot after you left. I didn't notice it had stuck to my foot until I reached the kitchen. I cleaned it up as best I could. I don't think the card inside is damaged."

The spidery scrawl across the front of the envelope would have told me who sent the card even if I hadn't recognized the grapefruit essential oil Dame Lawson wore in lieu of perfume. "This can't be good."

"Who's it from?" He continued stuffing his face. "There was no return address."

"This is Dame Lawson's handwriting."

Boaz choked on his next swallow. "What does that old bat want with you?"

"I have no idea." I smoothed my thumb over the sealed flap and wished it could stay that way. "I'm not sure I want to find out."

Sandwich forgotten, he prowled closer. "Do you want me to open it?"

"It's not a bomb. It won't explode in my hands." Unless she hexed it...

Boaz grunted once.

I replayed my words and winced. "I didn't mean—"

"You can say bomb around me." He chuckled. "Explosion. Boom. Bam. Blam. All good. I promise."

Ducking my head, I took the out I was given. That's when I

noticed him scuffing his boot, the ribbon from the giftbox Volkov had given me trampled underfoot. Boaz must have been snooping when I got home and dropped it in his rush to pull together his innocent act.

"You're lucky I wasn't going to recycle that."

"Volkov caught me off-guard." He snatched up the grungy ribbon and slapped it across my palm. "I didn't know there were other guys sniffing around you."

His honest surprise that another man had shown interest in me stung my already smarting pride. Clearly the thought I might have a boyfriend had never crossed his mind. Had he believed all he had to do was open his arms for me to fall into them?

Though I *had* primed him to believe that, I still snapped, "I'm not a freaking fire hydrant."

A snort ripped out of Boaz, and I briefly wondered how Amelie felt about being an only child.

Light as a breeze, he snatched the envelope from my hand and tore into the letter. I had fallen for his ruse hook, line and sinker. I ought to know better by now. Delighted I was such an easy mark, he lifted it high over his head so I couldn't reach it even when I jumped, and read it out loud. "Your presence has been requested at the inauguration ceremony for..." A frown knitted his heavy brow. "The Society has named a new Grande Dame."

"Who?" I snatched the invitation while he was too stunned to fight back. "Clarice Woolworth Lawson."

Maud's not-so-younger sister was rising to power, and Dame Lawson was offering me a front-row seat.

Learning I was indebted to the Grande Dame had chilled me to my marrow back when I'd thought the vampire meant Abayomi Balewa, the woman who sentenced me to Atramentous, had freed me. But the timing of his visit and now this announcement dropped ice cubes into my bloodstream.

Dame Lawson cast in the role of savior was as unlikely as Boaz taking a vow of celibacy.

"Come on, Squirt." Boaz hooked his arm behind me and guided

me down onto a couch in the living room. "This must be a formality. There's no law saying you have to accept."

"Accept." Hysterical laughter bubbled up the back of my throat. "The last time I faced the Society..." I clamped a hand over my mouth and ran for the downstairs bathroom, where I emptied my stomach. I knelt there dry heaving for several minutes before a cold washcloth pressed against the base of my neck. "Go away."

"You gave me the stomach flu when you were eight by throwing up in my face when I picked you up and swung you around the room too fast. We're past this."

"Privacy?" I rasped.

"Pretending you're okay when you're clearly not. Don't do that. Not with me."

The order would have rolled off me like water off a duck's back had I not detected his genuine worry.

"I visited Odette." I braced my forehead against the toilet seat. "I talked to her about...things."

Our conversation—about Mom, about Atramentous, about Volkov—had lingered too close to the surface of my thoughts for me to keep them down at the mention of Dame Lawson's big promotion.

"I'm glad." He refolded the rag to give me a cooler spot. "She's a good confidante for you. Not as stellar as me, but not a bad second choice."

"Friend, Tilt-A-Whirl, mechanic, breaker-and-enterer, and now confidant." I marveled at the size of his ego. I don't know how he managed to cram it into the bathroom with us. "You can't be every-thing to me."

"How do you know?" The cool weight at my nape vanished. "You haven't let me try."

"I did let you try," I contradicted him. "You just weren't interested."

"You were a kid." He scoffed, offended. "You should be glad I wasn't interested. What kind of pervert would that have made me?"

"I still thought I loved you." Heaving a groan, I propped my legs under me and wobbled to the sink to brush my teeth with my finger and a squirt of sample-sized toothpaste scrounged from the medicine cabinet. "It still hurt when you didn't love me back."

"I've always loved you, just not the kind of love you wanted from me." His fingers trailed the side of my arm. "You were like a second little sister to me. Forgive me if it took time for me to shift gears and stop seeing you in those ridiculous pigtails you used to wear. And that rainbow jumpsuit? Gods, that slayed me. You were the cutest thing."

I met his eyes in the mirror. "Somehow this is more embarrassing than vomiting in front of you."

"I don't know where this is going." He wrapped one heavy arm across my shoulders in front, his forearm hot against my collarbone. "I don't know if it's going anywhere at all." He kissed the side of my head in brotherly concern. "But the love? That part we've got down pat. You gripped my heart in pudgy fingers the morning I caught you hurling mud pies at Amelie, and you still haven't let go." Another kiss, this one softer, warmer, but still chaste. "It's the rest we have to figure out. If you want to try."

For a single moment, I caved to an old weakness and leaned against him. His grip tightened across my shoulders, pressing my spine against the wall of muscle at my back. Cradled in his arms, I was safe and cherished, and both those things made my chest ache after having gone so long without them. But the cost of gambling with this man could be losing this easy flirtation between us. I had never looked at him as a brother, but I had always considered him family, and the risks outweighed the rewards in my book.

"Stop perving on me and let me go to bed." I broke his hold and exited the bathroom. "*Alone.*"

"Spoilsport." He strolled to the front door but hesitated on the threshold. "Grier? Burn that invitation. Pretend you never saw it. That woman lost all rights to call you family or expect your support when she didn't speak up for you at your sentencing."

Having nothing to add to that, I left him to say his goodnights to Woolly and wandered into the kitchen for a glass of warm milk before bed. Visiting Odette had left the center of my chest raw and aching, and I longed for what had once been a cure-all.

"I'm going to kill him," I muttered at the fridge, which Boaz had stocked with all my favorite junk food in addition to a few practical staples. A sticky note clung to a package of cheese slices, and I peeled it off the label. Block letters spelled out the cost of my groceries. "U O ME LUNCH."

Shame curled in my gut as I accepted his offering. His concern warmed me, but I hated him thinking I was a charity case. First the bike and now this. Tomorrow I would have to set him straight. But tonight... I poured myself a tall glass and nuked it to perfection with a sappy grin in place.

I was on my way upstairs with my treat when I spotted the plastic bag on the counter. I poked it with a finger, revealing an opened package with one cuttlebone left and a bag of seed twisted off with a sandwich tie. Another note clung to the packaging. I read it out loud, though I was sure Woolly already had the scoop. *"You take worse care of that zombie bird than Macon did. I found him zooming around your bathroom crapping everywhere. I cleaned up the mess and put the little turd in his cage. You can thank me later. I will accept dirty pics as payment. Left you something to pose in."*

I tossed his note aside and skidded into the living room to find Keet dozing in his cage. Boaz had positioned the stand near the picture window overlooking the rose garden, exactly where I'd intended for him to go. It's not like Keet required seed or water to live, just the occasional drop of blood, but he seemed to enjoy the catharsis of cracking seeds, and some of it must be going down the hatch since he pooped enough to be an ostrich.

Wary of what other gifts Boaz might have left me, I jogged upstairs and shoved open the door to my room. I'm not sure what I expected. Lace. Silk. Something highly inappropriate. A scrap of fabric that wouldn't cover anything. What I found was an olive drab tee that smelled like him and could wrap around me three times. The reminder he knew what it was like to wake from fractured memories with a scream lodged in his throat soothed my earlier irritation enough that I shucked my top and slid into his, snapped a picture and texted it to him. No caption. Anything I could think of now felt too much like an invitation, and I'd already received one too many of those for one night.

FIVE

I woke in a nest of twisted sheets on the floor in my usual corner. Guess not even Boaz's shirt was enough to ward off the dreams. Oh well. It was the thought that counted. Woolly, usually the first one to prod me after an episode, left me blissfully alone. But then again, I was taking her advice and talking to people. That must have been enough to earn me a gold star for effort.

The clatter of dishes jarred me, and I leapt to my feet, pulse thundering in my ears. "Woolly?"

A hiss escaped the floor register, a sigh of disappointment that I thought she would let in trouble.

But she had welcomed a vampire. And Boaz, whose middle name, I was pretty certain, was Trouble.

Maybe it was time to educate the old girl on the meaning of stranger danger.

After pulling on a bra and a pair of pajama bottoms, I shoved open my door and padded into the hall. That's when the dueling scents hit me. Coffee. Onions. Cheese. Three of my favorite things. I trotted downstairs into the kitchen and came skidding to a halt.

"Amelie." Not the Pritchard sibling I'd expected to see. "What is it with your family breaking into my house?"

"Grier? Is that you?" She hunched her spine, pretended to gasp and wheeze, and used the spatula as the world's shortest cane. "It's been so long. I thought you'd forgotten about your old pal Amelie."

"It's been like—a day." I crept past her to sniff whatever she was cooking. "And I've been busy."

"Clearly." She plucked at my shirt. "Please tell me I don't have to make this breakfast for three." She lifted a halved cherry tomato off the cutting board and held it against my flaming cheek. "Hmm. Cherry tomato red. That, my friend, is the color of guilt." She bit into the slice then yelled, "Guilt! Get your guilt here! Grab it while it's hot and fresh, people."

"Boaz left me the shirt." I clamped a hand over her mouth. "He wasn't still in it."

"I don't need details." She pretended to heave. "Really, I don't."

I took the plate she offered me then poured us both mugs of coffee and carried it all to the bar.

"What brings you by so early?" I took a bite of garden omelet and groaned. "Not that I mind if you want to do this for me every night."

"You only think it tastes good because you've been living on oatmeal. Trust me, no one else will eat my cooking. You leave a few eggshells in *one* time, and suddenly you've earned a spot on *Worst Cooks in America*." She tucked into her meal. "I wanted to make sure after everything that's happened you're still okay with taking my shifts tonight."

"I gotcha covered." I waved away her concern. "Did you find out where you're going yet?"

"Nope." She glared at her fork. "I asked my folks again, and they fed me more super-secret Pritchard family gobbledygook."

I shifted in my seat, uncomfortable. Amelie noticed and pounced.

"What's got you so twitchy?" Her nose wrinkled. "Unless my brother is the reason you can't sit still on a hard surface. That you can take to your grave."

Glowering at her, I resisted the urge to defend my honor and stabbed a tomato instead. "I heard the Society is about to name a new Grande Dame."

"Boaz told me about the invitation." Amelie shoved her plate of half-eaten food away. I couldn't tell if she didn't like her own cooking or if the topic had turned her stomach. Either way, I was making eyes at her omelet. "She's got balls to issue you an invitation. I hope they turn blue waiting on you to show up to her soiree."

"Will your family attend?" Her mother, Annabeth Pritchard, served as matron of their family. The voices of Low Society members might not be heard as clearly as those of the High Society, but the swearing-in of a new Grande Dame was meant to bridge the gap between classes. "You can take notes and report back to me."

"I doubt I'll go." She shrugged. "I'll ask my folks for the highlights."

"What about Boaz?" He looked good in a penguin suit, even if he hated acting grown-up long enough to tie his patent leather shoes.

"None of us want him set free in a room full of people who turned the other cheek while you were sentenced." She wrapped her hands around her warm mug. "He's spent five years learning how to kill, and our parents want to keep his itchy trigger finger scratched in other ways."

Her comment swept chills down my arms. "What exactly does Boaz do for the army?"

"That's classified," he growled from the doorway. "Amelie, it's time to go."

"Really, Woolly?" I kicked the back of the bar with the ball of my foot. "Do I even get a say in who comes in my house?"

The lights flickered and died until the only sound left in the kitchen was the hum of major appliances.

"You forget, she *is* the house." Boaz crossed to me, his eyesight keen in the dark, and tugged on the sleeve of my shirt before grazing my flannel-covered thigh with his fingertips. "This is a good look for you, but the idea was to wear only what I left you."

"All I saw was the T-shirt."

Leaning close, he breathed me in, and his breath tickled the shell of my ear. "Exactly."

"Ugh." Amelie carried her dishes to the sink then fed her omelet to the disposal. "I'm out."

A horn honked loud enough to convince me Boaz had left the front door open. "Have they given you the scoop?"

"Nope." He rolled his eyes. "They won't even share the location, so we're all riding together."

"The family that conducts dark rites together stays together?" I shoveled in another mouthful of omelet. "Don't sacrifice too many virgins. Your parents probably had to special order them from out of town now that you're back."

"There's only one virgin I'm interested in sacrificing," he purred.

The skin on my face ignited like the surface of the sun, and I was grateful for the darkness. The jerk might see my expression, but he couldn't pick out the red splotches rouging my cheeks.

"You are not sheathing your ceremonial dagger in my—" I finished lamely "—sheath."

"You're so cute." His teeth closed over my pulse. "I could eat you up."

"I'm a virgin, not an idiot. I grasp double entendres just fine."

"I bet you do."

Spinning the fork on my palm, I jabbed him in the abs, and he jumped back while I cackled. "Shoo fly, don't bother me."

"You're a cruel woman, Grier Woolworth." He clutched his gut like I'd disemboweled him instead of checking him for doneness. "You're lucky I like claws. The more you scratch me, the worse the itch gets."

Short blasts from a car horn had him cursing under his breath.

"Maybe you should consult a dermatologist." I smiled as sweet as you please. "Or maybe a vet since you've developed some odd cat fetish? Or would that require a psychiatrist?"

"We'll finish this later." He darted in and ruffled my hair. "Later, Squirt."

I bared my teeth and hissed at him just to hear him laugh his way out the door.

Sadly, my antics didn't amuse Woolly. She remained stubbornly silent while I rinsed the dishes. Mourning the loss of Amelie's omelet, I put away the supplies littered across the counter. I reserved a few slivers of tomato and carried those into the living room. Keet, diurnal by nature, was snoozing on his perch when I popped in to check on him and left him with his treat.

The skin at my nape prickled when I stepped out onto the front porch, and Woolly didn't rouse herself to protest against my exit. Usually I got a slamming door or flickering porchlight—some outward indication she was in a tizzy over me leaving.

The absolute stillness disturbed me enough I reached for the wards on instinct. A skull-rattling pain sliced through my scalp, and I gasped through the resonations that almost sent me crashing to my knees. The normally radiant song of her consciousness had quieted until I had to strain to make out even a note, and still she hadn't cried out in those final moments. Maybe because she couldn't.

An oily blackness clung to the back door, seeping underneath and spilling across the hardwood planks.

This was no temper tantrum. The wards had been breached. Woolly was... She was... Silent.

I took a running start and jumped off the porch into the yard, keeping a mental eye on the intruder. I shoved into the carriage house, retrieved the key and battled with the smallest trunk to retrieve Maud's bag. This time the trunk behaved, so I set the bag on its lid and opened the ink to dip the brush for the sigil required to deepen my perception. Not waiting for it to dry, I pocketed the ink and the brush then charged back into the house.

The greasy taint stained the door leading down into the basement, but a quick check of its knob assured me the wards sealing off Maud's private laboratory remained secure. She had refreshed the wards protecting her sanctuary each night with blood straight from the vein. I doubted anything could crack the magic seal—I couldn't—but it made me uneasy that this *thing* had tried.

Glimmers of spent magic sparkled out of the corner of my eye. Under the sigil's influence, the intruder left a shimmering slug trail of dark energy. I painted a few sigils for safety on my arm, but that was all the protection my weakened powers offered.

A panicked chirrup caused my heartbeat to skip, and I bolted into the living room to face the intruder.

Or not face him. He didn't have one. A mass of undulating robes whipped in an unfelt breeze. The wraith sensed me and whirled, its hood as empty as eternity. In his fist, he clutched Keet. Droppings oozed through his spectral fingers, but he didn't seem to mind.

"Release him," I ordered, advancing on the wraith. "Let him go, and I won't banish you."

I didn't have the strength to banish a wraith, but the wraith's master didn't have to know that.

Rather than back down, the creature pulled a smoking envelope from the depths of its robes and passed it between the bars of the empty cage. Before I settled on a plan of action, he popped Keet like a snack into his absent mouth and vanished in a whirl of black mist.

"Keet."

I spun in a circle, my mind touching on every corner of the collapsing wards, but I already knew what I'd find.

Keet was gone.

I SPENT the better part of an hour restoring the wards and rousing Woolly from her drugged slumber. The fact my *house* could be knocked unconscious terrified me. Whoever had controlled the wraith had managed to slip inside with a nasty bit of work that over-lapped one of the weakened points in the wards.

I snapped pictures of the combined sigils the intruder had used to gain access so I could show Odette later, then scrubbed the foul ink until red bubbles frothed through my fingers. The anchor wards surrounding Woolworth House were carved into the stone of her foundation. A little bit of blood shouldn't have overpowered inset patterns woven together by a master necromancer, but these had, and I worried this was more proof the old girl's strength mirrored mine.

At least my puny magic wasn't at fault for the breakdown in communication between Woolly and me. As it turned out, someone had eroded key points in the sigils that had slowly eaten away at our link until the only time I registered the interference was when I made a focused effort to check the wards.

Flicking the light on my phone, I started the grueling process of examining the foundation. I didn't have to look far before I spotted the first missing sigil, gouged from the stone with sharp claws. Great. Permanent damage. How was I supposed to repair this? It's not like I could lift up Woolly and slide a new slab under her.

I found five more missing sigils that corresponded with the thinning of the wards I'd been sensing over the past several days. For now, the best I could do was dip my brush and swipe on fresh symbols. Those would keep until it rained, or at least until the dew faded them.

After examining the patchwork wards with a critical eye, I decided they would do and capped my ink.

As much as I hated leaving Woolly while she was vulnerable, I had to honor my promise to Amelie. We both needed our jobs, and being Haints paid better than anything else we could do while keeping our night-owl schedule.

I trudged up the steps and entered the house. "Will you be okay for a few hours?"

The foyer chandelier dimmed to near blackness before surging.

"You have nothing to be ashamed of." I patted the doorframe. "This is my fault. I should have pulled my head out of my butt sooner." All that wallowing hadn't gotten me anything except a violated home and a stolen pet. "If I had taken the minor attacks more seriously, I might have noticed the damage to the sigils before the wraith..." I spun on my heel, thought trailing, marched to Keet's empty cage and fished out the envelope. "Why am I not surprised?"

A nearby floor register ticked on and set a curtain wriggling in anticipation.

"It's from Dame Lawson," I told her, and opened the envelope with care. "Guess I didn't RSVP fast enough for her." I skimmed the first line then read the rest aloud for Woolly's benefit. "Dearest Grier, I do hope you'll reconsider my previous invitation. Being named the Grande Dame of the Society for Post-Death Management is a momentous occasion, and I expect all my family to be in attendance. That includes you. Our relationship has been strained these past few years, but I hope to rectify that soon. Proof of my good intentions should be evident by now. You are standing in your own living room, reading this letter, are you not? You can thank me for that with your presence."

The tinkle of crystals in the chandelier laughed at her gall in claiming me now that I'd been exonerated.

Again, I rolled the vampire's warning around in my head. What did Dame Lawson want from me? What did *he* want? Why did anyone want anything from me at all when I had nothing but the clothes on my back and the roof over my head to my name?

Dame Lawson hadn't just dispatched one of her lackeys to leave her calling card. Whoever the architect of this infiltration was, he was brilliant. And the energy, now that I'd had time to reflect, had definitely been male.

With those grim thoughts circling, I walked into the kitchen, scooped up the invitation, and dialed the gas burner high on the stove. Then I took Boaz's advice and burned them both to cinders.

The floor register gusted air in a relieved sigh as I swirled the ashes down the sink.

"We ought to be safe. For now." A tired exhale parted my lips. "They got what they wanted. A hostage."

The letter hadn't mentioned poor Keet, but it would have been incriminating if it had, and you didn't get to be the Grande Dame by making such rudimentary errors. The message was clear. Her wraith postman had done his job well, proving she could get to me and mine inside the wards, inside the house. But why she would demand my presence at all stumped me.

I was a half-trained assistant with no title and no prospects. The Society had already added my inheritance to their coffers. They had seized control of my assets at my sentencing. Woolly had been the only thing I fought tooth and nail to keep. At the time, she had been flush with Maud's power, and no one but me could have given her to another master without her consent. So, really, that had less to do with my wishes and more to do with hers.

A sliver of fear pierced me through the heart. What if that was the game? Letting her rot these past few years without a necromancer tending her wards? Woolly was weak, a shadow of her former self, but she would fight a new master to her death, of that I was sure. But did the Society care?

Woolly was more than a house, more than my family. Her basement was a library full of books written in Maud's own hand. Her entire brilliant career, every experiment, every memory, every theory, penned in leather-bound volumes. The collection was priceless, and the magical locks protecting her life's work could *not* be shattered without Maud's blood. And that was long gone.

"I'll be back as soon as my shift ends," I comforted the house. "You remember how to use the phone?"

The landline was a luxury I almost couldn't afford, but the connection to me soothed her.

"Call if you need me." I checked to make sure my cell was fully charged. "I promise I'll come straight home tonight. No pit stops."

The phone in my hand blared Miranda Lambert's "The House That Built Me," and my heart cracked open wider. She didn't want me to go. For once, her paranoia was founded. But that didn't change the fact that I couldn't hole up here forever. We needed money to keep the power on and the pantry stocked. And though I would never say so to her, Dame Lawson had proven I was no safer here than I was out in the wide world.

"I'll start making inquiries, see if I can't find someone willing to help me repair the foundation." Odette was my best bet. Others would ask more of me than I could give. "Just sit tight."

The old house creaked a pitiful sound that stoked the fire smoldering in my belly.

"Everything is going to be okay," I promised her, and I hoped it wasn't a lie.

Leaving her unguarded made me feel just as helpless and alone as Dame Lawson had no doubt intended.

The ride to work blurred, and the tours dragged into eternity. Tips were low, more salt in the wound. I couldn't blame my victims, though. Tonight my heart wasn't in spooking people, not when I had been so thoroughly spooked myself, and it showed. On my way out the door, I paused to beg a favor of Neely then cut a path through the gloomy parking lot.

I pulled up short when I noticed a man inspecting Jolene with a covetous eye. No, not a man. A vampire. The one whose warning had come too late. "Not you again."

"I had one of these once." His pale fingers stroked the leather seat. "A long time ago."

"Good for you." I jingled my keys in my palm. "Step aside." I wasn't about to get close to him while I was defenseless. "I need to get home."

"Have you given any more thought to what we discussed?" He glanced up, quicksilver eyes flashing. "You seem like a nice girl, and I don't like breaking pretty things."

"That escalated quickly." I balled my fists to hide their trembling. "Is this a *three strikes, you're out* kind of a deal?"

"You received an invitation." He sidestepped answering me. "Are you going to accept?"

As well-informed as he appeared to be, I didn't see the harm in telling him the truth. "I don't have much choice."

"The inauguration is in two days." He scuffed a black cowboy boot on the pavement. "I'll give you twenty-four hours to decide if my master sends you a car and driver or if he sends me instead."

"Clan Volkov has offered me an alliance with their heritor." The thin bluff was all the protection I could muster. "Danill won't be pleased to hear another clan is threatening an interest of his."

The vampire smiled, fangs on display. "I can hear your mother in your voice."

The barb struck home. "How do you know my mother?"

"There are a lot of things I know about you, Grier. Maybe I'll tell you a few of them sometime." He tipped the brim of an imaginary hat and strolled across the lot into the shadows. "Night, ma'am."

Wait.

I had to snap my jaw shut to keep the word from escaping, but my arm shot out all on its own, fingers curling with the urge to call him back. It was a trick. It had to be. Mom had no family left, and Maud and Odette were the only friends she had mentioned. This male was a predator, and he read in me a weakness he could exploit. That was all.

I climbed on Jolene and sped away before curiosity got the better of me.

Woolly gusted a sigh of relief in the form of rattling floor registers when I walked through the front door.

"All's well?" I padded to the empty birdcage and stared at the swing like that might bring Keet back. "No trouble while I was gone?"

The floorboards groaned a nervous affirmation.

"I'm going to walk the perimeter." I pocketed the bottle of ink and the brush just in case. "I want to get another look at things before I call it a day."

The front door stuck a bit on my way out, but she let me go. Three hours later, dawn was a pink smudge on the horizon, and I was still clearing away the brittle vines and lichen covering the foundation to better see the etched sigils when the gate creaked behind me.

"What are you doing out here?" Amelie drifted closer. "I figured you'd be in bed by now."

"Not that I mind you skulking through my yard at dawn when you think I'm asleep—" I grunted as I stood "—but do I get to know the reason?"

"Boaz." She hiccupped a sob. "He's been drafted."

"Drafted." The word, so unexpected, stumped me. Try as I might, I couldn't draw a straight line between that word and his name. "But he's already in the army."

"No, not the army." She wiped her cheeks with the backs of her hands. "The sentinels."

Cold sweat beaded down my spine as memories of black-clad enforcers prowling darkened hallways surfaced. Batons in hand, they'd clanged the metal rods against the bars, against fingers, often breaking them, when inmates woke from their stupors long enough to plead for mercy that was never granted.

"They draft from the Low Society to fill their ranks, but he was passed over when he was eighteen." Crossing to me in a daze, she rested her head on my shoulder, and I wrapped my arms around her. "We thought he was safe."

"Until he came home fully trained," I finished for her, a shudder in my breath.

I ought to be used to fate kicking me when I was down, but this... I just got Boaz back. I didn't want to lose him again so soon.

"Mom got a letter a few days ago. I brought it to her while she was dusting, and she broke the crystal bowl Gran got her as a wedding gift. It slipped through her fingers while she read." As the matron of their family, the news would have gone to her and not him. "Turns out Boaz wasn't given leave. He was discharged. The paperwork got pushed through right after he left. He didn't believe it until he called his commander to verify."

The Society had ended his career with a letter, and he would despise them for that. Like he needed another reason.

"They won't station him at Atramentous," she said, like that made this any better. "He protested when you were taken. He was arrested twice. Bet he didn't tell you that." She gave a watery laugh. "He was on a watch list for a while. That's why our folks encouraged him to join the army. They wanted him as far away from the Society as possible."

"That idiot," I murmured against her hair, my heart swelling.

"He really is." She sniffled. "But he's an asset, and they're willing to overlook his record."

I bit my lip to keep from asking again what exactly the army had had him doing, but she wouldn't rat him out, and he wasn't ready to share.

"What do your parents think?" I held her at arm's length. "Can your mom...?"

"No." Her bottom lip trembled. "She told us tonight she's been fighting it for the past two years, since before he re-upped. She thought that might keep him out of their clutches, but it's no use. Dad has a sterling service record, and Boaz followed in his footsteps. You know how big the Society is on bloodlines. They expect families to stay pigeonholed."

"Plus, he can't cause them trouble if he's somewhere they can monitor him."

Amelie went quiet, and again I wondered what I was missing.

As much as I had looked forward to spilling my guts when she got home, I couldn't dump my problems on top of hers while she was one sob away from shattering. My troubles would keep for another day.

"Want me to walk you home?" I dusted off my knees and my hands. "I can regale you with tales from the tours you missed, including that goth bridal shower." I didn't wait for an answer but flung my arm around her shoulders and aimed us toward her house. "I had to confiscate a dead pigeon from the maid of honor. I don't know where she got it. I didn't ask. All I could think was I didn't want to witness her biting its head off or worse."

She leaned her head against mine. "I always miss the good stuff."

I escorted her home, and she stole another hug before vanishing inside the house.

"Grier," a weathered voice rasped. "Do you have a minute?"

"Mr. Pritchard." I whirled toward the driveway and the older man standing there. "Hi."

"Amelie told you the news." His sigh conveyed his thoughts on the draft. "We worried this day might come. Boaz is a good man, a good soldier, but he's reckless and pigheaded and bighearted too. It's a dangerous combination."

Unsure what response he wanted from me, I stood there and listened while he vented.

"They're going to send him away. There are no prisons near here that require his...specialty." He shifted his weight from one foot to the other. "You three have always been as thick as thieves, and I know this is going to be hard on Amelie and on you."

"Yes, sir." On that we agreed. "Boaz is one of my best friends. I'll miss him."

"I'm glad to hear you call him a friend, that things haven't..." he coughed once into his fist, "...progressed."

Oh, to be a specter and able to turn invisible at will.

"We only have to look as far as your house to find him these days." He spread the fingers of one hand. "I just don't want to see either of you get hurt. Long-distance relationships are hard. You can ask his mother about that. She didn't see much of me for the first three years of our marriage. I came home a stranger to a stranger. We had grown up, grown apart, and it took a dedicated effort on our part to mend our relationship."

Theirs had been an arranged marriage, one of the few good matches I could name, but that left them no choice except to mend those bridges. Divorces were taboo among Society members. Lifetime estrangement from spouses were far more common, and the details much juicier besides.

A cold stone dropped into my stomach. "I see."

"Me too," Boaz drawled from behind me. "Thanks for the pep talk, Dad. Grier and I can take this from here."

Father and son entered a staring contest over my head, and I got the feeling Mr. Pritchard lost since he backed down first. Turning on his heel, he marched into the house with a stiff set to his shoulders. The class divide had kept the Pritchards from embracing me as they had Amelie's other friends. Factor in my raging crush on Boaz, an attachment Maud had been willing to humor so long as it wasn't reciprocal, and I got how they might have viewed me as a ticking time bomb of teenage hormones.

It just sucked they were apparently still waiting for me to go *boom*.

"Walk you home?" He offered his arm like a gentleman. "I could use the exercise after being cooped up in a car all night." I hooked my arm through his but kept a respectable distance between us. After we crossed the property line, he murmured, "So."

"So," I said in agreement. "When do you leave?" I forced myself not to haul him closer to prove he was still here. "Did they give you an estimate or...?"

"Two weeks."

"Two weeks."

"Is there an echo out here?" He jabbed me in the ribs. "Stop feeding me my words and dish out some of your own."

"You want the truth?" Asking was a formality. I already knew his answer.

"Always."

"I hate that you're leaving. I wish you could stay. I don't want you to go."

"You're going to make me blush." He tugged me closer until our sides were flush. "If I'd known the draft was what it took to win you over, I would have volunteered a long time ago."

"Liar." I snorted a laugh. "You keep trying to twist things around, but *I'm* the one who nursed a crush for like ten years. You probably wouldn't have noticed I was gone if I hadn't sprouted boobs there at the end."

"That's not true. What happened to you—" The muscles in his arm tightened beneath my hand. "Forget I said anything. I know you don't want to talk about it."

"I'm getting there." For the first time, it felt like that might not be a lie. "You better get back before your dad sends out a rescue party." I unlinked our arms. "Try not to be too hard on him, okay?"

"The old coot is trying to scare you off," he said, incredulous. "That is not okay."

"He's got a point." As much as I hated to see the hurt flash in Boaz's eyes, there was no denying that. "I can't leave Woolly, and you can't stay. Army or the sentinels, you have to leave either way."

After all these years of pining after him, I wasn't sure I had much more patience left in me.

I was done waiting for my life to start. I wanted to live while I could in case this taste of freedom soured.

"I hate when you use logic against me." Quick as a flash, he stole a kiss from me, just a brush of his lips that set mine tingling. "Good thing I'm too stubborn for that nonsense to stick."

"Y-you kissed me," I stammered.

"That's not a kiss." His knuckles scored a line down my cheek. "However, I am willing to demonstrate the proper method. With tongue."

My very first kiss, and from the glint in his eyes, he knew it too. *Jerk.* Yet he claimed he didn't count. Fine. Neither would I.

"Go home, Boaz." I shoved him back with a palm to his chest. "Next time, keep your lips to yourself."

"What fun would that be?" His cocky grin resurfaced. "You taste like cinnamon."

"And you taste like the breath mint you popped knowing you were going to put the moves on me."

"Ouch." He clutched his chest. "You wound me. Can't a man be both minty fresh *and* spontaneous with his affection?"

"Buh-bye."

I waved him off and headed inside the house. The empty bird-cage stood in the corner of the living room like an accusation. Keet hadn't been with us long this time, but his absence radiated through the silent room stained with a psychic oil spill from where the wraith had lingered while he left his message.

There was nothing left but to wait out the inauguration. When the bird poop would really hit the fan.

SIX

Cinderella was never going to be my favorite fairy tale. That whole scrubbing until your fingers pruned and blistered did *not* appeal. But, as dry and cracked as my hands were from all the rubbing, digging and scraping around Woolly's foundation, I glowed with a sense of accomplishment. I had been lacking a purpose since my return, besides the daily grind of survival, but it seemed I'd found a project to occupy me.

Woolly was getting a defensive overhaul. All I needed was a smidgen of guidance to get me started.

But a visit to Odette would have to wait. I had more pressing obligations this fine Monday night. As in, I planned to press Volkov for every scrap of information he could give me on my stalker. Who he might be, what he might want, what master pulled his strings. And how Mom fit into his equation.

With Amelie's help, I had dressed to thrill in a swishy sundress I hoped would win me points with Volkov. Figurative ones. Not fangs. She had piled my hair on top of my head in a half twist that left tendrils framing my face. A few deft strokes of concealer hid the bags growing darker under my eyes, and the gloss she swiped over my lips plumped what little I had to work with in that department. The matching ballet flats kept the look casual, but I hadn't been this done up in ages outside of work, and it felt good to be both girly and able to breathe at the same time.

I spun out the front door, humming a popular country song, and smacked into a wall of vampire.

"*Oof*" didn't sound sexy, no matter how dolled up you were.

"I thought we agreed to meet at the fountain." As per his texted instructions. I scooted forward and pulled the door shut behind me, not that it would stop Woolly if she wanted to invite him in later. "Did I misunderstand?"

"I was in the neighborhood..." The obvious lie caused his lips to curve with amusement when he noticed my budding scowl. "Perhaps it is more honest to say I made certain I was in the neighborhood."

A sleek black car awaited us at the end of my driveway, and the same thin male dressed in a black suit held open the rear passenger door. His jaunty chauffer's hat made me grin. "Ma'am."

"Fancy," I teased Volkov, who shrugged as though his wealth and my perception of it didn't bother him.

A male comfortable in his own skin. I admired that. Particularly since his skin was built to weather eternity.

I ducked inside and breathed in the new-leather smell. Forget eternal life, this right here was a perk worth not-dying for.

Volkov joined me, and I realized my mistake. His scent drifted around me, much more potent in an enclosed space, and my gut clenched. I was eyeballing the bench seat and wondering if he had ever gotten friendly with a "just friend" back here, when he scooted until our thighs brushed and put his arm behind me.

At my side, I gave the bangle a subtle shake like it was a glow stick in need of activating.

"Where does the tour begin?" His fingertips toyed with my shoulder, and he released a contented sigh as the car pulled out into traffic.

The more he relaxed, the tighter I wound until I couldn't stop my leg from bouncing. "This isn't a date, is it?"

"Do you want it to be?" he flung back at me.

Do you want to date the nice vampire would eventually segue into *Do you want to feed the nice vampire,* and the answer was, "No."

"Then we will remain friends." He frowned down at our proximity and gave his head a little shake. "My apologies." His fingers circled my wrist, his thumb stroking the skin, the veins, under the bangle. "The sight of blood arouses." A growl roughened his voice. "The sight of you wearing mine..." He loosened his fingers one by one, as if the effort cost him, and rested his palm flat on his thigh. "I was unprepared for the effect."

"It's fine." I tried not to think about how we still pressed together from hip to knee. At least now my stomach had settled. "How about we get things started?" I swallowed my nerves and donned my tour-guide persona. "I can't say I've narrated a driving tour, but I'm sure I can manage." I twisted a bit to give myself a few precious inches of breathing room and picked the first landmark I recognized. "See that pub? It's a favorite of all the locals. You don't find too many tourists there. Too smoky, too loud and too wild on ladies' night."

"You sound as if you're speaking from experience."

"Did I mention the likelihood of them carding you goes lower as your hem goes higher?"

Following Boaz like a love-struck puppy had given me one heck of an education in more ways than one.

Volkov raked his gaze over me, assessing. "How old are you?"

Curiosity pulsed behind the words, and I wondered how often he interacted with my kind—or humans for that matter. Necromancers commanded respect. Humans, on the other hand, were food, their lives too short for most vampires to take notice of them.

"Twenty-one." Old enough to barhop without the fake ID for a change.

"So young," he murmured.

"How old are you?"

"Thirty-five," he admitted. "Does that make you uncomfortable?"

"Age is just a number between friends," I assured him, unwilling to consider the true issue.

"So it is." His rich chuckle rewarded me. "Can I ask if I'm your only friend with a sun allergy?"

"You can, and you are." I fiddled with his bangle, which snapped his gaze to my wrist. Slowly, before I compounded my faux pas, I slid my hand out of sight to avoid the temptation to fidget. "I do, however, have a stalker of the undead variety."

With Volkov pressed so close, I felt his thigh muscles tense. "What do you mean?"

"A vampire was waiting for me when I got home from work the night I met you." I outlined our conversation and his threats from the parking lot too. "Any clue who he might represent?"

"Without a name, it's impossible to guess." He drummed his fingers on his knee. "You're a valuable asset, Grier. All the clans with means will be in contact with you in the coming days. Of that I'm certain. It could be that this male represents a clan without the funds or clout to win you over by traditional means and seeks to intimidate you."

"Do I get to know why everyone wants a piece of me all of a sudden?"

"It's not my place." Frustration turned his comment bitter. "You'll learn soon enough, and when you do, you'll understand why an alliance will be beneficial to you, and why remaining unallied will only encourage more such incidents."

Thinking back on what Odette told me, I had to be certain he and I were on the same page. "You're talking about me marrying for protection."

"Yes."

"And you're okay with your master offering you up on a silver platter?"

"You're beautiful, kind and intelligent. I could do far worse." He sobered. "Do you understand how the vampiric clan system operates?"

"I understand basic vampire biology and how the undead caste system works. The rest wasn't a concern of mine. I was being trained as an assistant and not as a practitioner."

A peculiar expression swept over his features before he smoothed them. "Last Seeds are a caste unto themselves, but we are loyal to the clan that bred us. For me, that was Clan Volkov. I'm the first Last Seed my line has produced in centuries. I will outlive them all, and that makes it my sworn duty to oversee the protection, growth and wellbeing of the clan. As the youngest born vampire, I am the heritor, but one day soon, I will be named master."

I gulped audibly, and his eyes tracked the motion as my throat worked. "You've got the wrong girl for the job, Mr. Volkov."

A clan master's wife I was not. I could barely take care of myself, let alone hundreds of undead.

"Danill," he insisted. "You're young, but you're strong. I would be proud to have you at my side."

"Until I turned old and gray," I mumbled. "I'll be honest here. I'm not sure I could handle aging while you stay young and gorgeous. I'm not a vain person, I don't think, but it would poison me from the inside out if I had to know you were entertaining younger, more beautiful women on the side."

"Our vows are sacred." He shifted to look at me head-on. "Accept my offer, and you accept me for who and what I am as I will accept you for who and what you are. I will be yours until your dying breath, and I vow I will never injure your pride or your heart."

"I was just granted my freedom. I can't toss it away without a good reason, and you can't give me one."

"I am under orders I can't break." His gaze skittered to the window. "No matter how much I might wish to gain the advantage with you, I am bound to silence."

A concern niggled at the back of my mind, and it popped out

before I could filter my mouth. "Heritors are answerable only to their masters...and the Grande Dame of the Society."

"See what I mean? Intelligent." His slow smile held a razor's edge. "You are also correct."

Black spots danced in my vision at what he wasn't telling me. The Grande Dame had anticipated the offer his master and the others would make, and she must have put orders in place to hobble their efforts as much as possible. Meaning she intended to make an offer herself. Not good. Not good at all.

I took a moment to study his profile while his attention was fixated elsewhere. "Will you attend the inauguration tomorrow night?"

"I have no choice." Catching the slip-up, he amended with, "It's my pleasure to witness history in the making as the first Grande Dame of my generation is named."

I snorted out a laugh. "You sound about as happy as I am to be going."

"Born vampires aren't allowed much socialization outside our clans until we reach our majority. You're the first necromancer I've engaged in conversation. Are your kind not the community-minded group they present themselves to be?" His bland delivery informed me he was well aware of what dangerous waters he treaded. "Isn't that the point of calling themselves a Society?"

"We have a *Grande Dame*." I shook my head. "Necromancers are all about the prestige. The Society for Post-Death Management sounds more upscale and corporate than Will Raise the Dead for Cash, Inc."

A rich, dark laugh broke from his chest. "You have more reason than most to resent their antiquated hierarchy."

"They aren't all bad. The High Society is the most ridiculous. The Low Society is more relatable."

"Interesting," he mused. "I would have thought being raised by Maud Woolworth would have ensured the exact opposite."

"I came into the culture late in life by their standards. My formal education started when I was five, which put me years behind my High Society peers. Factor in my public school education, which exposed me to humans and Low Society as my classmates, and I grew into too much of my own person to conform."

Stubborn as the day is long—*just like your mother*—that was Maud's favorite lament.

"Plus, Maud was not the conformist type. Dame Lawson despaired of me, the orphan her sister had adopted. She was determined the Woolworth heir act like a lady. She doesn't have any daughters, only her son, Linus. She played with me like a doll until she grew bored with her attempts at taming me. She stuck bows in my hair I ripped out when her back turned, and I wore shorts under my skirts so I could strip them off after dinner and run outside to play. Maud just laughed and told her sister *girls will be girls*."

"You are not close to Dame Lawson then?"

"No."

There was nothing more I could say about her that wouldn't plunge me into the abyss. All my memories of that woman were strung on a thread that tied to the same fixed point in time, the worst night of my life, her recent antics included. What started as rage over what she'd ordered done to Woolly morphed to grief over Keet's abduction which spun my thoughts back to the last time I'd faced her in the Lyceum along with the other society dames and matrons.

I hadn't come out on top then, and I doubted I'd climb to new heights tomorrow. All signs pointed toward new lows being in the forecast. At least I would get my bird back.

Perhaps sensing the taut wire of my temper vibrating, he set about defusing my anger. "What can you tell me about that building?"

Though it took a moment to relocate my tour-guide persona, I reapplied her within seconds, a trick learned from Amelie.

"The Black Hart was built in the early 1800s. It went by another name then, White Sparrow's Tavern." The spiel tumbled out with practiced ease, and I took comfort in the cadence of the story.

"Patrons swear the building is haunted by the original owner, Brutus Sparrow, who bricked his mistress up in the basement when she tried to leave him. Folks claim he loved her so much that when she made amends with her husband, he slit her throat and walled up her corpse so he could keep her forever. Even now his wails of grief at having killed the love of his life can be heard on clear nights. And a few have even seen her wandering the halls, dressed in a filmy white nightgown slicked with blood from the gash in her throat."

"What about that one?" Volkov indicated the mom and pop grocery store where I liked to buy fresh fruit. "Surely there can't be horror attached to such a wholesome place."

"You would be wrong." I took his dare merrily. "The same family has owned the property since the 1920s. A Cat 1 hurricane hit Beaufort, South Carolina, in September of 1928, and it produced more than a foot of rain that caused significant flooding in Savannah. Only this end of town escaped unscathed. Everything from River Street down was underwater, including the hospital. Newspaper clippings tell us that since the market was the largest structure standing, it was cleared out and cots were brought in to aid the victims." I wiggled my fingers at him. "According to the current owners, some mornings they go in to open the store and find lights on and objects moved by the restless spirits who perished there and the brave souls who fought to save them."

"Remarkable."

"This town is mired in creepy. All old cities are if you dig deep enough."

"I don't mean the town." His fingers brushed my arm. "I mean you."

"Friends don't let friends flatter unnecessarily." I popped his hand. "Bad vampire."

"I braced for the worst." He made a vague gesture. "I expected you to be…"

"Bitter? Reclusive? Insane?"

"Yes," he agreed with a wince.

"Finish your thought." I waved him on. "I can take it."

"I came to you prepared to sacrifice myself for my clan, but I see now I was a fool to doubt my master's wisdom. What he asked of me is no sacrifice at all."

"I'm broken, Danill." As a maybe friend or possible ally, I owed him that truth. "I'm held together with bubble gum, and the next time life chews me up and spits me out, this sanity thing might not stick."

He clasped my hands between his much larger ones. "I can't protect you from the teeth—life grinds us all down—but you will discover in time I am exceptional when it comes to sticking around."

"We're friends until you do something jackassy that makes me break up with you. Or I do." I extricated myself from his grasp before I gave him the wrong idea. "There's a solid fifty-fifty chance one of us will blow this."

"I'll take a fifty-fifty shot over none at all." He settled back against the seat, content. "Who will you bring with you to the inauguration? The friend I met?"

"Boaz?" I imagined him on my arm, his warmth thawing the chill in my heart, but the image flickered into him vaulting from the amphitheater's lush marble floor into the stadium-like seats, where he'd strangle the new Grande Dame with her own pantyhose. "No. Definitely not." I had already lost him to the draft. I wasn't about to let him commit treason. "I plan on going stag."

"Would you consider a formal escort rather than a date?"

"Call me paranoid, but I'm ninety-nine-point-nine percent sure tomorrow night will spell my doom in all caps." A date, escort, whatever, would also get in the way of her negotiating with me for Keet's safe return. "You don't want to get mixed up in this, not when she has pull with your clan and can make your life miserable until she kicks the bucket."

"What is one century in the span of my lifetime?" The tips of his fangs, lengthening with his desire to protect—probably another side effect of wearing his blood as a fashion statement—pressed into his bottom lip. "Let me prove my worth. Let me show you the value in my offer. Let me give you, at least for one night, the comfort of having a clan at your back." His voice lowered. "You don't have to face her alone, and unlike your friend, I can behave." He rolled a wide shoulder. "Within reason."

Arriving with Volkov on my arm would make a statement, and it would be nice not to face the firing squad alone.

"Okay." I stuck out my hand, and his engulfed mine when we shook. "It's not a date."

SEVEN

My stalkerpire failed to put in his threatened appearance, but that likely had more to do with the two slabs of beef Volkov ordered to stand guard at my front door the rest of the night and into the next day than any change of heart. Neither male would meet my eyes, but when I checked on them before bed, they addressed me with a quiet reverence that unsettled me.

Apparently my value was a well-known commodity to everyone. Except me.

Or, I had to allow, it was possible they merely protected that which their heritor deemed valuable. They might have done the same for any woman who found herself in Volkov's crosshairs. How awkward that must make dating for him. I could stand the cage he'd lowered around me for now, until I got my answers at the inauguration, but I would suffocate beneath such precautions over time. Having known the inside of a cell intimately, I had promised myself never to return to one. No matter how well-intended the protection might be.

Plus, it was downright humiliating when the bodyguards stampeded up the stairs and bulldozed into my room at dusk after they heard me screaming in my sleep. Waking up to two vamps—fangs out —hissing at shadows in my room was almost worse than traversing the dark and twisting dreamscape of my mind.

Well, I had warned Volkov I was broken, right? Maybe evidence of exactly how shattered would send him running.

An *all's well* chime rang out, and I fought a losing battle with a grin as my company arrived.

"Damn, girl. This is your house?" Neely gawked on the front porch. "It's gorgeous."

"Thanks." The porchlight near him flickered the tiniest bit as Woolly preened, and I cleared my throat loudly to remind her not to show off in front of our very human guest. "Come on in."

"What's the deal with your bookends?" he asked once the door shut behind him and his rolling bag. "They look like bodyguards." His eyes rounded. "*Are* they bodyguards?"

I winced and told a half-truth. "The guy I'm dating is overprotective."

And the vamps, after my screaming episode, had refused to budge from their posts during Neely's visit. They were already dead. It wouldn't have killed them to hide in the bushes for a couple of hours.

"Are we talking celebrity protective? Political-figure protective?" He glanced over his shoulder like he could still feel their eyes on him. "Or are we talking mob protective?" He lowered his voice. "Do you need help? Tug your earlobe once for yes and twice for no."

"*Neely*." I burst out laughing. "Danill Volkov is a lot of things, but a mob boss is not one of them." I twisted the truth, an ugly necessity around humans, yet again. "A strange man was spotted on my property after our first date. Considering who he is, he's concerned for my safety is all."

"*Volkov?*" he squeaked, dropping his bag's handle and grabbing me by the shoulders. He shook me until my eyes rattled. "Are you insane? Volkov House is a shrine to that family's obsession to acquire what they want at any price. And that was just a charred pile of lumber."

Chills blasted up my arms for reasons I couldn't pinpoint. I was aware of the house's bloody history, and I had an inkling of Volkov's clout, though it would help if I could access Woolly's basement to get at the library, but Neely's perceptiveness had switched on a light in my head that wouldn't fade anytime soon.

Before I wrapped my mouth around a defense of Volkov's honor, Woolly chimed again. This time there was a trill of excitement in the sound I hoped Neely would blame on bad wiring.

"Hold that thought." I scrambled to the front door, half-expecting to find one of the siblings Pritchard, but a third vampire stood on the porch wearing a familiar jaunty hat with a garment bag slung over his shoulder. *It's official. Woolworth House is infested.* "Hi. Can I help you?"

"Mr. Volkov sends his regards, miss." He slid the bag down his arm then offered it to me. "And this."

"What is...?" Through the peephole near the zipper, I spied silky blue fabric. "He bought me a dress?"

"Apologies, miss, if this seems too forward." He extended his arms farther, careful not to reach across the threshold. "The invitations went out late by the usual standards, and he worried you might not have had an opportunity to shop for the occasion."

Or the funds for a dress as extravagant as my former rank required. None of the gowns in my closet still fit. Not even a corset could save me. Borrowing from Amelie had been my only option, but the simple cut and serviceable materials were the Low Society equivalent of a uniform, albeit a lovely one, and I would have stood out like a sore thumb amid the High Society glam.

With one thoughtful gesture, Volkov had spared me from cutting remarks hidden behind jewel-encrusted hands and mocking laughter they wouldn't have bothered to hide at all. I didn't want to like him for it, not when I knew he had an agenda where I was concerned, but I appreciated his thoughtfulness all the same.

"Tell Mr. Volkov I appreciate his generosity." I accepted the bag before the driver could drape it over my shoulder to be rid of its responsibility. "I look forward to seeing him tonight."

The driver executed a tight bow, turned on his heel and left.

I shut the door and bounced off Neely's chest. The little eavesdropper.

"He bought you a dress." Neely snatched the bag and hung it on a coat hook. "You don't find him dressing you a tad bit, oh, I don't know, *possessive?* Have you ever watched *Pretty Woman?*"

"I'm broke, not a hooker." I shouldered him aside and glided down the zipper. "Volkov is saving me from embarrassing myself—and him—by showing up in hand-me-downs."

A clatter drew my eye to the kitchen. Amelie stood there with a rose from my garden in one hand, its petals the same pink as the dress she'd loaned me, and one strappy shoe dangled from the other. Its mate must have slipped through her fingers when I insulted her generosity.

"Guess you won't be needing these." Voice tight, she tossed the rose on the coffee table and collected the fallen shoe. "I'll be around later in case you want to talk when you get home."

"Amelie..." I reached for her, but she bolted, the door slamming behind her. "I didn't realize she was there."

"She knocked on the back door while you were talking to the driver. I didn't think you'd mind if I let her in." He crossed the room and lifted the rose to his face. "She took the back way around so she could trim a boutonniere for your date."

I hung my head as shame washed through me. "I didn't mean it to come out like that."

The difference in our classes had never mattered to me. I didn't mind the dress so much as I hated that I couldn't provide for myself, let alone on the level I had grown accustomed to as Maud's heir. Borrowing reminded me of all I had lost, but this... There was no excuse for hurting Amelie. None.

Maybe I had lied to Volkov if all it took was a handful of sequins to show me Atramentous hadn't cured me of my vanity after all.

"She's your best friend." Neely returned to me and tapped me on the nose with the silky rosebud. "She'll forgive you. Just don't give her time to stew, and make sure you take her up on her offer."

"I will," I promised, staring out the windows at the rear of the house like I might catch a glimpse of her.

"Let's see this dress." He nudged me with his shoulder. "We have two hours to get you ready for your date, and I don't even know what I'm working with yet."

"You do the honors." The unveiling didn't seem as enticing as it had a minute ago.

"You don't have to tell me twice." He plunged his hands into the open bag and hauled the dress out with one smooth flip of his wrists. Silver and gold beadwork studded the sleeveless top portion, which rose in an elegant high collar while the royal-blue skirt flared in filmy layers. A matching silk wrap draped the left shoulder. The breath he sucked in mirrored mine, and he cackled at a note pinned to the bodice. "I believe this is for you."

"*Red is my favorite color,*" I read aloud, "*but blue reminds me of the night we met.*"

"Aww. That's so sweet," Neely cooed as he lifted out a silver evening bag. "Maybe Grill should be a thing."

"Grill?"

"Grier and Danill?" He rolled his hand. "Honestly, it's like you know nothing about fandom."

"Five minutes ago, you were telling me crazy is hereditary, and now you're shipping us?"

"Crazy *is* hereditary." He held up a finger. "But look what I found in the bottom of the bag."

"Oh." My fingers curled to touch the strappy silver kitten heels. "Those are nice."

"Nice? *Nice?*" He wiped his thumb across my bottom lip. "Sorry, you had a speck of drool there."

I batted his hand away with a snort. "Okay, so I have a weakness for strappy shoes with sensible heels."

"And I have a weakness for men who put their credit cards where their mouths are."

A fresh shiver zinged through me. Thinking about Volkov's mouth gave me chills, and I wasn't sure they were the good kind. Amelie bit me once after I stole the last cupcake at her seventh birthday party, and I cried for hours. How much worse would full-grown fangs be? And then there was the sucking...

"Come on." Taking my hand, he hauled me into the downstairs bathroom to get started. "Let's tame that bird's nest you call hair."

NEELY REFUSED to let me sneak a peek in the mirror while he worked. After I tried one too many times, he moved us to the kitchen table as punishment, going as far as to draw the blinds so I couldn't catch my reflection either. He trusted me to paint my own nails. Mostly because he decided since he didn't have polish to match my dress that I would have to make due with a clear coat, which he seemed certain even I couldn't botch.

An hour into my makeover, the guards changed. Volkov texted me so I wouldn't worry when I found unfamiliar faces outside the door, and also so Woolly wouldn't evict them on reflex. So far she was tolerant of Volkov and his entourage, which made me more curious than ever why the old house had a soft spot for him. Had Maud known him? His clan? Had she resuscitated one of them? More than one?

Again I wished I could access the basement and research how all this fit, but not even the weakened wards had diminished the strength of the binding on that particular door. Whatever secrets Maud had concealed down there, and there must be thousands scribbled on notecards and tucked like bookmarks into journals, she had wanted to take them with her to her grave.

An hour after that, Neely pronounced me finished and escorted me to the parlor, where an antique mirror leaned against the wall stretching from the floor almost to the ceiling. The woman staring back at me reminded me so much of those old pictures of Mom I had to study the light fixture until I was sure no tears would roll down my cheeks and ruin my makeup.

My hair had grown long during my incarceration, but I'd chopped it off below my shoulder blades with a pair of scissors after I was released. Neely had trimmed those ends before weaving a messy fishtail braid that started where my hair parted on the left and created a thick band that he had woven into an over-the-shoulder style before curling the wavy ends. I'd skimmed enough of Neely's magazines at work on slow nights to recognize the smoky eye treatment responsible for highlighting my wide, tawny eyes. The glossy lips and under-stated makeup gave me a healthy, natural glow that made me radiant.

"You are a miracle worker," I murmured. "I knew you were good, but this is— Are you sure that's me?"

"At work, you're a character. I try to tailor a look to each girl, but it's still an act." He rested his hands on my shoulders and smiled at me through the mirror. "For this, you get to be you. Just a version of you who's had twelve hours of sleep and whose go-to look doesn't always involve a messy bun that resembles the aftermath of a bomb going off on top of her head."

"Thaaanks."

"You're welcome." He grinned like an imp. "Now, let's see how your beau did guessing sizes."

Used to getting indecent with Neely, I stripped down to my panties and bra and let him help me step into the dress. Volkov flat-tered me a bit by purchasing a size too small, but Neely swore at the zipper until he had me contained. Not for the first time, I thanked my time spent as a Haint for teaching me breathing was optional. The shoes fit like a dream, but I kept a pair of waders strung on a hook off the side of the porch for when the spring and winter rains puddled in the yard. He could have gotten an idea of my size from those. I preferred that rationale to him having a foot fetish.

"Keep eating to a minimum, and you ought to be fine," was Neely's final assessment.

However the night unfolded, I doubted I'd have an appetite once Dame Lawson finished with me.

"I owe you for this." I clasped his hands. "How can I repay you?"

"Do you know not all the girls even check their makeup? They couldn't care less how they look or what I've done with them. Others can't be pleased no matter how I try. You're the exception. You're always happy to follow my lead, and you trust me to make you shine." He squeezed my hands. "That's all I need. This..." he swept his hand down my body, "...is soul food for the artist in me."

"Well, be that as it may, I'll try not to feed you too often." I released him before he noticed my sweaty palms. "I don't want to take advantage of our friendship."

That fast my thoughts spun back to Amelie, and a fresh pang of misery stung me. She ought to be here, I felt almost naked without her, but it was my fault she was missing the big send-off.

The front door opened without warning, and I sucked in a sharp breath that made me dizzy in my already restricted gown. There were only two people to whom Woolly had given carte blanche, and one of them would be nursing hurt feelings until I apologized. That left the one person I really, really didn't want to see me dressed up like I was playing princess.

"Damn." Boaz darted his eyes from detail to detail like he couldn't take it all in at once. "You're gorgeous." He gave himself a mental shake. "Jolene ain't gonna cut it tonight, Squirt. Not in that dress."

Or at least I think that's what he said. I was too stunned by the crisp black suit tailored to fit his wide shoulders, the gleam of dress shoes instead of scuffed boots. His wild hair was tamed into a neat crew cut that must have happened within the last half hour since he hadn't mussed it yet.

The pale-pink rosebud threaded through the buttonhole of his lapel left me feeling two inches tall.

"I must have missed the memo." He flicked it when he caught me noticing. "I thought you were borrowing Amelie's pink dress."

I wrapped my arms around myself, wishing for the shawl. I wanted to hide the gown that had inspired awe a minute ago but now caused my stomach to cramp. "What are you doing here?"

"I can't let you go alone." He shoved his hands into his pockets. "I promise to behave."

I choked on a laugh. "I don't believe you."

A throat cleared, and we both winced at having forgotten Neely was in the room with us.

Boaz had that effect on me, always had, probably always would to some degree.

"Boaz, I'm sure you've heard Amelie mention Neely. He works his magic on the Haints each night." I tugged one of my curls, and he glared at me until I lowered my hand. "He was kind enough to help me with my hair and makeup."

"Boaz Pritchard." He stuck out his hand and winked. "I'm your new biggest fan."

"Neely Torres." He blushed when they shook. "Amelie said you're a holy terror, and that I should run in the opposite direction if we ever met."

"Amelie is my kid sister. She tends to exaggerate where I'm concerned." In that moment, Boaz was pure Southern charm. "I'm not so bad once you get to know me."

"He's right," I agreed, earning me a startled glance from brown eyes. "He's worse. Much worse."

"You shouldn't listen to her either," he mock whispered. "She's had a raging crush on me since kindergarten. I used to have to run laps around the playground just to keep this little monkey off my back."

Considering he was right, I didn't have a conversational leg to stand on. *Jerk.*

Woolly chose that moment to quaver out another excited chime, and Neely ducked his head, looking like he wanted to be anywhere other than here. I didn't blame him.

"Expecting someone?" Boaz studied my attire, and I heard the pieces clicking together in his head. "You have a date."

"An escort," I corrected.

"I saw the—" he caught himself "—guards."

"There was an incident the other night." I kept it vague, knowing he would have leapt down my throat for keeping secrets if Neely hadn't been acting as a buffer. "Mr. Volkov left me protection as a deterrent."

"He did, did he." The skin beneath his left eye ticked. "That's him at the door?"

"Pretty sure," I murmured, staring at my hands.

"I'll let myself out the back. I wouldn't want to ruin your grand entrance." He nodded at Neely. "Nice meeting you."

Another chime, a questioning note, rang out as Boaz stormed through the kitchen and into the garden.

"Chin up, sweetheart." Neely draped the shawl around my shoulders then gathered his supplies and rolled them behind him into the living room as we approached the front door. "The rest of the night can't go worse than this."

Oh, if only that were true. This—this was just the first misstep in a night that promised a big fall.

What would Amelie think when she saw Boaz dressed to the nines with nowhere to go and no one to go there with? What had he been thinking showing up unannounced? What was he thinking now? He must have realized the dress came from Volkov. Did that have him wondering what else the heritor might have given me to sway me to his side?

Draped in opulent gifts from Volkov, I felt bought, owned, and the real fun hadn't even started.

EIGHT

The insistent doorbell snapped me out of my shame spiral. Nothing changed the fact I had to attend the inauguration. Dame Lawson had sanctioned a wraith attack on my house, and I planned to hold her accountable. Somehow. And then there was Keet. Was he the bait luring me into a cage of her own design? Did she plan on forcing me to negotiate for his return? Or would she hand him over if I performed the act of dutiful niece on her big day?

Snorting, I somehow doubted I'd wriggle off her hook that easily.

"Are you ready?" Neely positioned his rolling bag near the door then beamed. "You're going to knock 'em dead, Grier."

Half of them were already dead, but it's not like I could tell him that if I wanted him to keep breathing.

"Yep." I gripped my silver clutch in front of me. "Let the dog and pony show begin."

Neely tsked at me but opened the door with a sweeping gesture to reveal Volkov dressed in a black tux molded to his frame. His hair was swept back away from his face, and a pucker creased his brow when he spotted Neely. But when his gaze slid past my friend's shoulder onto me, the only sign of his irritation vanished as if it had never been, and his slow smile radiated approval at what he saw.

"*Solnishko*, you are breathtaking." He placed his hand over his heart. "Are the dress and shoes to your taste?"

"You chose well." I gave a little twirl at Neely's urging. "Thank you for your generosity."

"By accepting my gifts, you have given me the pleasure of caring for you. I wish to show you that it can always be this way between us." He delivered the line with enough sincerity to impress the orator in me. "Tonight I will be the most envied man in the room." His smile grew sharp. "I can hardly wait."

"Okay, cats and kittens, this is where I exit stage left." Neely tamed a flyaway with a quick twist of his wrist. "Have fun."

"I don't believe we were introduced." Volkov eyed Neely with an intense expression. "I'm Danill Volkov."

"Neely Torres." He gave a little wave. "I work with Grier at Haint Misbehavin'."

"He's a genius with hair and makeup." I bumped shoulders with him. "He was kind enough to come over and help me get ready."

"Then I'm in your debt." Danill reached into the front pocket of his suit and withdrew an honest-to-God money clip and began peeling off bills. "What do you charge per hour?"

The sight of all that money had Neely's mouth flopping open and shut. "This was a, uh, favor."

"You should be compensated for your time." He pressed a wad of cash into Neely's limp fingers. "A favor done for Grier is a favor done for me."

"Grier?" Neely wheezed, eyes wide. "I..."

"You earned it." I patted his cheek with a tad more force than necessary to snap him out of his shock. "You ought to be getting home. Cruz will worry."

"Yes." He gripped the handle on his bag, and Volkov stepped aside to let him pass. "Thank you."

Volkov inclined his head, waiting until Neely got behind the wheel of his car before facing me. "He's human."

"Maud took care to make sure I understood the human world." These days I wished she had given as much thought to educating me about our own. "I don't view them as lesser, only different."

A peculiar look crossed his features. "Was I wrong to give him money?"

"Would you have noticed him at all if I hadn't included him in our conversation?"

"With you in that dress?" He spoke with absolute conviction. "No."

"Mr. Volkov..."

"Danill, please."

"Danill," I conceded. "We come from very different walks of life. You're used to having a bustling staff. I get the impression they're background noise for you. That's not the case for me. Even when Maud was..." Throat tight, I tried again. "Maud was paranoid. She hated having strangers in the house, and she refused to hire domestic help. She raised me to be independent. No maid or butler or cook. Only a driver, and Gus didn't hang around the house. Maud had to phone for him."

"It bothers you that I overlooked your friend."

"Forget I said anything." I smoothed down my skirt. "My upbringing was peculiar by anyone's standards. I didn't know where I fit before, and that hasn't changed. Honestly? I'm more confused than ever about my place in the world. So how can I lecture you about being the product of your culture? At least you're secure in your identity. I envy you that."

"We all envy that which we do not possess," he countered. "Shall we?"

A soft laugh huffed out of me. "I just noticed you didn't come inside. Scared?"

"Having experienced your hospitality once, I regret to admit it unnerves me to find myself completely at the mercy of a being I do not understand and cannot sway to my side through traditional means."

"True." I stood on the threshold. "Woolly's love can't be bought. Her trust must be earned."

"Would she allow me inside a second time?" He presented the question as if I were the determining factor.

"There's only one way to find out," I teased.

"Perhaps another time." He glanced at the heavy gold timepiece on his wrist. "We have just under an hour before the festivities begin. We should be in our seats prior to the commencement. I want time for my guards to sweep the crowd before you're recognized."

Chicken, I almost teased. But this was real and getting realer by the minute. I was returning to the Lyceum where I would face off against Dame Lawson and the others who formed the bedrock of the Society.

"You know what to do," I told Woolly, and my cellphone buzzed once. "Good girl."

I took the arm Volkov offered me, and the locks *snicked* behind me.

The driver dipped his chin and opened the door for us. I settled on the backseat, and Volkov joined me a moment later, this time keeping a foot of distance between us. Clearly he was on his best behavior tonight.

The drive to the Lyceum took forever and no time at all. The car rolled to a stop, and we exited on the steps of city hall. The massive limestone building loomed overhead, its clock tower a shadow against the cloudy night sky. The domed roof and cupola, each gilded with twenty-four-karat gold leaf, would have glinted in sunlight, but it wasn't glittering now.

A black SUV parked behind us and ejected six guards. Two eased into the shadows and vanished. The other four swarmed us.

We entered in a cluster through the front doors under the guise of attending a private meeting. Inside the quiet was absolute, the only sound the click of my heels. I'd visited cemeteries more alive than these empty halls.

"This is a formality, Grier." Volkov steered me toward a bank of elevators. "It will be over soon."

"Guess you can hear my heartbeat, huh?" Each vicious thud threatened to shatter a rib. "Or can you smell my fear?" Under my breath, I mumbled, "I should have hosed myself with perfume."

Etiquette drummed into my head had prevented me from doing more than swiping on deodorant. Vampires' heightened senses meant even light fragrances left them with pounding migraines after a few hours of exposure. The polite thing was using unscented products when anticipating prolonged contact.

"You've chewed the lipstick off your bottom lip." He zeroed in on my mouth. "I scented blood, not fear."

"Neely is going to kill me." I fumbled in my clutch for the tube of emergency tinted lip gloss he'd anticipated me needing. "Would you mind?" I dipped the brush into the bottle and passed him the wand. "I'm afraid if I make it to the bathrooms, I'll hide and never come out."

"I'll do my best." He swiped the tip gently over my bottom lip, and the broken skin stung. "There." He drew back to admire his handiwork. "Good as new." He snapped his fingers, and one of the guards appeared at his side. "What do you think?"

The male spared me the briefest of glances. "She is flawless, sir."

Volkov's final inspection lingered far longer. "She is that."

Heat flooded my cheeks as I tucked away the gloss, certain I would need it again later.

We entered the elevator, Volkov and me pressed into one corner by the four guards positioned between us and the door. He toyed with the bangle he'd given me, his fingers blazing hot trails over my wrist. The guards used a key to open the control panel and pushed the button for the subbasement that held the Lyceum.

"Is this normal for you?" I whispered. "All these guards?"

"No." He caught himself taking liberties and lowered his hand.

"Our laws demand I keep two guards with me at all times in public, but they're not usually so intrusive. The rest are a precaution."

"No hints?"

"Afraid not."

I blasted out the deepest exhale my bodice allowed. "Can't blame a girl for trying."

"Soon we will be allowed to speak candidly," he assured me. "Then there will be no secrets between us."

I pasted on a smile to cover the knee-jerk urge to contradict him. We all kept secrets. Some out of kindness, some in anger, and others to protect ourselves. But I doubt he'd meant me to take him literally. White lies wove the fabric of the Society, after all.

The elevator slowed and then stopped, and so did my breathing. The doors opened on a rush of tinkling laughter and murmured conversation, and the guards fanned out in the bright hallway. The male nearest us gave a nod, and Volkov led me from the booth onto a glossy expanse of dark crimson tiles, edging into black, the colors so rich they evoked the image of freshly spilled blood starting to congeal. In our lines of work, I supposed the red-on-black decor hid a multitude of sins.

An elderly man wearing a simple gray suit spotted Volkov's entourage and cleared his throat. "Danill Volkov, Heritor of Clan Volkov, Last Seed of Marcus Volkov, and his lady friend."

Relief cascaded over me. Entering on his arm was intimidating enough without my name being broadcast throughout the amphitheater.

Silence greeted us as Volkov led me to the circular stage where the aggrieved and the accused stood to receive their judgment before the Society. There was no other way to enter the Lyceum except to cross the dais. Each step blasted chills down my arms as though someone were walking over my grave.

Before us sat an opulent box seat for the Grande Dame's use. Two silver chairs sat to either side of what might as well have been a throne, the seat golden, gem-studded and as ostentatious as it got. I had to wonder if it wasn't a holdover from a time when necromancers had been treated as god queens. Pretending there was history to the piece made it more palatable. Maybe I could spend the next few hours concocting a macabre history for it that I could weave into the story I recounted to Amelie.

A half step below this level, a short balcony railing separated a seating area reserved for the lowest rung on the ladder. Made vampires watched us with covetous eyes that flickered black with hunger. On the level above them sat the Low Society matrons. The women cackled and chatted and seemed to enjoy the chance to catch up with one another. I scanned their faces, but Matron Pritchard was absent. The next tier was reserved for Last Seeds. Fewer chairs filled that space, and none of them were occupied. Two shadowy figures I recognized as Volkov's missing guards checked each chair, each spindle on the railing, each nook and cranny where danger might lurk.

Volkov and I stood there, exposed on the stage, the heat from the bright lights breaking me out in a sweat. I risked a peek at him from the corner of my eye, and his smugness tipped my mouth into a frown. The attention made my skin crawl, but he was lapping it up as his due.

For a male in his position, I suppose this adulation was normal. For me, it was pure torture.

The final row, its adornments brushing against the ceiling, was reserved for the High Society. Unlike the friendly chatter of the Low Society matrons, the High Society dames each kept their own council. A few whispered behind their hands, but on the whole, they gave the impression they had somewhere else they'd rather be, when this ceremony was the social event of the year. More like the decade. Perhaps even this century if Dame Lawson was particularly long-lived. Gold and gemstones dripped from their ears, fingers, necks and wrists. The elaborate beading on their gowns must have weighed fifty pounds, and I had no doubt each design was an original.

Volkov applied slight pressure on my arm, and I snapped my

attention back to my own party as I was led to a set of stairs. All those sharp eyes as you strolled to the darkened stairwells made the skin between your shoulder blades twitch as if half the Lyceum's occupants had daggers trained on your spine.

Two guards walked ahead of us. The staircase was tight, but Volkov remained by my side, and I was grateful for his strength to lean on. The final two guards trailed behind, sandwiching us between a wall of muscle and fang. The two guards who had cleared the area nodded a greeting to Volkov. They dipped their eyes in a show of deference to me that felt undeserved.

We took our seats, positioned above the mouth of the tunnel with a direct view of the empty box where the Grande Dame, both past and future, would soon complete their ceremonial power transfer. Despite the pinch in my middle from where the gown cut into me, I took my first full breath since arriving in the Lyceum.

Volkov leaned close to avoid our conversation being overheard by any sensitive ears present. "You're upset."

"Not with you." He was who he was, and he made no apologies for it. "Nervous."

"Would you like a drink?" He gestured to the servers circulating with large platters filled with fluted glasses of bubbling pink liquid. "It might settle your nerves."

"Sure." Tonight I would take all the help I could get.

A guard appeared at my elbow seconds later. He must have fetched the drink prior to Volkov asking me. He was a master at anticipating needs, I'd give him that.

"Thank you." I accepted the drink and sipped. Tart lime and pink grapefruit hit my tongue edged with a slight bitterness. Or maybe that was the memory dredged up by the taste. "What's this called?"

I wanted to make sure I never ordered it again by accident.

Reading the pucker of my lips as permission to relieve me of my drink, Volkov accepted the glass and sipped. "A Long-Faced Dove." He laughed at my wrinkled nose. "Would you like something else?"

"That seems to be the only drink circulating." I clutched my small purse in my lap, snapping and unsnapping its clasp. "I can hold out a while longer." I offered him a weak smile. "Though I might need a drink when I get out of here."

If I got out of here.

"That can be arranged." Volkov settled back in his chair and started people-watching. "Do you have a favorite drink?"

"Not really." I'd turned twenty-one inside Atramentous, and getting sloshed hadn't been high on my priority list since my release. For one thing, alcohol was expensive. For another, it was an addictive balm that left you right back where you started from, just poorer for your trouble. "Amelie and I used to sneak into Boaz's parties back in high school. I had a margarita once. The girl he was dating at the time blended them like a pro, said it was her mom's favorite. I liked that."

"High school," he murmured. "You share more history with him than I'd realized."

"We grew up together—Boaz, Amelie and me." Not quite the three musketeers since d'Artagnan hadn't wanted to bone Porthos. "I had the worst crush on him back then, and he thought it was hilarious. Not exactly the reaction I'd hoped for, you know?"

"And now?" He kept his expression neutral. "Has time and separation changed either of your perspectives?"

"He's always going to be important to me, but the truth is, I don't know how much is just falling into old habits and how much is real." I smothered a grin. "Boaz is a terrible flirt, but he throws his whole heart into loving the person he's with at the time he's with them."

"Ah." Volkov nodded. "You're concerned any fling would be brief and the damage to your friendship lasting."

"Exactly that." I tapped the back of his hand where it rested on the arm of his chair. "Are you sure you're not a mind reader? You're the most perceptive guy I've ever met."

"Wouldn't that be a handy talent? No, I can't read minds, but I can read people." He indicated the bangle that kept me from curling up in his lap like a spoiled cat. "Lures are as individual as fingerprints. The worst hunter can feed and release their donor without doing harm with a bare minimum of training, but there is an art to giving a person the thing they want most that facilitates their full surrender, and the blood is always sweeter for their submission."

Submission was not my kink. Not that I had any kinks I was aware of. But if I did, I felt pretty sure that would not be one. Submission required a level of trust I might never be capable of cultivating with a man. Let alone a vampire.

Admitting he was a master manipulator, in any context, made me hyperaware of exactly how accommodating he had been since meeting me. How much of Danill was I seeing versus what the Volkov heritor had been ordered to show me?

A ripple shuddered through the crowd that saved me from having to formulate the appropriate response after hearing the predator next to me wax poetic on his love of the hunt.

"Ladies and gentlemen." The announcer's clear, high voice rang through the amphitheater. "It is my pleasure to introduce to you Clarice Woolworth Lawson, Dame Lawson, future Grande Dame of the Society for Post-Death Management."

I was perched on the edge of my seat without realizing I'd decided to inch closer to the railing.

The woman who strode forward could have passed for Maud from this angle. White hair swept up in a classic twist. Modest gown the color of wet blood with long sleeves and a square neckline. Practical heels that click-clacked, causing her abbreviated train to swish like a serpent's tail across the floor.

Not until she vanished in the shadows of the stairwell did I remember to breathe.

NINE

People thrust into appalling circumstances either learn to cope or they go mad. I coped with Atramentous through madness. The perpetual darkness, the drugs, the knowledge I would lie curled on that filthy floor until the day I died, beat me down until I almost embraced the hiss of the injector as chemicals spiraled through my bloodstream and swept me away for hours or days or months at a time.

There I learned how to retreat inside my head, and that's where I huddled during the inauguration.

Blind, I watched the proceedings. Deaf, I heard the vows spoken. Mute, I moved my lips on silent affirmations.

A warm hand on my arm made me flinch hard enough the legs of my chair scraped against the planks.

Volkov withdrew, giving me space to sink back into my body, but gestured toward the box.

The newly minted Grande Dame stood with her arm outstretched. Pointing. She was singling me out. Her mouth formed words, but I couldn't hear them over the thudding of my pulse in my ears. I looked to Volkov for a translation, but he kept his face carefully neutral while listening to her speech.

"She's asked you to take the floor."

I snapped my head toward him. "W-what?"

"It will be fine," he assured me. "My guards will escort you down and remain in the stairwell."

"Danill." For the first time, I used his given name without prompting, and it rushed out on a terrified whimper.

"I have no claim on you." He took my hand, his thumb sliding over his bangle. "I'm not allowed to stand with you without an under-standing between us."

The temptation to accept his offer of alliance beat under my skin. The only thing that stopped me from sinking to my knees at his feet and begging was the fact he had known this was coming. Whatever she intended, whatever was about to happen, he had strolled in here tonight armed with that knowledge. And he had refused to share it with me.

The same survival instinct that had kept me alive this long roared to wakefulness.

Volkov had already admitted he excelled in giving people what they desired most. Wasn't that what he had done for me? I craved safety, and he offered me protection in tiny bites that were easy for me to swallow. Guards at the house. An escort to the inauguration. Even the bangle made a powerful statement in that as long as I wore it, our dealings were one hundred percent consensual. For a person who'd had so little choice in her life, it made for a much more potent lure than his own.

All these guards, all for show. What good were they when I would stand on that floor alone?

"I have to do this on my own." Truth gave the words an extra punch of bravado I didn't feel. The wrap snagged on my chairback and slid off my shoulders as I stood. I didn't have it in me to retrieve it, and I waved off the guard when he offered me assistance. That left me holding my bag, and I wasn't convinced I could manage that either. "Hold my purse?"

"Of course." He offered a faint smile. "I'll be right here."

Putting one foot in front of the other, I exited into the stairwell and climbed down. The guards followed at a safe distance, close enough I could call out for them but not so near they quelled the roiling in my gut over the fact Volkov remained in his seat. A silent ultimatum.

I paused in the shadowed archway, sucked in a breath, and then I was striding forward to greet my fate.

The Grande Dame arranged her expression into a welcoming smile with a benevolent yet sad undertone.

"My darling niece," she murmured. "I'm so glad you came."

I curtsied, which seemed more prudent than snapping out, *What choice did I have?*

"Please join me in welcoming Grier Woolworth, everyone." Her strong voice projected to every corner of the room. A beat of stunned silence preceded a smattering of confused claps. "Many of you have asked why I chose to ascend to Grande Dame. The reasons are simple. Our justice system is flawed. I witnessed this firsthand five years ago when my niece was convicted of murdering my dear sister, Maud, and I am humbled to stand before you on this momentous night to witness true justice served."

A profound hush silenced the amphitheater, and my knees quivered beneath my skirts.

To her right, the former Grande Dame, Abayomi Balewa, flinched as if the words had stricken her, but she covered her reaction with a regal nod to her successor and joined my aunt to address the masses.

"There was no public trial held for Grier Woolworth," Balewa began. "The matter of her guilt was settled behind closed doors out of respect for Maud and her family, and out of necessity due to the privileged nature of her work for the Society." Her knuckles pushed against her skin where she gripped the balcony railing. "The evidence available at the time convinced us, convinced *me*, of Grier's guilt. The heinous nature of the crime demanded our highest punishment, and I meted out a penance of equal severity."

The Grande Dame looked on, wearing an earnest mask tinged with the exact right amounts of understanding and forgiveness. Two words I bet she'd have to Google for a definition.

"Within hours of Maud's death, her heir, the child she raised and loved as her own, was stripped of her title, her fortune and her freedom," Balewa continued, "and I will carry the shame of my actions for the rest of my life. That is why, after serving the Society faithfully for the last seventy-nine years, I chose to step down and relinquish my title." At long last her gaze settled on me, and there was nothing remorseful in her expression. "Tonight, it is my great pleasure to announce that my last act as Grande Dame is to restore Grier Woolworth to her rightful place within the Society."

Murmurs rumbled through the crowd, growing louder as the implications set in.

"You mentioned the available evidence convinced you of her guilt," a Low Society matron called. "What new information exonerated her?"

The present and former Grande Dames exchanged a loaded glance that resulted in my aunt stepping forward while Balewa reclaimed her seat.

"I never gave up hope that one day Grier might be vindicated. I never stopped searching for answers." The faint tremor in her voice was quite convincing if you overlooked the glacier coldness in her eyes. "A recent health scare—" she placed one hand over her heart "—turned out to be the key to unlocking the mystery."

Insidious whispers hissed from the dark corners. A Grande Dame admitting a public weakness was a bigger treat than catching beads thrown in Tybee Island's annual Mardi Gras parade.

"My sister was, as you all know, a brilliant practitioner. She was also enthusiastic in her pursuit of knowledge to the point of being careless with her own health." Unable to produce a tear, she ducked her head and dashed her fingertips under her dry eyes. "Upon reexamining the evidence from that horrible night, it has been determined that Maud died of a heart attack. It's rare, but not unheard of, and more common in necromancers her age. The Woolworth line, in particular, is susceptible. Our own mother, Nina Compton Woolworth, died of such an ailment. I myself am now under a physician's care to monitor my own condition."

A woman in the High Society balcony stood and waited until the Grande Dame acknowledged her with a curt nod.

"I saw the child marched into the Lyceum that night with my own eyes," she argued. "She was drenched in Maud's blood. What say you to that?"

"Grier was trained as an assistant, not as a practitioner, so your question is a valid one. Grier discovered Maud that night, and, in her grief, she granted Maud's dying wish." She gestured to the Low Society woman seated on her left, and the woman passed her a heart-shaped box with the heft of solid gold. "My niece was in shock when she performed the Culmination. You can imagine how traumatic that must have been for such a young girl, let alone one who had never witnessed the ceremony until she found herself duty-bound to complete Maud's last rites."

The woman inclined her head and sat. Or that's how I interpreted the movement from the corner of my eye. I was unable to peel my gaze from the ornate box the Grande Dame held in her hands.

Pain jarred my kneecaps, the room shot upward like I was back on the elevator, and I descended into nothingness.

"*Grier.*"

Someone called my name, but there were so many faces, too many faces, all staring down at me as I knelt there unable to stand, barely able to lift my head.

Maud's heart was in that box. Her *heart.*

Bile stung the back of my throat, and I clamped my teeth together to keep it down.

A gasp rose throughout the room when a man leapt from the

second balcony, landing in a crouch. He gritted his teeth when he stood and limped as he crossed to me, but I had never been happier to see Boaz in my entire life. I curled against his broad chest and sobbed into his starched shirtfront while the Society glared daggers at my back.

"It appears my niece is overcome by her good fortune," the Grande Dame announced. "You there," she called down to Boaz. "Escort her to my chambers."

"I got you, Squirt." He exhaled sharply when he stood but ignored his pain long enough to haul me to my feet. "Lean on me. That's it." He wrapped his arm around my waist and tucked me against his side. "I'll stay with you until they pry me off, okay?"

"Okay," I murmured, hiding my face against his ribs.

"Mr. Volkov would like to accompany the heiress."

The heiress.

Well, that was one mystery solved.

Feeling a hundred years old, I drew back enough to look into the eyes of one of Volkov's guards. "No."

That harsh syllable was all the fire I had left in me.

"You heard the lady." Boaz shouldered past the guard and held me close while we shuffled down a long, dark hallway. "New boyfriend is pushy, huh?"

"He's not my boyfriend." Right now, I couldn't imagine so much as accepting a ride home from him. "I'm not sure if he's a friend period."

We reached a doorway flanked by sentinels, and Boaz shouldered them aside as he had the vampire guards. Grande Dame Lawson waited for us in an oversized wooden chair positioned behind a blocky antique desk that dwarfed her. The eyesore belonged in a captain's cabin on a pirate ship, not in the hallowed halls of the Lyceum. Again, a few rogue brain cells paused to wonder at the origin of these incongruous bits of our history while the others scattered at the sight of the box centered before her.

"Grier, you look peakish." She indicated the single chair positioned across from her. "Sit." She snapped her fingers at a man stationed near the door. "Bring the girl a drink."

I melted into the chair on watery knees, and Boaz planted his hands on my shoulders to pin me upright.

"You look familiar." Eyes sharp, she raked her gaze over Boaz. "What is your family name?"

"Pritchard, ma'am." The dull, flat tone kept his anger well-hidden. "My mother is Matron Annabeth Pritchard."

"Ah. The neighbors." She reevaluated our closeness. "That explains it."

A sentinel appeared at my elbow and pressed a glass of icy water into my hand. I mumbled thanks and sipped to give my mouth something to do besides form the scream tickling the back of my throat.

"Grier is in capable hands." She flicked her wrist at the men in the room. "You may go."

"I want him to stay," I croaked.

Her lips mashed into a peevish line. "Are you quite certain?"

"Yes, ma'am."

"Are you trustworthy, Pritchard?" Her eyes narrowed on his face. "Can you keep her secret?"

Mine? Dread ballooned in my chest, my breath hitching. The only secrets here were hers. Right?

"I'm loyal to Grier, ma'am." He squeezed my shoulders. "I would never say or do anything to hurt her."

The room cleared until only the three of us remained.

"We shall see, I suppose." Leaning forward, she fixated on me while resting her forearms on the desktop, her fingers reaching out to strum against the box's lid, which she had positioned on her blotter for all to see. "You must be curious about your change in circumstances."

"I am."

"I know how my sister died."

That was all she said, all she had to say, and that put her one full step ahead of me.

All I knew was what I had been told, and I didn't believe a word of the charges brought against me.

The truth, whatever I had witnessed with my own eyes, was lost to shock, to time and to the drugs.

"You would have rotted in that prison if not for me. I showed Balewa the error of her ways. I convinced her of your innocence." The temperature in the room seemed to drop with her pretense. "I expect gratitude from you."

"Yes, ma'am."

"Are you that broken?" The question appeared legitimate. "Have you lost your wits entirely?"

Boaz tensed behind me, and I forced myself to meet her stare rather than watch her *tap, tap, tapping* her manicured nails on the gilded lid of the wretched box she made sure to keep in my line of sight.

"Ah. There you are. There's a spark left in you yet." Eagerness beat in her words. "I've had you watched since your release, and the reports were promising. I'm glad to see they weren't exaggerated."

"Why did you have me pardoned?" I reached deep and found a scrap of backbone. "Why am I here?"

"An interesting thing happened last year." She absorbed my shock that she'd kept tabs on me even in Atramentous without batting an eyelash. "An unsanctioned resuscitation, if you can believe it. Understandably, my contacts within the prison messaged me immediately."

How anyone kept as magically impotent as the inmates in Atramentous managed to raise an undead was beyond me. Not to mention the key ingredient was missing. "There are no humans in Atramentous."

"The diversity of your cellmates might surprise you." The Grande Dame continued illuminating me. "Necromancers, vampires and fae, yes. But there are also humans who have discovered us, who have threatened us with exposure, who have betrayed their lovers or spouses or children for fame or glory or wealth."

A chill settled into my bones that froze me to the spot.

"A new inmate, a vampire, suffered a bad reaction to his regimen and attacked a human in your group during your weekly exercise period." She steepled her fingers in front of her mouth. "You resuscitated him, Grier, with nothing but your own blood, a hint of magic, and the crudest sigils. Though I doubt he thanks you for extending his sentence from thirty or forty years into three or four hundred, I am, nonetheless, impressed."

"I didn't..." I tossed my head. "I don't remember..."

"I interviewed the witnesses myself. There can be no doubt. What's more, he's Deathless." She studied me for my reaction. "Do you understand what that means?"

"I've never heard the term, no."

"What you've created shouldn't be possible. The Deathless are made vampires with the longevity of a Last Seed but without their fertility limitations. They are capable of reproduction, and their children..." She drew in a breath that shuddered with pleasure. "They are true immortals, though their grandchildren are rumored to be mortal."

"You're saying two entire castes of vampires exist that aren't in any of our history books." None of the ones passed down to lowly assistants at least. "How is that possible?"

"There are only two documented cases of Deathless vampires rising. Any other records were destroyed when our Great Library burned in the 1300s. Surviving tomes are the private property of the Lyceum. Their care—and location—have been entrusted to the Elite, sentinels who are beyond reproach. They operate outside the laws of the Society to safeguard our history from those who might seek to alter it."

A secret history. *My* history. "Can I see them?"

"That's not possible." Her attempt at sympathy fell as flat as her tone. "They're stored in a climate-controlled facility somewhere outside the city. That's all I know, all any of us are allowed to know. The books come to us. We do not go to the books."

"What else can you tell me about the Deathless?"

"Only that five instances of them reproducing exists, along with eight examples of their mortal grandchildren. The bulk of the research on them has been lost." A thoughtful expression crossed her features. "That is why I'm considering pardoning your progeny in exchange for his full cooperation in our study of the Deathless condition."

Progeny. I had progeny, a man I didn't remember and doubted I would ever see again.

"What about me?" Thankful I wasn't alone, I reached up and covered one of Boaz's hands with mine. "How is this possible?"

"How much do you remember about your birth parents?" She prodded the old wound with careless fingers. "We believe the trait is passed through the paternal lineage."

"I remember small things about my mom, but there was only ever the two of us."

"You have no idea who your father is?"

"I was so young, and we were happy. Just the two of us." I shook my head. "The few times I asked if I had a father, usually after a play-mate brought it up, she distracted me with ice cream." Slowly, my eyes drifted back to the box. "I asked Maud, but she swore Mom had never told her. Her answer was always the same. That if he wasn't in my life, there was a good reason. That I should trust my mother's judgment."

"That is unfortunate." The Grande Dame digested this bit of news with a frown. "All I can tell you at this time is that your condi-tion is rare. The surviving texts all refer to the afflicted necromancers as being goddess-touched, favored by the three-faced goddess."

The urge to laugh tensed my shoulders at the thought of all those nights I prayed to Hecate when she answered with silence.

"This unexpected ability saved your life." She gave me a moment to absorb the subtle threat. "I have done you a great favor in restoring you to your former station. The announcement was made prior to this conversation as a show of trust. You must understand what this means."

"You want me to make more of them." But not too many. There was no prestige in being common.

"Don't sound so glum. You were heartbroken when Maud declared you were only fit to work as an apprentice. Well, this is your chance to be a full-fledged practitioner with a specialization no one else can claim. Wealth and fame are yours for the taking." She made a grasping gesture that ended with her fisted hand. "What more could you want?"

The truth for starters. "Did Maud know?"

"Without access to her library, we can't be certain." Her gaze unfocused as she stared at the macabre box. "She loved your mother very much. They were inseparable until Evangeline's family returned to France around her two hundred and thirtieth birthday. They kept in touch during the separation, but I didn't see Evangeline again until she showed up on Maud's doorstep after a dinner party with a child in tow. How much Evangeline confided in her, I can't say. I was the annoying younger sister and not welcome in their club of two.

"My sister was one of the most celebrated minds of our time. Even if Evangeline kept the truth from her, she must have known that once Maud took over your education, she would understand immediately that your magic worked in impossible ways. Perhaps that is why your mother turned to her old friend after an absence of so many years. Perhaps Maud robbed you of your rightful status and kept your education lacking in order to protect you. We may never know those answers with any degree of certainty."

Keet.

The first and only test Maud ever administered that required me to mix my own ink, using my own blood, and she'd let me believe I failed. She'd lied to me. One of the most powerful necromancers in existence had told me I was less, and I had believed her. Keeping me ignorant might have seemed like the ideal solution to her, but I was coming to the rapid understanding that only I could protect myself, and I had no idea how.

Exhaustion swept through me. All the fretting and waiting and pageantry had burned me out for the night. I wanted to go home. I wanted this to be yet another nightmare. At least I woke up from those. This—this new reality terrified me.

No wonder Volkov wanted me. Every clan would petition me to resuscitate their candidates. An alliance with me meant he would have a say in who was turned and in naming the price of their immortality. Here I thought my restored title and fortune might be factors, but I had sorely underestimated the scope of his master's ambition.

"I'm tired." I rubbed my forehead. "Can I sleep on this?"

"Of course, dear girl. I imagine this must all come as a shock." She pressed a button on her desk, and the door to her right swung open. The sentinel who entered did so carrying Keet in a small cage. The Grande Dame gestured to him. "I believe this belongs to you."

"Keet?" Boaz growled over my shoulder. "Why does she have your bird?"

"Insurance" was all I said, and I knew he understood when he stiffened behind me.

"When did this happen?" Boaz rounded on me. "Why didn't you tell me?"

I pinched my lips together. *Fiddlesticks.* I'd forgotten I hadn't caught him or Amelie up on the break-in.

Filling him in now, after the fact, did nothing to improve his mood.

"How can I protect you if you keep secrets from me?" His hands closed over my arms, and he lifted me from my chair. He was halfway to shaking me when the fury glazing his eyes cleared enough for him to recall our surroundings, the company we kept, and he lowered his voice. "You should have told me. I never would have let you—"

I lowered mine too as I extricated myself from his hold. "Exactly."

Ignoring the hulking man vibrating with rage at my elbow, the sentinel crossed to me and extended the cage. Keet, rustling his feathers at the movement, chirruped at me in happy recognition.

"Hey, fella." Vision blurring, I reached through the bars and scratched his head with my fingertip. "I missed you too."

"One more thing before you go," the Grande Dame called, circling her desk until she stood before me. "She would want you to have this." Boaz relieved me of the cage as she pressed the cold metal box into my hands. "She would want to return home."

The moisture evaporated from my tongue as my fingers closed over the terrible burden. "Thank you."

"We don't have to be enemies, Grier." She cupped my cheek in her palm. "I've made mistakes with you, and I'm sorry for that."

I locked my knees to keep from recoiling at her touch.

"Family sticks together." She kissed my forehead. "It's how we survive."

The cold weight of Maud's remains anchored me to the floor. Only the warmth of Boaz at my side thawed me enough that I could turn my back on her. The Grande Dame ordered the office doors opened, and we started our long walk down the dark hall leading back to the amphitheater.

"I'm sorry," Boaz murmured. "I was pissed you didn't mention the wraith. Woolly was attacked, and you didn't tell me. Your aunt kidnapped your goddamn zombie, for Pete's sake. You love that stupid bird."

We reached the elevators, and I stopped. "Look, it happened the night you found out about the draft. I wanted to tell you and Amelie, but I didn't want to make things even worse, and there was nothing you could do about it anyway."

"You still should have told me." He palmed the back of my head and reeled me in for a gentle hug. "I hate that I made you feel Volkov was your only option."

"It's more complicated than that."

"Next time, let me be there for you." He released me when the doors rolled open. "That's what I'm here for, okay?"

A burst of warmth kindled in my chest at the offer. He could be such an overbearing knuckle-dragger sometimes, but his heart was in the right place. A good woman might be able to train him up right one of these days, and more power to her. With the paths of our lives diverging yet again, I didn't waste time hoping that job might fall to me. The odds, it seemed, had never been in our favor.

TEN

B oaz texted a friend who traded keys with him on the steps of city hall, and we climbed into a borrowed sedan that smelled like stale fries. I still hadn't seen his new ride, but I heard its throaty growl a few streets over as his friend took her for a spin. Our neighbors must *love* his new purchase.

I cocked an eyebrow at him. "You must think you're pretty smooth."

A smile glinted in his eyes. "Comparisons have been made between me and babies' bottoms, yes."

"Thanks for the ride." I leaned my head against his shoulder. "Thanks for being here tonight."

"Anything for you, Squirt," he rumbled. "You're my best girl."

A quiver rippled through my lower stomach at his tone. Of all the times he'd called me his best girl, I had never once believed he meant it, but I was having trouble not taking him—and the wide palm he wrapped around my thigh—seriously.

"You aren't making this any easier," I murmured, thinking on his father's warnings.

"Good," he said without an ounce of remorse. "I'm tired of easy."

Those words ranked up there in my top ten list of things I had always wished he would say. Now that he had, I had no idea what to make of them. So I breathed him in and didn't make anything of them at all.

All too soon, we paused at the end of the driveway while the automated gates swung open, and I released a pained groan. "I'd hoped Volkov would take the hint when I didn't ask him to wait for me."

"I'll handle him." Eagerness sharpened Boaz's expression as he rolled up to Woolly and parked. "You need to rest. I'll make sure he understands that."

"I appreciate the offer, but he's not going to quit until I tell him no." I lifted my wrist and shook it side to side. "Besides, I have to give this back to him."

"How much does he know about you?" Boaz asked in a quiet voice.

"I don't know," I admitted. "He refused to share his intel. He let me get blindsided tonight."

He mulled over that. "Is that why you're refusing his offer of alliance?"

I jerked upright and met his stare. "How did you—?"

"I'm not a total idiot." His gaze skimmed down my body, over the dress Volkov had given me. "He's stamping proof of ownership all over you. The dress isn't half as bad as the jewelry. There's only one reason why he would give you a weapon against him, and that's if he was trying to win you over with trust."

"Can you do me a favor?" I slid the crimson bangle over my wrist, shuddering at the warmth it had leached from me. I wished I could chuck it at Volkov as a distraction while I bolted for the house, but running from predators only turned you into prey. "Don't let me make a total fool of myself out there."

"I've got your back." He reached over me and palmed a stake from the glovebox. "Do what you need to do."

We exited the car together, leaving Keet in the floorboard and the box on my seat, but I walked ahead of Boaz to greet my former escort. "I wasn't expecting to see you again tonight."

"I wasn't sure how long the Grande Dame would keep you, so I came here to wait. I hope you don't mind." He gestured toward Boaz. "I assumed your friend would see you home. It appears I was correct."

"Do you want me to get rid of him?" Boaz tossed the stake end over end in his hand. "Say the word, and he's gone."

Volkov scoffed in his direction, amused that Boaz would pit himself against a Last Seed and expect to come out on top. "I only came to make sure you were all right. It's my duty as your escort to ensure you arrived home in the same condition as when you left."

"I'm fine, thank you, but I've come into some information tonight that changes things." I extended the bangle toward him. "I appreciate your offer, but I can't accept it at this time. There's too much uncertainty in my future for me to factor in one more unknown."

"Tradition demands you keep it as a token of my esteem." He spread his hands, palms out, and stepped back. "I am forbidden to pursue you should you return the gift." He looked to Boaz for confirmation. "It is an absolute refusal. I will accept it, of course, if that's your wish. But I hope you will keep me in mind for a while longer, until you've had time to adjust to your new circumstances."

"He's telling the truth." Boaz shrugged when I checked in with him. "The courtship ends when the avowal is returned." He held Volkov's stare. "However, there's no rule that says you have to wear it while you're making your decision."

I tucked in the smile twitching on my lips and conceded the point. Fine. So maybe I wouldn't shake off Volkov tonight. But Boaz had found me a loophole. I could keep the bangle as an escape hatch for the day the Grande Dame pressed me too far into a corner. Not an ideal solution, since it meant I had to keep tap-dancing around Volkov, but if I could find another means of nullifying his lure without depending on his gift, I could seize the upper hand in any future negotiations.

"All right. I'll keep the bangle for now." I didn't put it back on, and Volkov let his mask slip a fraction in his irritation. "I don't want to make any irreversible decisions until I've had time to weigh my options."

Volkov inclined his head. "Perhaps I could persuade you to—"

Boaz placed a proprietary hand at the small of my back, and Volkov's lip twitched in a snarl.

"Not tonight." I stepped away from Boaz to show that while I wasn't with Volkov, I wasn't with him either. "Maybe some other time."

Volkov took a step that mirrored mine. "Grier."

"She said no." Boaz didn't raise his voice, didn't shift his weight forward, gave no outward indication he was primed for battle. Except for his smile. There was something wicked and dangerous in the curve that set my pulse sprinting. "Back off, vamp."

Volkov bared his fangs and hissed under his breath. His guards, who had been content to watch the show up to this point, pushed off the car and approached us.

"This is my line," I warned Volkov, stepping between the vampires and Boaz. "Cross it, hurt someone I love, and there's no going back."

The threat had the desired effect, but I got the impression admitting I loved Boaz, no matter that it was mostly unrequited, had painted a target on his carotid.

The growl of a motorcycle approaching caught the guards' attention and shattered our stalemate.

"I'll be in touch." Volkov shoved his hands into his pockets. "Soon."

Boaz and I stood together in silence until their taillights flashed at the end of the street.

"He's going to be a problem," he predicted as he returned to the car to gather my things. "Vamps are hella territorial, and he thinks I hiked my leg on his hydrant tonight by bringing you home."

Of course he would remember the hydrant comment.

"We'll figure something out." I frowned at the limp he had concealed from the vampires. "For now, you need to go home and take care of your leg."

He grunted. "Don't start mother-henning me, Squirt."

"You're lucky you didn't break something jumping onto the dais." I shoved him gently. "Count your blessings."

Grumbling all the way, he bent down and dropped a kiss on top of my head as he passed off Keet and the box. "Don't think this means you can start bossing me around every day."

I batted my lashes at him. "I wouldn't dream of it."

A herd of wild buffalo would have made a quieter exit than Boaz's stomping. I got the feeling he wasn't thrilled leaving me alone for the night, but asking him to stay over wasn't happening. I had too much to process tonight without adding the temptation of Boaz sleeping down the hall from me to the mix.

Ready for this night to end, I took the stairs and sang out, "I'm home."

The porch light blazed in welcome, and I shuffled in with all my burdens as the door shut and the latches engaged until Woolly was locked up tight behind me. An air of expectation hung around me as she attempted to use silence to crack me, but I was a tough nut and onto her tricks. After all, I had taught her most of them.

"I'm sorry, girl." I rested my forehead against the door. "So much happened tonight, and I don't want to get into the gory details."

A floorboard groaned in protest.

"I'll give you the scoop tomorrow, I promise." I rushed to assure her I wasn't falling into old habits. "I just need to think for a bit. Is that okay?" The lights in the foyer brightened in assent, and I lifted the cage. "Look who's back."

The curtain near the window where Keet's empty cage sat rippled in excitement, and I transferred the little guy back into his own home. The smaller one I would toss out tomorrow to be on the safe side. Keeping any gift from the Grande Dame, no matter how benign it appeared, struck me as asking for trouble.

After trudging upstairs, I changed into Boaz's rumpled shirt and crawled under the covers in the cool darkness while my mind raced frantic circles around all I had learned tonight. At least I had confirmation of who I owed the favor. Now the question would be when did she plan to collect?

ELEVEN

I choked on a scream and scrabbled deeper into the corner. I was panting through the worst of the pounding heart and screaming adrenaline dump when I understood what had woken me. The doorbell. Woolly flipped on every light in my room and cranked them up to blinding levels to urge me to my feet.

I pulled on a bra and cutoff shorts before padding downstairs and pressing my eye to the peephole.

A short man decked out in a navy three-piece suit stood on my welcome mat. Green eyes flicked up to the fisheye lens, and he winked at me, aware he was being watched. His tan skin made the white sleeve of his shirt pop when he reached up to adjust the mop of black curls sliding across his forehead.

Woolly unlocked the door, and I pulled it open, careful to keep on my side of the threshold. "Can I help you?"

"Dame Woolworth?"

The impulse to glance behind me to see if Maud stood there twitched in my neck. "Grier Woolworth, yes."

Though, now that he'd mentioned it, I suppose with Maud gone, I was the current title holder.

"I'm Omar Hacohen." He extended his arm. "I work for the office of the Grande Dame."

"You don't say." I made no move to accept his hand. "What can I do for you?"

"For me? Not much." The leather portfolio he slapped against his thigh bore the insignia of my financial institution. "This visit is all about what *I* can do for *you*."

"Uh-huh." I cocked an eyebrow. "You're not trying to sell me a used car, are you?"

"Ouch." He gave an exaggerated wince. "Do I really cast off the snake oil salesman vibe?"

Yes. "A little."

"We got work to do, girly. You want to do it out here or in there?"

I wasn't in the mood to invite a stranger working for my aunt into my home, so I joined him on the porch and shut the door to give me something to lean against. "Out here is fine."

"Access to your funds were granted earlier today." A heavy packet with my name emblazoned on it was the first thing I saw when he flipped open the folio. "You have a new debit card in there along with all your new account information."

The urge to rip into the packet and hold that rectangular piece of heaven in my hands twitched in my fingers. The promise of financial solvency had me salivating harder than the time I spied on Boaz skinny dipping with his friends.

This was more than the ability to keep the lights on and the fridge stocked. With access to my inheritance, I could afford a specialist to repair Woolly's foundation. More than that, I could erase all the years of neglect from her creaking floorboards to her leaking windows to her peeling paint. I could give the old girl a facelift that would make her the envy of the town.

"Before we get to all that," Mr. Hacohen said, pulling a pen from the pocket of his single-breasted jacket, "I got some forms for you to sign."

Forcing myself to block out the stack of papers that would turn my world upside down for the third time—or was it the fourth? I was starting to lose count—I tried for nonchalance so he wouldn't see I was ready to tear the activation strip off my new debit card with my teeth.

Reinstating me took the better part of two hours. Just a few dozen initials, thirty or so signatures, and I was once again a woman of means who could afford all the Honeycrisp apples she could eat. Heck, I could invest in entire apple orchards to ensure an unlimited supply.

"Pleasure doing business with you," Mr. Hacohen said, slapping his folio closed. "One of my cards is in your packet. You need anything, call me. I'll be handling your case."

"Does that make you a lawyer?" He hadn't told me exactly what he did for my aunt, after all.

"Girly, it makes me a hell of a lot of things." He ruffled his springy hair. "I need to get back to the Lyceum to file these. Enjoy the rest of your night."

"Night," I called to him, cradling the packet against my chest. "Thank you."

Mr. Hacohen lifted a hand as he slid behind the wheel of his car. I waved and went back in the house.

Though I had a shiny debit card burning a hole in my pocket, I wasn't about to play hooky. Better than most, I knew fortunes could change hands on a dime. I owed Cricket for hiring me on the spot, no questions asked, after I vanished on her last time. I would have been begging scraps from Amelie's table if not for Cricket's willingness to extend me a second chance.

Oh, no.

And the award for worst friend in the world goes to...Grier Woolworth!

Between the news of my reinstatement and the confrontation with Volkov, I had forgotten Amelie. My best friend, and I hadn't spared her a second thought as I climbed into bed and left her to wait up on me.

Surely Boaz must have... But it wasn't his job to clean up after me.

I retrieved my cellphone and dialed her up before I lost my courage.

"I don't have time for this right now," she answered on the second ring. "I'm late for work."

"I'm sorry I stood you up last night." I dumped the thick packet on the bar. "I should have called."

"Yes, you should have." Hurt throbbed in each syllable. "Boaz told me some of what happened. He said congratulations are in order."

The urge to ask what, exactly, he'd told her made me trip over a rug. Boaz was a lot of things. Mostly, he was a pain in my butt. But he was trustworthy and loyal, and he wouldn't betray me even to his sister. Not without a good reason.

"Can we talk about it tonight after our shift?" I wheedled. "There's a cupcake with your name on it at Mallow. My treat. I'll even spring for some of that hot chocolate you love."

"Mallow? Come on. That's not fair. I'm trying to be mad here." She huffed into the receiver. "How can I hold on to my righteous anger when you're offering me sugar?"

"Is that a yes?" It was *so* a yes.

"I want you to know I'm only agreeing to this because those marshmallows are hand cut, and the chocolate is seventy-five percent cacao."

"I can respect that." Anything to get my foot back in the door. "See you in a few." I pulled up my hair as I headed for the front door and slung my purse over my shoulder. My very light purse. *Fiddlesticks.* Volkov still had my wallet tucked in the silver purse from the inauguration. Guess I was obeying the speed limit tonight. "I'm off to work," I informed Woolly. "Call me if you need me."

A warm swirl of air tickled my bare feet as the floor register hummed with contentment.

Despite her cheerfulness, I expected a fight when I reached for the doorknob. A thread of suspicion unspooled within me when her usual resistance never manifested. I didn't doubt she was happy to see my social circle had expanded beyond Amelie over the last several days, but I hadn't expected her to want me to go.

Maybe this more self-assured Woolly was the result of Boaz dropping in so often he might as well start paying rent. Or Amelie traipsing around at all hours. Or Keet tweeting his head off in front of the picture window. Or the influx of new visitors. It was hard to tell what had been the tipping point, but her rooms were full of laughter and conversation. She had a family again. That's all she'd ever wanted. I was happy one of our wishes were so easily fulfilled.

I was still thinking on Amelie when I reached the garage and bumped into Boaz and the gleaming monster that must be his new ride. I loosed a slow whistle and circled the bike, admiring her curves. Much like Jolene, she was crimson and chrome with a dash of black for contrast. The two bikes could have been siblings.

"Hello, gorgeous," I breathed.

"Hi yourself."

"The bike," I clarified, not that it did much to wipe the smug grin off his face. "How's your leg?"

"Still attached." He caved under the intensity of my glare and gave me a report. "I've got some bruising and soreness, but it'll heal. Happy? It's nothing I can't handle."

Call me cynical, but I doubted he had gotten off that easy. The lines bracketing his mouth told me he was in pain but doing his best to mask the ache of impact on his left leg. "What are you doing here?"

"Don't sound so suspicious." He had the nerve to act hurt. "I came to offer you a ride to work."

"Thanks to you, I have a ride." I pushed the button on my fob to raise the garage door. "Besides, I have a date with your sister after work. No boys allowed."

"Here's the thing." He rubbed the base of his neck. "I stayed up last night thinking about...everything." He cut his eyes toward the shadows like he expected one to break off from the cluster and start gunning for me. "You're pinging on the vamps' radar. They might not know exactly what you can do, but I'm betting there's a reason Volkov popped up when he did, and I'm guessing that means the Grande Dame isn't the only one with contacts inside the prison."

"That makes sense." I leaned against the side of the building. "The guards are necromancers, but the inmates are all kinds."

"You get what that means, right?" Boaz waited for me to piece it together. "You can't go out alone. Not until the dust settles, and we know what we're up against."

Leave it to Boaz to lump us together. I might as well be an honorary Pritchard considering how he treated me as if I were one of their own. The feeling of belonging, well, it didn't suck.

"You can't babysit me. That's not fair to you." I fingered the fresh plastic in my pocket, newly activated, and considered him. "I could hire you. Plenty of military and law enforcement guys do security."

He snorted like I'd told the most hilarious joke ever. "Get on the bike."

"You're not the boss of me." I followed up that zinger by planting my feet and refusing to budge. "I'm not going to take advantage of you."

"Crush my dreams, why don't you."

"Can you be serious for five minutes?"

"I want to take care of you." His eyes narrowed to irritated slits. "What's wrong with that?"

"Nothing." I wilted at his exasperation, hating how he viewed my craving for independence as rejection. Boaz smothered me because he loved me, I knew that, but I was tired of accepting his handouts without ever giving anything back. Even tonight, when I ought to hop on and avoid risking a ticket, I couldn't unstick my feet without saying my piece. "I just want to take care of myself for a change."

"We can get you there," he said after a minute. "But you have to crawl before you can walk, and, Squirt, you're still on your back with your legs kicking in the air like a flipped baby turtle."

Amelie was right. He really did have a weird fixation about getting me on my back.

"Gee, thanks." I glowered at him. "I'm humbled by your faith in me."

"You want your independence? Fine." He grinned, a slow and feral thing. "Earn it. Work with me on self-defense. I'll have time to teach you the basics before I leave, and I'll hook you up with a former army friend. Taslima." He sighed at my finger quotes around the word *friend*. "I didn't have sex with her. She shot me down. So you already have that in common. Taz can keep the classes going."

Working all night and then coming home to a butt-whooping from Boaz before dawn? I could think of a million things I'd rather do, but not a single one I ought to choose over what he was offering. I had too much riding on my ability to fend for myself to turn up my nose at his offer.

"Well?" he taunted, and stuck out his hand. "What do you say?"

For better or for worse, I shook his hand. "You've got yourself a deal."

TWELVE

Boaz dropped me off a half-dozen steps from the front doors of Haint Misbehavin', like I could manage to get in trouble between him and the entryway. I wasn't sure if I ought to be insulted six feet was as far as he trusted me or grateful I didn't have to risk another late-night rendezvous with my stalkerpire.

"Shift ends in six hours." I climbed off the bike. "I'll catch a ride with Amelie to Mallow. Are you headed home?"

"I'll be around," he said vaguely. "Got your phone?"

"Yes, Mom." I patted my cross-body purse. "I have ibuprofen in case of headaches and bandages in case of blisters too."

"Good girl." He let my sarcasm slide right off him and twisted his mouth up into a smile that promised nothing but trouble. "Have fun."

Worried about what that smile promised, I hurried inside and bumped into Amelie.

"Was that Boaz?" She craned to see over my shoulder. "I thought I heard that stupid bike of his."

"He gave me a ride."

Her nose crinkled. "How literal are we talking?"

"For the millionth time, I'm not having sex with your brother." Or any sex at all, despite the ridiculous injection of testosterone my life had received. "But since you spend so much time imagining us bumping uglies, if our uglies ever do bump, you'll be the first person I call with *all* the juicy details."

"You could have just told me to keep my nose out of your business."

"We're practically sisters." We had been stuck like glue since I came to live with Maud, way before my boy-crazy phase made me forget about that time I caught Boaz eating his own boogers on a dare. Mostly. Okay, so not even hormones could erase some horrors. "That makes it my solemn duty to inflict as much emotional distress and mental anguish on you as humanly possible."

"If that was your plan, then you succeeded beyond your wildest dreams."

Voices drifted down the hall from the room where Neely held court, meaning we had a few minutes until our turns with hair and makeup. Amelie led the way into the women's parlor, and we started pulling on our costumes. Her gown was buttery yellow and complemented her golden-blonde hair and warm, brown eyes.

The room bustled with the other female Haints prepping for the long night ahead, so we kept conversation light and didn't talk about any of the things that mattered until Neely called for us.

While Neely worked on Amelie, I thumbed through a few of the magazines he kept scattered around his workspace. Several sported blank sticky notes over brunette models with builds similar to mine, confirming my suspicions that I dressed so poorly he had resorted to shopping for me in his head as a form of therapy.

A petite woman edging toward fifty popped her head in the room. Dressed in a black satin swing dress straight out of the fifties, with her blonde hair pinned in victory rolls, Cricket was less Southern belle and more rockabilly in mourning.

"Neely," she mouthed around an unlit cigarette. "Enough with the primping. Amelie, get your butt in my office." She snapped her fingers. "Move it."

Being a good little employee, Amelie hopped straight to her feet and followed Cricket out.

Neely guided me into the chair then leaned around the corner to make sure the coast was clear.

"I didn't want to say anything in front of Amelie, but I've been dying to ask." He vibrated with excitement. "How did your date go with Volkov?"

"It was..." *life-changing, terrifying, amazing,* "...not bad. He's a decent guy."

Decent in the vampire sense of the word, which was not quite the same as the human one.

"That hardly sounds like a declaration of undying love."

Undying. Good one. "I haven't known him long enough for him to inspire more than the occasional hot flash."

Honestly? I wasn't sure how much of that was true attraction versus the lure, and I might not ever be.

"Chemistry is important." He tapped my nose with the end of his brush. "It's not as important as mutual respect, financial solvency or humor, but it's up there. It's been my experience the better you know a person, the more connected you feel to them, and the more attractive they become to you."

Comforted by the tickle of soft bristles over the bridge of my nose, it struck me why these sessions appealed to me when I was ultimately too lazy to learn how to apply more than mascara and lip gloss. Neely's medium might not be ink, but his brushes had been the only ones on my skin for the longest time.

"What about Boaz?" Neely shot me a look that dared me to deny we shared a spark. "The polite thing to do would have been to go with a man on each arm. They both put so much effort into impressing you. Seems a shame you had to choose. Why let one go to waste?"

"I'm not starting a harem." Though a blond and a brunette wasn't a bad place to start...

The grapevine would be buzzing after last night with rumors

circulating about whose arm I arrived on and whose car I left in. None of that factored in Boaz's swoon-worthy save either. I would have appeared quite the social butterfly, or worse, when nothing was further from the truth.

All I needed was for the pearl-clutchers and uptight suits with daughters of a marriageable age to think I was collecting eligible bachelors from all levels of Society. That would win me allies. Or, you know, a knife through my kidney.

"This is a judgment-free zone." He started twisting my hair into a thick braid. "So I expect you not to judge me when I say you should get out there and see what life has to offer before you settle down with one guy for the rest of your life. You're young. Have some fun. Break some rules."

Most days it felt like I had broken enough rules to last a lifetime. "How much did life offer you before you settled down?"

"Enough," he said with a sharp exhale.

I met his gaze in the mirror. "Is everything okay?"

"People just suck sometimes."

Recalling Cruz's hostility, I had to ask, "You'd tell me if you were having problems with someone at work, right?"

"You need this job more than I do." He squeezed my shoulder then reached for the curling iron. "The last thing I'd do is let you step in this flaming-hot mess."

Warmth flooded my chest that he would place my financial problems above his own equally serious ones, but that was just Neely. He had no idea this job was now a hobby for me, and selfish as it might be, I didn't want him viewing me in a different light. Everyone else was already sizing me up for their own purposes. Until I put in my notice or Amelie blabbed, I was content to be my old ramen-slurping self where he was concerned.

But, as the saying goes, with great power comes great responsibility, and I wasn't about to let this abuse go unpunished.

"Let me know if you change your mind." I gave myself a once-over when he stepped back to admire his work, understanding more now than I had last night what Neely meant when he said this was my character look, not my *me* look. "I'm off to spook the pants off my victims."

"Just make sure you go through their pockets before you donate them." He gave me a saucy wink. "Bring your waterproof parasol. There are showers in the forecast."

"Ugh." The odds for more than a good misting must be low or else Cricket would have put the kibosh on tonight's tours. Cancellations weren't for our benefit, naturally, but for the preservation of the dresses, suits, hats and parasols, and to save on her dry-cleaning bill. "Good thing I'll be leaving with Amelie. I hate riding Jolene in the rain."

A shudder rippled through him. "I don't know how you can stand to ride her at all."

"Bikes are freedom."

"Motorcycles are what happened when a man looked at a perfectly respectable bicycle and thought, *How can I transform this into a flaming death machine?*"

A laugh sneak attacked me, and I wheezed through the corset. "It's not for everyone, but still. Don't knock it until you try it. Bring Cruz to my house sometime. I'll give you guys lessons."

His demeanor softened. "He would look good in leather."

"See?" I swished toward the door. "It's a win/win."

On my way past the bulletin board, I pulled down the envelope with my list of victims and skimmed the details on each group. Fifteen in one and eight in another. A grumble worked its way past my lips before I remembered tips weren't do-or-die tonight. Armed with that comforting thought, I headed to The Point of No Return.

"Excuse me, miss," an all-too-innocent voice drawled behind me. "I'm a last-minute addition to your tour. Here's my ticket."

I stopped walking and started counting backwards from ten. "Boaz, what do you think you're doing?"

"Cricket said your groups were light tonight." He pressed a torn stub into my hand. "She was thrilled to sell me tickets for back-to-back tours." He rubbed his hands together. "Let's see what you got."

Mentally, I rerouted the later tour so he wouldn't have to trudge along the same path. "I expect you to behave."

"I'm a paying customer." He slapped his palm over his heart. "Whatever happened to *the customer's always right?*"

"That only counts for actual customers and not annoying big-brother types."

With a twist of my wrist, I stuck out the parasol I'd been using as a walking stick, a habit Cricket abhorred, out in front of him. Busy watching the swish of my skirts, Boaz tripped and stumbled into an awkward crouch on the pavement.

"Oh, sir. Are you all right?" I projected my voice to reach my victims and cranked up the charm. "I do apologize. Please forgive little ol' me. I hope you aren't injured."

"No harm done." His smile promised retribution. "Can you give me a hand up?"

It was a trap. It had to be. I did *not* want to give that man my hand while he had that look in his eyes, but we had the crowd's attention now, and there was no going back. "Of course."

He stood without applying an ounce of pressure on me and brought my hand up to his mouth where he pressed a lingering kiss into my palm then closed my fingers over the spot his lips had caressed. I angled my body away from the group then rolled my eyes so hard they whirled like tops.

Still in character, I bobbed in a neat curtsey, reclaimed my hand and strolled toward the gathering. Several of the women sized Boaz up with slow perusals, wetting their lips like they couldn't wait to taste him. A few of the men puffed up at the shift in attention away from them, but their chests deflated upon noticing I was the sole target of Boaz's lethal charm.

Lucky me.

We set out after I gave the booze talk, Boaz leading the pack, and

I guided us down one of my favorite routes, the one that passed a haunted brewery open to the public on the weekends.

"The Clark family owns the Black Dog Brewery. The bar is street level, and there's a fantastic garden out back. I highly recommend the stuffed jalapenos, but I've heard good things about their burgers too. The downstairs is under renovation at the moment, and it's got its own creepy history, but tonight we're going to focus on the two stories above the bar that are so haunted the ghosts refuse to allow the renovations necessary for the business to expand."

I got a few interested murmurs out of that one, so I pushed ahead.

"The last time Mr. Clark attempted to have the second floor brought up to code, he got calls from his furious workers demanding compensation for their ruined equipment. Apparently, several guys had left their larger, and therefore more expensive, power tools upstairs overnight, and when they came back the next morning, all the windows had been thrown open—even the ones painted shut—and their drills, saws and nail guns had been tossed out onto the street."

"That can't be true," a gruff man argued.

The teen boy next to him smirked. "What? You don't believe in ghosts, man?"

"No." He shifted on his feet, uncomfortable in the spotlight. "I don't believe that thousands of dollars' worth of power tools would still be on the street in the morning."

Tittering laughter rippled through the crowd, and I joined in. "I can't argue that logic."

"How do you know this stuff actually happened?" a girl asked from under the boy's arm. "Are y'all given a script or something?"

Unlike my annoyance with out-and-out skeptics who seemed to book tours for the sole purpose of making the guides' nights miserable, I could appreciate a healthy dose of honest doubt.

"Each guide is required to study the history of the locations on every individual route. That information is pulled from books, old newspaper clippings and the internet." I gave what I hoped was a winning smile to the man who asked the original question. "We're all guilty of exaggeration to create a juicier story." I held up a hand to forestall their next questions. "*But*, and this is an important *but*, the bare bones are true. Go home. Google. You'll find all the information I covered tonight and so much more."

"Cool," the teens murmured in sync, cementing my assumption of their coupledom.

"Any more questions?" I must have done something right because the crowd shook its head in unison. "In that case, y'all can follow me right across the street to the oldest restaurant in Savannah."

"You've got them eating out of the palm of your hand," Boaz murmured near my elbow.

"Stepping into a role is freeing." The job helped me feel normal for a few hours a night. As much as any Southern belle spewing grisly horror stories for tips can be called normal. "It's a fun job."

"Amelie's always loved it." He appeared thoughtful. "She's going to miss it when she graduates and picks up full-time work in her field."

"Once a Haint, always a Haint." I twirled my parasol. "She can always pitch in at Halloween if she starts pining for the good old days."

"Hard to believe she'll have her MBA in a few years." He shook his head like it might help him absorb the fact his little sister was growing up. "A Master's in Business Administration. What will she even do with that?"

Jealousy, that old green-eyed monster, reared its ugly head, and I'm ashamed how long it took me to defang. I hated that petty side of me. Hated how I envied Amelie's bright future. Hated being so screwed up I kept enabling the cycle.

We had always planned on sharing a dorm room, or maybe getting a small apartment off-campus, but that hadn't happened. Obviously. Living at home had to be saving her a ton of money, though. So there was a bright side in there. And it's not like it was her fault that when I held the future we'd planned against the one I'd been handed, I fell short.

I'd earned my GED after a few weeks of classes, but there were gaps in my formal education as well as my necromantic one. In a prison where parole was a pipe dream and the inmates were drugged until all they could string together was drool, the Society wasted no funds on bettering us. And, with Amelie nearing her final stretch, I had no hope of catching up to her.

Just the thought of being the new kid again...

"Marketing," I answered after too long of a pause, quoting the answers she'd given me when I'd asked the same question. "Accounting. Management. Computer information systems, whatever that means."

"I have an associate degree in criminal justice."

"Really?" I glanced over at him. "I didn't know that. Congrats. I bet the pics of you in your cap and gown—" I tried picturing him all solemn and dignified. Instead, I remembered the catastrophe that had been his high school graduation. "Did you wear clothes under the gown this time?"

His eyes crinkled at the corners. "That's between me and the goddess."

I burst out laughing. "That's a *no*."

"Cut me some slack." His wounded act failed courtesy of the mischief glinting in his eyes. "I'm trying to impress you here."

Impress? Boaz had been as naked as the day he was born under that gown, and he wanted me thinking long and hard about what I'd missed out on. Emphasis on the long and the hard. That part of Boaz's anatomy had ceased to be a mystery the day he walked on stage, accepted his diploma with one hand and hiked up his gown to moon the crowd with the other. To this day, I'm not sure if I ought to be thankful I didn't get the full moon, or if the side-peen I glimpsed was somehow worse.

Exhibitionism was apparently a turn-on for him. Shocker.

A prickling sense of unease swept over me as we neared the restaurant, and I slowed my pace.

"Keep walking, Squirt." Boaz waited for me to catch up to him. "They won't make a move in front of so many witnesses."

They? Three men played checkers on the swayback front porch. When we got within five yards of them, the tallest one lifted his head, met my gaze and winked at me. "It's my stalkerpire. Looks like he brought friends."

"Stalkerpire?" He chuckled before patting a chest pocket on the leather jacket he hadn't removed. "Don't worry. I brought friends of my own."

Stakes? There were no laws that said you couldn't arm yourself against other supernatural races. But the Society found the notion of self-defense so unseemly as to punish those who got caught brandishing weapons sharper than their wit.

They were under the mistaken impression that, as the race who created vampirism, vampires were somehow beholden unto necromancers. While that might be strictly true, and most were respectful enough, the perfume had faded from that rose long ago. Vamps didn't appreciate being treated as second-class citizens, but the Society never let them forget their place, as evidenced by their subfloor seating at the Lyceum.

"What are the odds of this not ending in blood?" I whispered out of the side of my mouth while smiling back at my victims, hoping they believed the lie they saw written on my face and ignored the clanging of their inner warning bells. Running from a predator was a bad idea. It turned those warning bells into dinner bells real quick. "I need to get these people to safety."

"These people are your safety." Cannon fodder was what he meant. "These guys have been following us for the last five blocks. That they got here ahead of us is a bad thing, Grier. It means they're learning your routes."

Hunting me like feral cats with one mouse to split between them. "Why didn't you say anything?"

"There's nothing you could have done, so why worry you?"

His logic was sound, and I got why he'd kept his mouth shut, but his attitude reminded me so much of Volkov at that moment I was amazed when smoke didn't pour out of my ears. Protecting me was one thing. Coddling me was another. I didn't care if my only choices were exsanguination or exsanguination with a side order of kidnapping, I wanted to make that call for myself even when the answer was obvious. I wanted the courtesy of being asked instead of having my fate decided for me. Again.

"I'll do what I can to drag out the last three stops, but we need to hash out a plan."

"I've got it covered," he assured me.

"I bet you do." I stormed off to begin my recitation. Though my skin crawled when I turned my back on the vamps, I trusted Boaz to save me from becoming a pincushion. "This is the Rumrunner, founded back in 1789 by the pirate..."

The vamps gave up all pretense of playing their game to listen in and sneer at us. The crowd got restless, their hindbrains twitching without understanding why, and I hurried through the rest of my talking points. As my group hit the sidewalk heading toward a more residential area, with brighter streetlights, they shook off the worst of their unease.

"Why were those guys being so rude?"

I located the speaker—the teenage girl—and took a moment to pause and address the group. "The sad truth is some locals get their jollies by heckling guides and their groups. I don't see the appeal, but it happens at least once a week. I'm sorry it happened to you."

At least the skeptics I got. They wanted a forum to voice their contrary opinion, and they were willing to pay money to one-up a guide peddling the opposite of their beliefs even when it ruined what should have been a fun outing for everyone else. A total waste of cash, if you asked me, but whatever.

Locals showing their backsides, though? That I didn't get. Sure, the Southern-belle thing might be a tad ridiculous, but that was half the fun. Ghost tours were a booming industry in towns with a claim to a bloody heritage. We helped the tourist trade. We kept history, albeit the gorier side of it, alive. Where was the harm? Why the hate?

Of course telling my group that vampires were stalking us was more likely to end with my faux victims becoming actual victims when they swarmed the vamps and started quizzing them on their undead lives and asking the usual questions about how one went about getting bitten. Receiving the bite was easy. Heck, there were vampire restaurants where they chose willing humans right off the menu. But much like the misguided warg lore claiming one bite would turn you into a slavering wolf on the nights of the full moon, a vampire bite wouldn't turn you immortal either. Neither would drinking their blood, though I did once see a human get high that way.

Want to become a vamp? You need a willing necromancer, a signed contract, and a verified money transfer before that happens.

The group shuffled, eager to keep moving toward the lights. These victims were getting the short end of the stick tonight between the tool debate and the leering vampire debacle. I sensed a few of them were ready for this to end so they could go back to their hotels, and I hated their evening had been a downer. We breezed through two stops when the crowd remained listless. The vamps had trailed us. I could sense them in the prickling of the fine hairs down my nape. Or maybe that was my imagination running wild.

We reached The Point of Hey You Made It Back, and the crowd dispersed in an eager rush. Boaz ushered me inside then set off toward a cluster of shadows pooling under a Bradford pear tree heavy with white blossoms. Amelie met me in the hall dressed in jeans, a tee and sneakers. Wasting no time, she shackled my wrist with her fingers.

"We're going out the back." She hauled me toward the rear exit. "Boaz is distracting them for us."

"I can't leave. Cricket would murder me if I left in one of her gowns." I pulled against her. "And I still have one tour left."

"Not quite." Neely swaggered from his makeshift salon and struck a pose in the hallway. His dark-gray trousers looked painted on, but his matching frock coat hid a multitude of sins, and his cravat, tied with an intentional air of negligence, made him appear quite the dandy. The stovepipe hat he doffed in our direction completed the ensemble. "I have one tour left."

I let Amelie drag me a few more steps. "You don't have to do this."

"Sure, I do." He shoved up my skirt in the front, untied the bow cinching the hoop skirt in at my waist and shoved the frame down around my feet like a coiled Slinky. "That's what friends are for." He drew back and inspected me. "That'll do. This way you'll fit in the car."

"Thanks, Neely." I kissed his cheek. "You're the best."

"Yes, well, your boyfriend's tip paid for Cruz and me to rent a cabin for the weekend up on Stone Mountain. It's the least I can do."

Caving to Amelie's sense of urgency, I followed her out the rear exit. "What about your tours?"

"I'm done. Remember when Cricket pulled me into her office? She was telling me the private tour I had tonight cancelled. The bride has mono." She herded me toward her car. "With Neely covering for you, we're both off the hook."

"What did you tell him?" The truth wasn't an option. "Why does he think I had to ditch?"

"I didn't have to tell him anything except you needed a favor."

Stupid tears wavered in my vision. Neely was a good egg.

"Where are we going?" I climbed in her car and waited for her to join me. "I'm guessing Mallow is out of the question."

"Boaz said to get you home." She cranked the engine then sped out of the lot, hands white-knuckled on the wheel. "We can have burgers delivered if you want. I don't have anywhere to be since I'm off early. For once, I don't have any studying to do either. Classes don't start back until next week." She glanced over at me. "It's been forever since we spent more than five minutes together."

"Burgers it is then." I pulled up the app for our favorite pub and started ordering. "To molten lava cake for dessert or not to molten lava cake for dessert?"

"How is that even a question?"

When she was right, she was right.

THIRTEEN

The delivery girl almost beat us to the front door, and I could have kissed her rosy cheeks once the smell of hand-cut fries hit my nose. Food made my situation seem less dire. Food that I could now pay for without counting out lint-covered pennies I dug from under the couch cushions would taste even sweeter.

While I swiped my debit card through the girl's card reader and tacked on a fat tip to encourage her to zip out here the next time I ordered, Amelie carried the bags into the kitchen and set up our feast.

"I picked up the Oregon Trail card game last week," I said while bumping the door shut with my hip. "Do you want to see who can die of dysentery first?"

The Oregon Trail was the first video game I had ever played. Amelie had a brother, so she was no stranger to the virtual landscape. Being an only child with a caretaker who was known to grumble over the switch from horse and buggy to automobiles meant the anti-quated program on our school computers was my first exposure to gaming. Though Amelie would bust a gut laughing if I called it that out loud.

"Maybe after we eat?" She stuck her face in the bag and inhaled. "That game always makes me hungry."

"Me too." I rubbed my stomach. "I always run out of food first."

We settled on our usual stools and passed out the grub, not wasting time on things like manners before digging in with moans of approval.

"Boaz told me you've been reinstated as the Woolworth heir," she said around a bite of hamburger. "It's nowhere near enough for what they put you through, but it's a good start. I assume that means they forked over your inheritance too?"

"They did indeed." And it could all vanish again in the blink of an eye.

"Have you considered setting up an offshore account," she asked too casually.

"I haven't even checked to see how much is in there, so that's a no." I laughed off the suggestion until I caught her expression. "You're serious?"

"Promise you won't tell my lunkhead brother about this?"

"Cross my heart."

"He coped with you being gone by planning prison breaks, and I might have gotten wrapped up in the logistics with him a time or two. He had all these contingency plans outlined, but I kept circling back to how expensive it would be to live your life on the run, and it got me thinking about your inheritance. Maud was old school. Remember how much she hated checkbooks? Forget credit or debit cards." She shook her head. "What kept me up nights was thinking if she'd diversified instead of lumping all her cash in one bank, and a Society branch at that, you might have been set. Offshore accounts are the best option, and I do mean multiples, but normal human banks would offer you some protection too."

"You think I might be in a position where I need this one day." Hard to blame her when I felt the same.

"I think the new Grande Dame has a vested interest in you, and until we know what that is, you're in danger." Seeming to have lost her appetite, she set down her food. "You don't want to draw her attention if she's watching your account." Considering the Society had established it themselves, that was a given. "But withdrawing a little here and a little there and using it to pad your contingency plan seems like a solid idea to me."

Chest bowed with pride, I was seriously impressed with her advice and felt like more of a heel than ever for begrudging her the education she had worked so hard to earn. "Boaz and I were wondering what you planned on doing with your MBA. I'll have to let him know you're using your education to mastermind cushy lives for fugitives."

"Hey." She dusted off her shoulder. "Somebody's got to do it."

After inhaling a handful of salty fries, I noticed we had nothing to wash them down with and stood. "Do you want some tea or lemonade?"

"Tea, please." A text message chimed in Amelie's pocket, and she pulled out her cell and skimmed the screen. "Boaz lost the vampires."

I flicked a glance at the front door like they might be polite enough to knock first before devolving into fist-banging and more threats. "Have they realized you sneaked me out yet?"

"I'll ask." Her fingers blurred over the keys. Before she hit send, the phone rang. "I'm not slow," she snapped in the voice reserved for her brother. "I have short fingers." She listened for a second. "Grier is right here, safe and sound. No— Are you crazy? Wait. Don't answer that." She thrust the phone at me. "You deal with him."

"What is your damage?" I asked through a mouthful of juicy burger goodness.

"The vamps scattered after the late-late tour departed," he panted, footsteps hammering in the background. "They must have gotten the tour schedule from Cricket. She wouldn't think anything of a victim requesting a specific guide. That or they've been watching you long enough to figure it out on their own. Either way, it's bad news. The leader peeled off when you didn't lead the nine o'clock tour, but I spotted him circling the block in a black Escalade. When the midnight group left and you were nowhere in sight, the whole crew ditched."

"Do you think they'll come after me at home?" My stalkerpire wasn't shy about trespassing.

"I'd bet money on it." Metal clinked in the background. "Be there in a few."

"See you when you get here." I ended the call then exhaled. "Boaz is on his way."

"What about the vampires?"

"We might have company." I packed up my food and shoved it in the fridge for later. While I was up, I took a moment to check the jury-rigged wards, but their low-level hum indicated they were holding firm. "Let's hope Boaz gets here before they do."

Amelie's hand lifted to her throat, and she rubbed the skin there with her fingertips.

A knock on the door interrupted me before I could pour us drinks, and we exchanged wary glances.

"Sit tight," I told her and stalked across the room where I peered through the peephole. Volkov grinned at me, his usual guards flanking him, both armed to the teeth. Blowing out an exhale, I rested my forehead against the door. "Looks like we have backup."

Volkov might be pissed about how things played out last night, but he wouldn't burn any bridges until I gave him back his bangle. Still, I double-checked with Woolly. "Is it safe?"

The chandelier crystals tinkled like laughter.

The door swung open under my fingers, and Volkov lifted a gauzy scrap of royal-blue fabric. "This was found in our box. The courier from the Lyceum returned it to me since we arrived together." The silver purse full of my ID was clutched in his hand. "And this I forgot to return to you last night."

"Thank you." I pocketed Amelie's cell for a minute while I reached out and snagged the purse. "I meant to text you to arrange for a pickup, but I got distracted. You saved me a trip."

In my haste to welcome our potential allies, I'd forgotten one critically important detail. The part about how Volkov wasn't technically my ally.

His fingers latched around my wrist where my bangle wasn't, and he dialed up his lure to smolder. Warmth spread up my arm, through my chest, past my jaw, until sparkles danced across my field of vision. Heat pulsed low in my stomach, and I smiled at him, tipsy, as the purse thudded at my feet.

One slow pull, and I stood in the circle of Volkov's arms before I registered making the decision to move.

A lightbulb flashed over my head. The vampires. They were the ones who had tampered with Woolly's wards, tweaking them, testing them, until she allowed one in the house. And I had been too weak to notice them severing our connection until it was too late.

No wonder Volkov hadn't risked coming inside again. The potential of me locating the damage and repairing it now that I had access to Society resources was too high.

The porchlight flashed in panicked bursts until the bulb fizzled from the overload, and the porch went dark. That explained why my lightbulb moment had been literal.

"There's someone I would like you to meet." He nuzzled me, the rasp of his beard delicious against my skin. "Will you come with me?"

"Grier," Amelie cried out. "Don't—"

One of the guards lunged at her, smacking against the invisible barrier filling the doorway, and she screamed.

"Come with me," Volkov coaxed, the scent of him effervescent in my blood. "Would you like that?"

"Mmm." I curled against his chest, breathing him in, and let him guide me down the stairs. The driver tipped his chin at me and opened the rear passenger door. Another male sat across from me, our knees brushing. A trill of fear shot up my spine, and my heart rate spiked. "I remember you."

"Shh." Volkov joined us, hauling me into his lap with gentle hands. "Pay him no mind."

"We should have done this from the start," the male sighed, his voice husky and deep. "I wasted a week of my time on recon when you could have hooked her from the start and saved us all this trouble."

His voice sounded so familiar... I angled my head for a peek at his face, but Volkov cupped my jaw and turned me back to him. Try as I might, I couldn't look away from the storm gathering in his thundercloud eyes.

"I had hoped to earn her trust." His thumb kneaded the thin skin over my carotid. "I wanted a willing partner."

"You can make her willing." The other male cracked his knuckles in rapid succession. "After a few months, she won't know the difference."

A flicker of panic tripped my pulse, but Volkov used his scent to ease my fears.

"The master should have left this matter up to me." His fingers traced the high curve of my cheekbones. "I could have made her see reason. All I needed was more time."

"Is that why one of my guys spotted her wearing that necromancer's shirt to bed?"

A growl pumped through Volkov's chest that rattled my teeth. *"Mine."*

The vibration soothed me, and I snuggled closer against him, burying my face in the curve of his throat.

"Dial it down a few notches." The other male coughed a few times. "Or I'll have to crack a window."

The words no sooner left his mouth than fists pummeled the glass near my head. A man with warm, brown eyes, his lip snarled up in a promise of retribution, bellowed my name. I lifted my hand in a tiny wave that Volkov stilled by pressing my fingertips to his lips.

With his skin on mine, his scent in my lungs, I slid into a sleep too deep for the banging to disturb me.

FOURTEEN

The glittering chandelier overhead blasted my pulse up into the stratosphere.

It was all a dream. Part of the nightmare. I'm home. In the foyer. That's my chandelier.

"Woolly," I murmured, lips dry and tongue thick.

"Miss?" A willowy brunette who looked no older than me bustled into the room with a pressed suit hanging from each hand. The door standing open behind her appeared to lead into a closet filled with similar outfits and a rack of coordinating shoes and accessories. "Oh, dear, you are awake at last. How marvelous."

The room, which was not my foyer, swam into slow focus around me.

Rose-pink walls. Gleaming white furniture. Shimmering gold accents.

Bookcases crammed with children's books lined two of the walls. Dolls slumped on every available surface, their porcelain faces sullen, all hope lost that tiny hands would ever lift them for play again. A hard lump under my hip produced a plush rabbit with a sculpted face. A dozen other stuffed animals in varying colors and sizes littered the queen-sized bed, walling me up in the center of the mattress.

All those eyes staring at me... *Creepy.*

A shudder rippled through me when I shoved upright and ended up palming the porcelain face of a bear. I knocked it away and wiped my hand down my shirt then startled. "Where are my clothes?" I clutched at the pink flannel button-down pajama top I wore and gaped at the matching pants and fluffy socks that completed the ensemble. "Who dressed me like this?"

"Oh, I did." The woman hung her burdens on the back of a door then faced me and...curtseyed. That's when what she wore registered. A pink dress, the same color as the walls, tickled her ankles. She wore a frilly white lace apron over the top, like frosting on a strawberry cake, and an equally ridiculous cap over her hair. "I told the master you were too grown for the likes of all this, but he insisted you use your old room, and one doesn't argue with the master."

"My old room?" Clearly, all the sugary pink was rotting her brain. I had never seen this pastel prison before in my life. "Where am I?"

"Oh, miss." She wrung her hands and glanced toward the door. "Please don't get worked up again."

Again? What was that supposed to mean?

A well-aimed kick sent plushies flying and gave me room to scoot down to the foot of the bed. My legs dangled, the mattress stacked so high she might as well have been calling me Pea. As in *The Princess and the...*

"Who are you?" I hopped down, saved from slipping on the hardwood floor by the grabby soles of the socks. "Why am I here?"

"I'm Lena, miss." Scurrying around the bed, she bundled the plushies in her arms. "This is where you belong. Where else should you be? What a silly question."

With her occupied on the far side of the bed, I ran straight to the door and tried the handle. *Locked.* Had I really expected anything less?

"You've got the wrong girl." I flew to the window and jiggled the latch. *Locked.* Who used a keyed lock on their freaking windows? "This is so very far away from where I belong." Or was it? She never had answered my question. How close was I to home? To help? I gazed out the window at the expansive grounds, the manicured gardens and the encroaching forest that stretched as far as the eye could see. "Where is this place?"

"This is your home. The master has awaited your return for ever so long, miss."

An arrangement of white roses sat on a desk beneath the window, their perfume turning my wish for home into a physical ache. I pretended interest in the flowers while weighing the gilded vase. It was metal, not too heavy, but perhaps sturdy enough. I dumped out the flowers, the water cascading over the desktop and splashing across the planks. I gripped the vase and swung it as hard as I could into the window. The metal thumped dully and bounced off the pane, slipping from my wet fingers to clatter on the floor.

Bulletproof glass.

"Dearie me." A fang pressed into her bottom lip as she rushed to clean up the mess. "He won't like this at all."

The sound caused a scuffle to break out in the hall, or maybe the window was rigged with an alarm. Either way, the door burst open, and Volkov prowled through, elongated canines on display until spotting first the mess, then the maid, and lastly me.

"Grier?" He breathed my name. "What happened?"

"Where am I?" I flattened my back against the wall. "What have you done?"

"Everything will be all right," he promised. "This is for your own safety, *solnishko*."

"Are you two deaf?" I screamed. "Stop ignoring me. Where. Am. I?"

"That information is classified. Pitch all the tantrums you like, no one here will give you that information." My stalkerpire strolled in with a grin. "Anyone who does won't live long enough for you to share it." He flanked Volkov, eyes on Lena. "Is that what you want? The death of an innocent on your conscience?"

I slid to the floor, pulled my legs up to my chest and rested my chin on my knees.

"Knock her out," my stalkerpire ordered. "Maybe the third time will be the charm."

"There's no need for that." Volkov squatted a safe distance away. "You'll behave, won't you?"

I stared straight ahead and kept my mouth shut.

"I am sorry," he murmured. "I wish things could be different between us."

When I didn't combust in a violent rage, Volkov appeared satisfied and stood. "Lena, send word if you require my services." His eyes met mine when he said, "The guards will know where to find me."

A warning. To let me know Lena was but the first obstacle should I attempt an escape.

The males left, and I kept on staring. Right through Lena, who had knelt while she checked my hands for cuts despite the fact my escape attempt was an epic failure. Even the thorns had been cut from the rose stems. Now the metal vase made sense. I doubt there was a single breakable object in my room with the exception of the dolls. That might do for a weapon in a pinch, but it wasn't going to help me escape.

A gasp broke free of my chest, and then another and another.

"Don't cry, miss." Lena rubbed my shoulders. "It will be all right. You'll see."

But my eyes were dry, not a tear to blur the room as my vision telescoped to a single pinprick of light.

The door is locked and guarded. The window is sealed and unbreakable. There are guards in the hall.

I was a prisoner all over again.

Lungs burning, I gulped oxygen until I choked from swallowing. Not enough. Never enough. I clawed at my throat, raking furrows in my skin. I couldn't breathe. The walls pressed closer, suffocating me.

Air whistled through my teeth. No use. It was no use. None of it. I was trapped. In this room and in my mind and in my body. I couldn't escape.

The speck of light extinguished, and I was thrust back into the darkness.

The cold seeps into my bones. The putrid stink of my own filth clogs my nose until I part my ragged lips and suck in rank air swirling near the floor where I press my cheek. A man whimpers nearby. He cries all the time. Doesn't he realize that only makes it worse? For all of us? Somewhere a woman sings in a language I've never heard, her voice ruined after a guard crushed her neck beneath his boot. She bit him. I think she wanted him to kill her. Instead she was whisked away to the infirmary, given a taste of clean sheets and warm food, then cast back into her dank cell to suffer the memory.

"You're home now."

For the life of me, I couldn't tell if whoever spoke the words meant them as a comfort or as a taunt.

"...FIVE YEARS IN ATRAMENTOUS..."

"...this room is hardly a prison..."

"...needs to breathe..."

"I will tell the master."

I rocketed toward consciousness and propelled myself right off the bed.

I stood alone in a different room, this one blessedly normal, a guest suite done up in soothing blues reminiscent of coastal waters instead of some twisted princess theme. No sign of Lena.

A warm swirl of night air gusted my bangs into my eyes as I gravitated toward a set of French doors someone had left propped open to let in a breeze. I padded outside onto a patio. When that wasn't enough, I kept walking until my toes sank in the plush grass. I bent down and tugged until I pulled up roots. The rich, earthy scent of soil grounded me.

I used to dream about places like this during the times when it made no difference in the landscape if my eyes remained open or closed. Gardens without walls. Sky without end. Moonlight on my skin.

Freedom.

But it was all an illusion. The boxwood maze that hemmed in my spacious yard backed up to a stone wall. An inch of exposed rock peeped over the top, ruining the fantasy. The sky might be limitless, but I wasn't as fortunate. The caress of moonbeams was a small comfort. While I was sleeping off my panic attack, or Volkov's remedy, they had transferred their new pet from her gilded cage into a terrarium made of stone walls and stars.

The thought made me laugh, though my throat was too raw for me to make a sound.

Bone-weary, I sat on the lawn and let my mind wander. Bits and pieces of my abduction slid around in my skull, but none of the pieces interlocked. The one clear image I salvaged was of Boaz as he pounded on the glass, his eyes full of wrath, the promise of a painful death carved in every line of his face.

What was he doing now? Formulating more of his plans? Knowing him, he'd implemented half of them before Amelie finished screaming my name. At least they had each other. And, apparently, a few years' worth of pent-up rage at the system that might help them cope if the worst happened.

The slight tremble in my bottom lip infuriated me, and I bit down until I tasted copper.

I will not break.

Maud was gone, a chunk of my life wasted, but I was still here. I had survived. I would survive again.

All I had to do was swallow down the fear clogging my throat, breathe through the band cinching tighter around my chest, and stay present. No hiding behind mental walls when reality got too hard.

Time to put my resolve to the test.

Where was I? I couldn't have been unconscious that long. Then again, I had no recollection of waking prior to the last one. How far had he put me under to erase chunks of my memory? What had happened to me during that time?

After conducting a mental inventory, I decided I felt fine. A small headache, some tightness in my chest and a few other aches and pains that could be blamed on a long sleep without switching positions. I studied my hands, the ones I'd never expected to hold a brush again, and wished more than anything that I could speak to Maud one last time.

What have you done, you wily old coot?

Burying her head in the sand wasn't like Maud. Better than anyone, she should have known ignoring a problem wouldn't make it go away. Maybe she had wanted me to be older before I faced this. Maybe she thought she could protect me. Maybe death had seemed so abstract after all her centuries of living that she had miscalculated how much time she had left. And then those precious few decades that remained had been snatched away. Whatever her plan, it was a bust now.

Sprawling on my back, I crossed my ankles and folded my hands behind my head.

I stared up at the sky until I couldn't tell one blackness from another as my eyelids closed.

FIFTEEN

Three days into my captivity, as best as I could tell, I climbed into the comforting void in my head and stayed there. Not even the enticement of the outdoors tempted me from under the covers. I saw no one except Lena, who fretted over me, tucking and untucking me on the downy mattress I had no strength to leave. The entire scope of my world had narrowed to the bed, and I had trouble thinking beyond its comforting softness. Even the nightmares left me alone to cuddle my pillow and drift.

That was their first mistake.

Allowing me to wake in bed night after night tipped me off to how wrong I had been acting, how wrong I felt. I hadn't fought them since that first night, and that wasn't like me. I was a survivor. Not this docile invalid who swallowed spoon-fed lies and asked for seconds.

I scrounged up the will to examine the floor under the bedframe on the fourth night. The lack of sigils meant magic wasn't the culprit. No, they must have gone a more traditional route and drugged me through food and drink. That was the only explanation that made sense.

Otherwise I would have literally been climbing the walls by now, and the boxwood would have made it easy. Knowing my luck, Volkov would have been waiting to catch me on the other side. Him or my stalkerpire, who I had yet to hear named. Was his identity as protected as our whereabouts? I was starting to wonder why that might be.

Lena had breezed through the doorway at some point. I wasn't sure how long she'd stood there, looking down on me while I daydreamed of escape, before I smelled steak with grilled onions and noticed her.

"Would you like me to help you up, miss?"

I turned my head toward her. "Can I eat on the patio today?"

"I don't see why not." Her left fang dented her bottom lip. "It's such a lovely night."

"I'll behave." I forced a laugh that sounded like the dying gasp from a corpse. "I need some fresh air."

A change swept over her upon hearing the word *air*. "Let me clear a path." Her movements blurred in their swiftness. Clearly, my panic attack had spooked them. "Just keep breathing. In through the nose, out through the mouth." She whisked the food out to the table I'd barely noticed my first night in the garden room and rematerialized at my elbow. "I can get Mr. Volkov if—"

"*No.*" I forced my tone to calm. "I don't want to bother him. I'm sure he's very busy."

"He's the master's right hand these days." She exhaled a breathy sigh. "Handsome too. Kind. Generous. Such a power for one so young. You're awful lucky to have caught his eye, miss, if you don't mind me saying so."

If you like him so much, then you can have him. "He makes an impression for sure."

How well he'd lied to my face, faked being my friend, acted like he cared that I have a say in our relationship sure impressed the heck out of me.

Accepting my backhanded compliment as earnest praise, Lena

helped me sit upright then swung my legs over the side of the bed. I wasn't sure I'd have the strength to make it across the room, but my feet never touched the floor. She scooped me up into her arms, carried me outside and deposited me in my chair, all without breaking a sweat.

"There now. That's much better." She straightened her apron, which was still white, but made of linen. Her uniform had mellowed from Strawberry Shortcake into more casual attire. A white dress shirt with capped sleeves paired with dove-gray skirt and ballet flats. "I'll go tidy up your room while you enjoy your dinner."

Steaks came precut these days. Couldn't risk me playing with knives, could they? I popped a tasteless cube in my mouth to show what a good girl I could be when I put my mind to behaving. "Do you think you could get me something?"

"I will do my best."

"There was a bunny plush in my other room." I spooned up the mashed potatoes and forced down the first bite. "I was wondering if you might bring him to me."

"That I can do." A happy laugh bubbled out of her. "I thought you might remember him. He was always your favorite. That's why I put him where you couldn't miss him."

What I remembered was waking up with his face imprinted on my right butt cheek. That was the extent of our relationship as far as I was concerned.

"He's cute." I sipped from my glass, the wine too smoky for me to determine if there was more to its taste than toasted oak barrels. "I wouldn't mind having some company, you know?"

A flicker of pity crossed her delicate features. "I'll have to clear it with Mr. Volkov, you understand, but he would do anything for you."

Except let me go. "Thank you."

"Of course, miss."

"Lena?" I infused my voice with equal parts curiosity and eagerness. "When will I meet the master?"

"I can't rightly say," she admitted. "He's a busy male."

Too busy to check in on his captive? He must be very busy indeed. Or, just maybe, he wasn't here.

That would explain why no one had done anything with me up to now.

While I mulled over what they wanted from me and why they hadn't tried hard to get it yet, I forced down my meal. I skimmed my gaze over the patio, searching for weapons or means of escape or inspiration. All I found was a single, perfect clamshell pressed into the otherwise immaculate expanse of concrete that left me wondering who this room's original occupant might have been.

The colors and the shell reminded me of Odette and her seaside bungalow.

Then again, considering the bizarre pinkscape in my previous accommodations, maybe each room in this estate was themed.

Lena changed my sheets and set out clean pajamas, humming a song so familiar I could have joined in the chorus. I almost asked what it was but figured she was as likely to give me a straight answer as she was to turn into a bat and fly across the moon.

I hadn't showered in almost a week, not that you could tell from my softly waving hair and moisturized skin. I was ninety-nine percent certain that I received daily sponge baths, a humiliation I was grateful to sleep through.

Finished with the main course, I dug into the chocolate mousse. The first bite dissolved on my tongue. Past that, I couldn't feel my tongue...or much else. The world spun faster when I turned my head toward Lena, but she caught me as I toppled from my chair and carried me back to the bed.

Hours later, I woke to find the hideous rabbit tucked in next to me like we were old pals.

Sleep pressed on me, a cool weight that suffocated, and my eyelids fluttered.

No.

Atramentous had taken years to rob me of my spirit. I wasn't caving again in under a week. I wasn't caving again *ever*.

Worried about noise carrying to my guards, I removed one of my fuzzy socks and tugged it down over the rabbit's head. Smashing his face against the edge of the wooden headboard was oddly satisfying. I peeled down the top and reached inside, choosing the sharpest, thickest piece of porcelain.

There were only so many places I could hide it where it might not be found. Not on me. My person wasn't sacred here. The sheets were out too. Those got changed each time I left the bed. The one constant was the French doors remained open at all times. One shard could go unnoticed out there.

Lethargy weighted my limbs as I swung my legs over the side of the bed. I tried standing but crumpled. The best I could do was hold the shard between my teeth, lips peeled back to keep from cutting myself, as I crawled on all fours into the yard.

While I debated where to bury my treasure, I noticed that same perfect seashell pressed into the concrete along the farthest edge. Careful not to bark my knees or palms, I inched forward until I could shove the pointed end into the dirt, leaving me a shallow edge to grasp when it came time to retrieve my new best friend.

Getting back in bed took forever, and I was drenched in sweat when my head hit the pillow, but sleep came between one blink and the next.

LENA WAS ARRANGING my breakfast out on the patio when I woke the next night with the rabbit curled against my side like I'd been snuggling him. I'd built up the sheet between us so I wouldn't get cut, but now it was time to get the creeper tossed out on his cotton tail.

Once the maid turned her back, I leaned over the edge of the bed and dumped the contents of my sock on the floor. The next phase of my plan was going to suck. Gritting my teeth in anticipation of the pain, I pulled the splinter-filled sock back on my foot, wincing as the fragments pierced my sole, and sat upright. With no small amount of glee, I dropped the rabbit, and the remainder of his face shattered on the planks.

"Oh no." Blood dripped from the end of one sock, so all I had to do was make a footprint to show how I'd gotten injured. "Lena, can you—?"

But Lena, being a vampire, smelled the blood and rushed to me before I finished the sentence.

"Miss, what happened?" Her small chest rose in eager pants, breathing in the coppery scent. "Your poor foot. Wait right there."

Docile as a lamb, I did as I was told while attempting to look sad about the bunny's untimely death.

A short woman dressed in pressed khakis and a cable-knit sweater rushed into my suite, took one whiff, and her fangs punched out of her gums.

"Blath it all," she lisped. "I do apologize, mith. I'm newly turned."

I wriggled farther onto the mattress. "Should you be in here?"

"I'm in complete control," she assured me. "Except for these. They theem to have a mind of their own."

"Here, ma'am." Lena passed her an opaque glass. "This will help."

The woman drained the contents, which stained her upper lip crimson, before passing it back and flashing a fangless smile. "Thank you, Lena."

"Dr. Heath will be your personal physician going forward," Lena explained. "Isn't that lovely?"

"You had a doctor made for me?" I was only half-kidding.

Undead general practitioners weren't exactly rare, but they weren't terribly common either. Plenty of physicians had the funds to be converted, but few practiced in their afterlife. Most lacked the restraint. The few who possessed the ironclad self-control required ended up blood sworn to a clan for the whole of their afterlife, their sole job tending its human members.

"Not hardly." Dr. Heath chuckled. "I already paid my dues,

thank you very much. I spent every dime of my husband's life insurance policy on making sure I didn't join him."

What could I say to that? "That's...nice."

"Let's have a look at that foot." She rolled the sock down and passed it to Lena, who fetched a trash bin to toss it in. "We'll have to clean this for me to find the slivers. I need a bowl of warm water." She made a circular gesture with her hands. "Large enough she can soak her whole foot."

"I'm sure there must be something." Lena strode to the bathroom with purpose. "Give me a moment."

"Sure thing." Dr. Heath watched her go before inclining her head and murmuring under her breath, "Stay strong, Squirt."

Certain I must be imagining things, I stared down at the top of her dark head. "What did you—?"

"Here you are." Lena placed the requested bowl on the floor at the foot of the bed. "Hold tight to me, miss." She gathered me in her arms. "Let's move you down here so I can get cleaning."

Desperate for another moment alone with the doctor, I grasped at straws. "Can we do this outside?"

"Not enough light, I'm afraid." Dr. Heath cut me a significant look. "This will have to do."

Had I imagined what she said? Was my mind playing tricks on me? How could I ask for confirmation without making it obvious? If I had imagined her cryptic remarks, then I couldn't risk inflaming Volkov's paranoia. And if I hadn't, then I couldn't risk Dr. Heath being captured and interrogated.

The warm water stung my cuts as Lena guided my foot into the bowl. The two women stood there staring like it might pop off the end of my leg and bolt for the door if not for their laser focus.

"This is going to sting." Dr. Heath put Lena to work holding a penlight while she picked out each tiny sliver. "These are all shallow. You won't need stitches. You're lucky this isn't much worse."

"It was an accident," I lied smoothly. "I forgot about the rabbit and knocked it off when I threw back the covers."

"I'm going to recommend you soak this foot nightly." She glanced at Lena. "Just give her extra time in the tub. That will be fine."

"Miss hasn't been well enough for the tub." She cast me an apologetic look. "I'll have a larger bowl brought up and—"

"Would you like to bathe?" Dr. Heath asked me point-blank. "Trust me. I have a healthy appreciation for sponge baths, they're a staple for patients with impaired mobility, but I see no reason why you can't start working on your endurance." She must have read my confusion. "I understand you've been unwell recently."

"Yes." The crimson swirls in the water drew my eye. "I suppose I have." I flicked my toe in the center of one, disturbing its curve. "A bath would be nice."

Waking secure in the knowledge I hadn't been manhandled while I slept would be even better.

"Good." She grinned while Lena worried her bottom lip with her fang. "That's settled." The doctor rose and wiped her hands clean. "Your foot will be tender for a couple of days, but you're fine to walk as much as you want."

"Thank you." I curled my fingers into my hand to keep from reaching for her. "Dr. Heath—?"

"The gardeners are planting out front," she announced over me. "Perhaps you'd like to visit them for a while since you enjoy spending time outdoors? A change of scenery would do you good."

"I would love that," I breathed, too excited by half.

"Miss isn't allowed outside the manor." Lena edged between us. "The master has forbidden her to leave her suite for her own safety."

"These are dangerous times," she agreed with Lena while staring over her shoulder at me. "Still, if you ever get the chance, you should visit the front gardens. The rose beds are lovely this time of year."

Our gazes held for a long moment, until I nodded that I understood, even if I wasn't certain that I did, that I could trust what I was hearing and seeing was real and not a hallucination tormenting me.

"Thank you for your assistance, Dr. Heath." Lena shifted to block the doctor's view of me. "Forgive my impertinence, but you ought not plant ideas in her head. I'm afraid I must ask you to leave so she can recover from her ordeal."

The tremble in Lena's voice piqued my curiosity. All the doctor had done was agree with her that danger to me existed, hilarious when you considered they were currently the biggest threat. Her comment about the gardens was even more benign. How had either of those offended?

"I'll be right back, miss." Lena glanced back at me. "We'll get you fed and maybe have a walk."

A bitter laugh rose up my throat, and I climbed back in bed, the one place I could go and be left alone while I turned over the doctor's visit in my mind.

Feed me, water me, walk me like the pampered pet I am. Who held my leash? Who was my master?

How did I gain access to that front garden? And what—or who— awaited me there?

"Are the rumors true then?" Footsteps announced Dr. Heath's retreat. "Has the Society launched an inquiry?"

"You'll have to speak with Mr. Volkov about that, ma'am." Lena hustled after her, the soles of her shoes a soft hush of sound. "It's not my place to speculate, and you'd do well to follow my example."

The door opened and then closed behind them. Lena would return with a fresh breakfast tray eventually, but for now... An inquiry. With six little words, the good doctor had given me a surefire cure for what ailed me.

She had given me hope.

SIXTEEN

Lena must have tattled on Dr. Heath. That's all I could figure when nights passed without a follow-up visit from her or any other doctor. I put each one to good use. I picked the scabs on the worst of the cuts to keep the scent of fresh blood in my room. Dangerous, yes, but also necessary for what came next. Lena, who was now in charge of bandaging my foot, had grown as numb to the scent as a cakeaholic who worked in a bakery.

When the night finally came that she didn't shake out my clothes after drawing me a bath or smooth her hands across the mattress in search of rogue pieces of porcelain, I set the second phase of my plan into action.

I went through the motions, a perfect robot, and climbed into bed before dawn with a fresh bandage on my foot.

Hours later, when the house had fallen quiet as its occupants drifted off to sleep, I climbed off the mattress, hit my knees, and crawled out to the patio. I found the shard by feel and almost cried with relief that it hadn't been discovered.

I plopped down in the grass and brought the shard up to my hair. I sawed off a three-inch hank then tapped the cut ends on the concrete like I was straightening a stack of papers. Once I had an even, blunt edge, I wrapped my used bandage longways to make a sad excuse for a handle. I regarded my makeshift brush with a critical eye. It would have to do. I might only have this one chance. I had to make the most of it.

I picked my tender foot until blood flowed, dipped my brush, and painted a delicate sigil for healing onto my stomach. A prickling sensation spread from my gut out into my limbs, proof the magic was working. That one minor rebellion was all I dared for now. Twisting my hair up into a bun, I hid the jagged edges then threaded the flexible brush into the center. After replacing the shard in the dirt, I crawled back into bed.

I hadn't prayed to Hecate since Maud died, but my lips formed her name as sleep tugged me under.

AT DUSK, I choked awake on a scream that brought Lena running. Dressed in polka dot pajamas, her hair swinging in a braid down her back, she skidded into my room followed by two snarly guards.

The males began a thorough search of the room while she fussed over me.

"Miss?" Lena dashed to my side, her wide eyes raking over me. "What's wrong?"

Sweat plastered my nightgown to my chest, so I hiked the covers up to my chin. The nightmare had slipped through the cracks and dragged me thrashing into awareness, a sign I was truly waking up from the drugged haze.

"A spider," I croaked. "It was...dangling..." I swiped my fingers through the air, "...in my face."

One guard snorted while the other shook his head.

"It must have come in from outside." Her weight shifted like she might stand. "I can shut the doors if you'd like."

"No," I rushed out. "Thank you. I'm fine. It just surprised me."

"Are you sure you're all right?" A crease formed on her brow. "You look a tad damp. Are you hot?"

"Yes." I grabbed hold of that excuse with both hands. "That must be what woke me."

Lena peeled the comforter down to the foot of the bed. "Do you want to sit up for a while or—?"

"I'm pretty tired." I faked a yawn and snuggled into my pillow. "See you at breakfast."

Catching my yawn, she covered her mouth. "See you then." Her eyes popped open wide. "Oh. I almost forgot. I have some wonderful news for you."

"Oh?" So far, I hadn't been allowed news of any kind. This didn't bode well.

"Perhaps I ought to wait until breakfast. I don't want to ruin your rest with too much excitement."

"I'm a sound sleeper," I assured her. They'd made certain of that.

"The master returns tomorrow night." She gripped my hand and squeezed. "He'll be so proud of how well you've adjusted in his absence."

"Tomorrow night?" That didn't leave much time.

"Don't fret, miss. After breakfast, I'll bring down clothes from your old room. We'll find you something to wear that's sure to please him. We want you to look your best when you're presented."

I lived in pajamas these days. How odd would it be to wear real pants? And shoes? "Presented?"

"All new clan members must be presented to the master and his council."

I bit the inside of my cheek to keep from snapping at her that I was a necromancer, an heiress, and the last Woolworth. Whoever this master was, he couldn't absorb me into his clan without the Grande Dame's permission to dissolve my house, and he could hold his breath until his face turned blue waiting on that. Strained as our relationship might be, the Grande Dame would never consent to erasing her sister's legacy. Not to mention she would never place such a rare and valuable commodity as my blood in the hands of vampires.

"Oh, miss, you must be so thrilled." She leaned in close and whispered, "Ariana, she's the upstairs maid, confided that last week, when she tidied Mr. Volkov's bedroom, she spotted a black velvet box on his nightstand."

Gooseflesh pebbled my arms. "Really?"

"Oh, yes. How romantic." Eyes closing in bliss, she almost swooned. "I bet the master asked Mr. Volkov to wait, but now that he's coming home, things will move faster. Mark my words."

"I'm not sure how I'll sleep after hearing all this," I teased while telling the absolute truth.

"I should have waited until breakfast. I meant to, honest, but you've had so many questions. I thought you would rest better knowing they'll all soon be answered."

"Thanks..." I bobbed my chin, pretending my head was too heavy for my neck, "...Lena."

As far as she knew, I was still drugged to the gills. She must think I was paddling as hard as I could to remain conscious. Wouldn't want to miss any other big announcements. Faking the slide into oblivion required zero effort on my part considering I'd had so much practice. My lashes fluttered, my lids drooped, and my lips parted on a restful exhale.

Lena fell for it hook, line and sinker. She ushered the guards out into the hall, and the door shut with a quiet *click* behind them.

Alone in my room, I stared up at the ceiling. I gave the guards a good half hour to forget all about little ol' me and settle into their routine. I had no idea where Lena slept, but judging by the fact she had responded first—and in her pajamas—I was guessing her room was next door to mine.

Once I was certain the coast was clear, I flipped back my covers and pulled up my shirt. The sigil from last night had sweated off, but so had the worst of the lethargy from the drugs. I sat upright without so much as a stitch in my side and planted my feet on the floor with no problem. Standing gave me a twinge, but it was doable. Walking, though. That required supreme effort.

Part of the issue was the lingering dizziness, but the long stretch of inactivity wasn't helping matters. How long had I been here? More than a few days. Longer than a week. A month? I'd lost track of time somewhere along the way. I had no idea how long formal inquiries lasted, but I had no doubt that was the reason I had been spared the master's attention so far.

Lena being Lena refused to give me the date or even tell me the day of the week. How much did she understand about what was happening? What did it matter? She wasn't blind. She saw me languishing day after day after day and had ample opportunities to help me. Instead she placed her hand gently on top of my head and shoved me back under any time I began to surface.

Not this time.

I shuffled over to the wall and braced on that so I could walk laps around the room. It was daylight outside when I finished, but the quaver in my leg muscles burned almost as much as the spark of hope still smoldering in my chest.

EXHAUSTION TREMBLED through my limbs as I sprawled in bed, but I was afraid to risk napping. Arachnophobia had worked once, but I doubted Lena would buy that excuse twice without it costing me. All I needed was to make it this far then stumble when she decided the lesser of two evils was locking me in at night to save me from parachuting spiders.

Rustling noises in the hall were my cue to lower my eyelashes and angle my face away from the door.

From the corner of my eye, I watched one of the guards smile at Lena as she ducked under his arm and scurried to set up my breakfast on the patio. He was still grinning when he pulled the door shut and locked it behind her.

Arching my back, I stretched and murmured a sluggish, "Good evening."

"How are you feeling?" Lena rushed to my side. "Would you rather eat breakfast in bed?"

"I can handle the patio," I assured her then wrinkled my nose enough to do Amelie proud. "I'd rather you changed my sheets in case that spider is still crawling around in here."

Lena chuckled at my expression. "Very well, miss. As long as you're sure."

Used to the routine by now, I lifted my arms, and she scooped me against her chest and carried me to my seat. Any humiliation I'd once felt about being toted around had burned out long ago.

"I'll be right inside if you need me," she assured me.

"Thanks, Lena."

Deciding what to eat and how much was like playing Russian roulette. Breakfast and lunch never left me zoned out like dinner, so I figured it was safe to pick at the mixed fruits. I got most of the strawberries down before pushing away my plate. The water tasted fine, but I sipped all the same.

I was staring at the seashell pressed into the concrete when Lena came for what I called a pulse check.

"You didn't eat much." Lena examined the leftovers. "Was the fruit not to your liking?"

"I keep thinking about what you said earlier." I pressed a hand to my stomach. "I'm nervous about meeting the master." I ducked my head. "And about what's in that ring box."

"Ariana has the patience of a saint," she swore. "I wouldn't have been able to resist peeking."

"Have you put any more thought into what I should wear tomorrow night?"

"I do have some ideas." She hesitated, uncertain if I actually cared about her opinion. "Would you like me to show you?"

"I want to look my best." I offered her my hand. "I might need help getting back in bed, though. Do you mind?"

"Not at all." She carried me back to bed and propped me up with pillows. "Wait just a tick, and I'll be right back with my top choices." Her smile widened. "Then we can talk about accessories."

"I can't wait." I reclined and held my pose until she left then murmured to the empty room, "It's going to be a *long* night."

No curtains rustled, no lights flickered, no swirl of heat embraced me.

I missed Woolly. I missed Amelie. I even missed Boaz, the jerk. And Keet.

With the training Boaz promised, I might have stood a chance against Volkov, but there had been no time. The Grande Dame had underestimated the vampires, how much they knew and the lengths they would go to secure me for their use, and I was paying for her miscalculation now.

I had no allies here, no friends. *Trust no one. Believe no one.* I had to keep my wits about me.

The only person I could rely on to get me out of this situation was, well, *me.*

And my sad excuse for an escape plan hinged on dropped hints, sloppy sigils, and the shattered nose from the smashed-in face of a rabbit.

SIX ROLLING GARMENT racks zigzagged across the center of my room. Two were dedicated to pants, three to blouses and one to shawls, jackets, and cardigans. Pushed against the wall were troves of accessories. A shoe cabinet cracked open to showcase everything from sandals to flats to neck-breaker heels. The jewelry chest, which Lena was currently digging through, sparkled like diamonds under the chandelier. Probably due to all the diamond-encrusted diamonds in there.

"What do you think, miss?" Lena held a strand of pearls in each hand, one white and one pink. "The pink is lovely, if you ask me, and it matches the pantsuit you selected." She tilted her head to one side and then the other. "The white is classic, and it coordinates with those peep-toe flats you liked."

Like was a strong word for how I felt toward any of her selections. Honestly, I didn't feel much of anything toward anything these days. "Let's go with white."

"All right then." She draped the modest strand around the neck of the mannequin she'd wheeled into my room, the form molded to my measurements, because that wasn't disturbing at all, and sighed over the finished product. "How lovely. The master will be so pleased."

The master could stick those pearls in his pipe and smoke them for all I cared. "What's on the menu for dinner?"

"I requested something light in case your stomach was still fluttery." She nudged the mannequin aside. "How does French onion soup with a fresh baguette sound?"

"Delicious." And difficult to mask the amount of food I wasn't eating.

"I'll go fetch your tray." Lena started wheeling the dummy out with her. "Be back in a jiffy."

"Can you leave the outfit? Just for now?" Still in bed, I held up my hands and made a frame with my fingers. "There's something I can't quite put my finger on..."

Uncertain, Lena stepped back to admire her handiwork. "You might be right, miss."

"Can I have extra cheese?" I asked to distract her from the mannequin. "Gruyère is one of my favorites."

"Whatever you like." Pleasure and relief mingled in her expression. "I'll be right back."

I waited until the doors closed then leapt out of bed and dashed for the clothes racks. I dug through every shade of pink known to man before finding one pair of simple, black slacks. I wasn't as fortunate with the tops. The best I could find was a dusky rose that could pass for brown in low light. The shoe rack was easiest. A pair of black ballet flats had caught my eye first thing. Rushing to the bed with my contraband, I ripped back the sheets then smoothed the clothes across the foot of the bed before climbing in and pulling the covers up to my chest.

Propped up like a princess, I awaited Lena's return. I didn't have to wait long.

"Here we are," she trilled. "I'll just set you up on the patio and—"

"I didn't get much sleep after the spider incident. Would it be too much trouble if I took dinner in bed?"

Stepping one foot out of this bed might cost me the outfit and the element of surprise if Lena fell back on her old habits. I couldn't risk her snooping, so I had to play up her expectations of me.

"You poor dear." She balanced the tray on the edge of the night-stand, folded down its legs, and placed it over my lap. "You must be exhausted." She tucked a lock of hair behind my ear. "Would you like to skip your bath?"

"Yes." I spooned in the first mouthful of soup, pretending to ignore the bitter slide down the back of my throat. "I can wake earlier and bathe before the presentation."

"An excellent idea," she agreed, then welcomed two guards into the room to help her trundle all the clothes back up to what she considered *my* room. "I'll be right back."

I spooned in as much as I could stomach without getting too woozy then put my acting chops to the test by reclining against my pillows and shutting my eyes. I kept the spoon threaded between my fingers for added realism, wishing she would let me keep it but knowing she would pry it from my fist.

Wheels squeaked, hangers clacked, and locks snapped into place. Gentle voices told me they'd noticed I'd dropped off and didn't want to disturb me. Whoever the master was, he had left strict orders for me to be pampered like a princess. One locked in a tower, but a princess all the same.

Warm lips pressed to my forehead, a motherly gesture, reminding me that despite Lena's appearance, I had no idea of her true age.

With practiced ease, she disarmed me and cleared away the dishes. Her soft shoes whispered over the tile, and the door shut on a sigh.

The temptation to nap dragged at me, but I only had one chance to do this before the master returned. Security was insane with me in residence. I didn't imagine that would change once he arrived. Masters were guarded even closer than heritors. Volkov had two shadows. The master could have six or more trained warriors in his entourage.

An hour passed as best I could tell, and then another. Anticipation itched under my skin, and I was ready for a good scratching. I eased out of bed on unsteady legs, the drugs turning my blood sluggish, and made my way to the patio. After locating the shell, I knelt and retrieved the shard.

"No going back now." Lena hadn't scented the bit of extra blood from the tiny sigil last night, but there was no pretending innocence after I made the first cut. "Hecate, be merciful."

Though the goddess and I weren't on great terms, she was all the comfort I had in this twisted palace.

Tugging my shirt over my head, I gritted my teeth and braced for the coming pain. I raked the shard across my ribs, and blood slid down my side. I tugged my hair free of its elastic band, and my makeshift brush tumbled into my lap.

I'd been deliberating on what sigils to pull from my arsenal for days. Most of the combinations I could draw from memory pertained to house wards. Sadly, I didn't know any for flight or invisibility, not that I was sure either existed, but they would have come in handy.

With bold strokes, I warded my body against attack. I wasn't sure the design would stand against a touch from Volkov, but it would be enough to ensure any bullets fired at me would miss, that kind of thing. Obfuscation made it harder to focus on me. Strength bolstered the power of the defensive wards and gave me a much-needed energy boost. Healing got inked down each thigh in bold strokes to help burn the drugs from my system.

Ten minutes later, I was covered in symbols, as many as I could wear without them overlapping. My side ached, but the wound had already closed thanks to the magic whispering over my skin.

Feeling more like myself than I had since the night I was taken, I rushed inside and dressed for my escape. I put the shard and brush in my pocket in case I needed them again then twisted my hair up on top of my head.

I blasted out an exhale and walked outside, across the rolling lawn, until I reached the wall. The infusion of strength made it possible for me to dig my fingers into the mortar between the stones and haul myself up despite how much I'd wasted away in captivity. I reached the top and straddled the wall, trusting in my obfuscation sigil to shield me while I studied the landscape and gained my bearings.

I had no idea what would happen when my feet hit the ground on the other side. The master might allow me my private garden, but security outside my room was tight, and it must be around the property as well. But how far could I get before—?

"Miss?"

I swung my head toward the open French doors leading into my room. Lena stood there in her pajamas, her hair a mess, her lips parted as she sucked in the night air over her tongue, pure terror in her eyes.

"Hold still." She rushed forward. "I'll help you down."

So much for my obfuscation sigil. Her keen sense of smell had fed her my exact location thanks to the freshly spilled blood.

Without looking back, I swung my leg over the wall and dropped. I hit and rolled the way Boaz had taught me when were kids and didn't have the sense to realize that his daredevil stunts—the ones I practiced alone to impress him with later—could break our ankles *or* our necks. I sprang to my feet and ran.

"There she is," one voice boomed.

"Stop her," another shouted.

"*Miss.*"

Blocking out their pleas, the barked orders, and the clomp of boots as the guards mobilized, I pushed my legs until my thigh muscles screamed. The mental snapshot I'd taken from high up on the wall guided me through two neighboring gardens and around the side of the palatial house. The front gardens were in sight when a magical charge rippled through the air and washed over my skin in a heated wave.

"*Grier,*" Volkov bellowed.

Adrenaline dumped in my veins, and my heart threw itself against its cage.

Please, Hecate. Please.

I skidded to a stop in front of the house and whirled in a circle, searching for the gardeners, for the roses, for any sign of what Dr. Heath had hinted waited for me here. I saw no one and nothing. I was alone, defeated. This was the extent of my plan, and it had blown up in my face.

Between the sweat and the friction, the sigils were rubbing off at record speed. Exhaustion dropped like a curtain before my eyes, and I fell to my knees.

A strange peacefulness swept over me as I tipped back my head, basking in the moonlight for the last time. I would not go back to that room, to that prison, and rot. I would not be sold into marriage, my body given over to a male for his use. Atramentous had broken a great many things in me, but I hadn't been violated in that way, and I had no illusions my luck would hold after Volkov wed me.

Bringing the ceramic shard to my wrist, I pressed down, breaking skin and freeing all the precious blood that had landed me here in the first place.

"Grier," Volkov panted, eyes wild until they locked with mine. "What are you doing?"

The row of ornamental trees rustled on my left. No, they were roses. Hedge roses. Without blooms, I hadn't identified them. A figure clad in black tactical gear strolled forward wearing a grin that chilled me to the bone.

"Oh, I don't know," he drawled. "My guess is she's so tired of playing house with a kidnapping son of a bitch she'd rather die than spend another second with you."

"Boaz?"

"Hey, Squirt." He winked. "Took you long enough. I've been lurking out here in the bushes for weeks."

"Grier, come to me." Volkov extended his hand toward me. "I will take you inside where it's safe."

Boaz snorted in his general direction. "I don't think so."

Wringing every drop of magic out of my sigils, I drew the strength to rise and bolted toward rescue. Volkov tackled me halfway, cranking up his lure until my eyes crossed, and I melted into a puddle beneath him.

"You are mine," he growled. "I will not let you go."

Blackness descended around me in a whisper of cool night air.

No, no, no.

I had to beat his lure. I had to keep my eyes open. I had to fight him off or lose myself forever.

I'm not going back. I'm not going back. I'm not—

Gunfire erupted in staccato bursts that made my legs quiver with the urge to run. Volkov jerked once then collapsed on top of me, crushing the oxygen from my lungs. Gasping for air, I shoved at his shoulders to roll him off me.

Screams and grunts erupted as bullets peppered the night. A few voices I recognized before they were silenced. The guards who had laughed at me about the spider. The males who'd trundled the racks of clothing in and out of my room only hours earlier. And lastly, a high-pitched shriek that raked nails down the chalkboard of my mind. I tried not to think too hard about that one.

Lena had followed me.

She wasn't following me anymore.

The dead weight on top of me vanished, and grasping hands lifted me onto my feet. I struggled against their hold until warm lips pressed against my ear and yelled over the commotion.

"It's me, Squirt. Relax. I got you."

I collapsed against Boaz, breathing in his familiar scent, and almost dissolved in his arms.

"I'm going to carry you," he called. "Just hold on to me."

"*No.*" I trembled in his grasp. "I can't—" I swallowed my panic, the remembered feel of Lena's arms under my legs and her arm hooked around my back. Carrying me, always carrying me, keeping me weak, helpless. I would never be helpless again. "I can walk."

"Okay, Squirt." He looped his arm around my waist, holding me steady while he examined my wrist where a deep gouge ought to be. He grunted when he found the wound clotted, a final gift from my failing sigils, then helped me limp a dozen yards away from where Volkov had fallen. "We've got a chopper on the way, and reinforcements are just over that hill. Can you make it?"

At the rendezvous point, five men dressed identical to Boaz bled from the darkened forest out into the open field and surrounded us. With a nod to him, they waited with us, watching our backs.

The *whomp-whomp-whomp* of helicopter blades slicing through the air kicked my heart into overdrive. Boaz shoved me into a seat before the landing skids touched down and strapped me in tight. He joined me, and the others filed in behind him.

Boaz flung his arm around me as the doors shut, tucking me against his side as much as the harness allowed. The chopper lifted into the sky, and my former prison shrank until only a speck remained. Not until the night was thick and black around me, a blanket of safety, did I let my eyes slip closed.

SEVENTEEN

The nightmare woke me. For once, that was a good thing. Probably. I hoped. I sat there with my spine pressed into a corner and my eyes screwed shut. I swallowed the foul taste coating the back of my throat. Herbs and copper. Nasty combination. Tears brimmed behind my eyelids while hope and fear collided in my gut. There was no going back once I opened my eyes. If it had all been a dream... If I woke to Lena staring at me...

"Woolly?" At the sound of my voice, the lights snapped on overhead, banishing my fears this might not be real. Warmth rolled in tracks down my cheeks, and I hiccupped when I said, "I missed you, girl."

The floorboards arched under my palms like cats eager to be petted.

"I'm sorry I left you." I pressed my cheek against the wall. "I didn't mean to go away."

However long I had been gone, it was too long.

Heat blasted from the floor register, its swirling warmth as close to a hug as the house had to offer.

The growl that rumbled through my stomach caused the curtains to flutter with laughter.

"Laugh it up." I elbowed the wall and immediately regretted my life choices. "You're not half as funny as you think."

While she chuckled at my expense, it hit me that I could eat, actually eat without fear, for the first time since Volkov snatched me. That was all the epiphany required to get me moving. Using the wall for support, I propped my feet under me. I made it two steps outside the bedroom before strong arms enveloped me. Boaz lifted me and spun me in dizzying circles down the hall.

"I thought you were never going to wake up." He planted a hot kiss on my forehead. "How are you feeling?"

"Physically?" I directed my focus inward and sought out each individual ache. I paid special attention to the faded pink line down my wrist, what should have been a nasty scar, but found the skin smooth. "Good."

"How about up here?" He knocked on my noggin gently then poked me in the chest. "And in here?"

"I'll let you know when I figure out that part," I promised. "Right now, it just feels good to be home."

"Where are you rushing off to?" He kept hold of my hand as I started walking away. "Got a hot date?"

"As a matter of fact, yes I do." I tugged on my wrist. "With whoever can deliver breakfast the fastest."

"I'm not sure that's such a good idea, Squirt." His grip turned to iron. "How about I cook instead?"

A flutter started behind my breastbone, a sharp breath hissing between my teeth.

Not again. Not now. Not when I'm home and among friends.

"It's okay, Squirt. You're home. Nothing can hurt you here." Boaz turned me loose and took a healthy step back, giving me room to breathe. "How about I sweeten the pot. How does breakfast in bed sound?"

"No." My gorge rose, and I shook my head until I teetered off balance. "Never again."

The stricken look on his face as he battled the urge to interrogate me eased the knot in my throat.

"Amelie told me to text the second you got out of bed." He reached for his cell. "Do you mind?"

"You really have to ask?" The true miracle was that she hadn't been camped outside the door beside him.

"Come on down, Squirt, I've got all I need in the kitchen to create the perfect welcome home meal." His thumb flew over the keyboard. "Frozen blueberry waffles and imitation maple syrup. The breakfast of champions."

Rolling my eyes with the knowledge he believed that, I took the stairs. Amelie must have already been on her way over, because I bumped into her on the bottom step.

"Grier." She flung herself at me and squeezed until I gasped for air in a good way. "I was so worried."

"Me too," I admitted, fresh tears wavering in my vision. "Are you ready to eat?"

"Eat?" Her nose wrinkled in Boaz's direction. "Tell me he didn't con you into waffles."

Woolly chimed before I got out my answer, and we moved our reunion to the living room.

The Pritchard siblings exchanged wary glances, and the foreboding sensation remained when I pressed my eye to the peephole in the front door and spotted Mr. Hacohen standing there in his trim, navy suit with a hand tangled in his corkscrew mane.

"This can't be good," I murmured, opening the door and frowning at the Grande Dame's messenger boy. "Yes?"

"You've been summoned." From the same leather folio as before, he pulled out a linen envelope. "The Grande Dame has sent me to fetch you."

"I'll need a minute." I shut the door in his face with no small delight and leaned against it, tearing into the envelope, which revealed what Mr. Hacohen had relayed almost verbatim. "I assume she wants all the details while they're fresh in my mind."

"How did she know you were awake?" Amelie scowled at the letter. "Did she bug the house while you were gone?"

"No," Boaz answered, and I didn't ask how he knew that was true, but I believed him. "Think about it, sis." He peered through the nearest window at the vibrant sunset. "Mom always gets her summons at dusk. The real surprise here is the Grande Dame let her sleep this long."

The scent of grapefruit wafted from the paper, and the sweetness cloyed. "Heard any updates?"

Boaz hesitated, which told me he was up to speed but wasn't sure I ought to be yet.

"I deserve to know," I said as I tore the card to shreds, "and I'd rather hear it from you than her."

"Thirty-four casualties. Twice that many popped UV capsules to keep us from interrogating them." The vampiric equivalent of cyanide pills. "Volkov is our only high-level capture. The other survivors were maids, kitchen workers or groundskeepers. The odds of them knowing anything are slim."

I ignored the clenching in my gut. "He survived?"

"Oh yes." The calculating smile stretching Boaz's lips made me shiver. "I made certain of it."

Amelie sidled closer and wrapped an arm around my waist to offer me support.

Finally, I was going to get my question answered. "Who is the master?"

"We don't know."

"How can you not know? Volkov was the ringleader. Doesn't that mean his clan was behind this?"

"The thing about Last Seeds is they last forever. Ancients, true immortals, grow weary of ruling their own corners of the world. They can sleep for hundreds of years at a stretch, and sometimes when they rise, their entire clan has disbanded, been absorbed, or just plain died out over time."

"Are you saying you suspect an ancient was behind my kidnapping?"

"There were five different clans in residence at that estate. None of them allied as far as Society records go. The Mercia heritor took his own life rather than let us get our hands on him. Whatever—or whoever—they were protecting, it's got to be big if clan masters are offering up their best and brightest to the cause."

"I should have tried harder." Lena was too loyal to her master. But there were others. I should have figured out how to widen my social circle and focused on weaker links instead of being one. "I had no idea the operation was so large."

"Neither did we. Not until we got a chance to examine what bodies remained."

Young vampires died very human deaths. Things didn't get weird until they passed the century mark.

"Legally, we had no proof you were behind those walls." His mouth flatlined. "You still had Amelie's cellphone on you when you were taken, but those coordinates only proved you were in the area."

"Rookie mistake," Amelie said, "not patting her down first."

"Old vampires are hesitant to embrace modern technology." Boaz made it sound like a good thing. "Their survival as a species hinges on an influx of made vampires who educate them about the current era. Volkov might be young, but he would have been sequestered in his clan home until about five years ago with people who remember Alexander Graham Bell's first telephone call, back in 1876, like it was yesterday." He rolled his shoulders. "Your abduction might have been an act of opportunity rather than one of forethought. I'm not saying it wasn't on Volkov's to-do list already, but your falling out the night of the inauguration might have bumped it up to the top."

"Why couldn't you isolate the cell's exact location?" Surely sentinels had the resources. "That's possible, right?"

"We're assuming Volkov's driver called ahead to announce their arrival, and one of the younger vamps on staff cautioned them to pat you down and dispose of any electronic devices on your person. They tossed your cell about thirty minutes away from the estate, but that still gave us a small-enough search area that, after consulting the property records at the Lyceum, it only took a matter of hours to tighten the net."

Hours to find me and weeks to extract me. Volkov had planned his trap well.

"The servant who answered the door belonged to one of the smaller clans, one who's never given the Society a reason to look at them twice. Their master denied us entry and refused to meet with us to discuss terms. Had we realized they meant an unrecognized master, we could have gotten a warrant to search the premises. As it was, all we could do was sit on our hands and pray you'd find a way out."

"Is that all?" I kicked up an eyebrow. "Dr. Heath made the front gardens sound mighty appealing. She mentioned the roses were particularly worth seeing." Speaking her name reminded me. "She was one of yours, wasn't she? How is she?"

"Yeah, Becky's in my unit." His face split in a grin. "She's an old pro at UC work."

"Your unit?" My knees almost buckled. "The draft."

"I've been active for about three weeks. Thanks to my years of service, it was more of a lateral transfer. No boot camp for me. They paired me up with Heath and put me straight to work." The twinkle in his eye spoke of his fondness for her, or for his new position, or maybe both. "Sentinel Elite work is a lot like being in the army."

"You're an Elite?"

"Don't look so surprised." He puffed out his chest. "HQ took one look at this package and had to have it. Story of my life."

"Color me impressed." And also suspicious. Very suspicious. Boaz had been dead set against joining the sentinels. Yet here he was, content and ranked much higher than any entry-level soldier could have dreamed. "Whose idea was it to infiltrate the estate? Yours or the Grande Dame's?"

"She might have suggested we make the op official." He worked his mouth like he was tasting something sour by giving her even that much credit. "She knew I was going in with or without sanction. Only the Elite has clearance for that kind of thing, so I offered up my services."

"Question."

"Answer."

"Smartass."

"Always."

"There are vamps in the Elite?" That seemed unlikely.

"No, but there's a solid market for magical augmentation." He snorted. "I laughed my ass off when Becky got her first stiffy. Took her hours to will it away."

"That explains her cover story as a newly-turned vampire. The scent of my blood gave her a dental erection."

"We figured it was a matter of time before you tried to ink your own sigils for protection." Boaz's conversational tone didn't fool me, not with that look in his eyes. "We put her in place as a precaution in case the temptation of your blood overwhelmed your guards' good sense."

"They didn't hurt me or feed from me." Easing away from Amelie, I edged toward the stairs, eager for a slice of calm before I got in front of someone who wouldn't back down from the hard questions. "I was treated well, all things considered."

"Volkov wouldn't still be alive otherwise," he promised. "Last Seed or not."

Well, okay then.

EIGHTEEN

y first order of business was tossing out every single pink thing I owned. Considering how much of my closet still belonged to fifteen-year-old me, that was a lot. A whole lot. I would have to make time to buy a new wardrobe now that I had the cash for it, but that wasn't a priority at the moment. The nicest thing I had left was the dress Volkov had bought me, which I stuffed into a trash bag along with the other clothes to donate. That left me in dark-wash jeans too loose for my waist and a niceish plum-colored sweater that hung off my shoulders thanks to the weight I'd lost during captivity. At least the matching flats still fit.

Doing my best St. Nick impersonation, I flung the bag over my shoulder and headed downstairs to meet the Pritchards.

Amelie sat on the couch next to Boaz. She stood when I entered the living room. "Can we talk before you go?" She fidgeted with one of the silver bands on her fingers. "I know Mr. Hacohen is waiting, but it won't take but a minute"

"Sure." I tossed Boaz the remote. "Turn on the TV and don't leave this couch."

I led her into the kitchen, and we each claimed our usual barstools.

"There are some things I've been meaning to say." She linked her fingers to keep them still. "When Volkov took you..." Her knuckles whitened. "I worried I might not get the chance."

"Let me go first." Hers wasn't the only conscience in need of unburdening, and all those days spent locked in my own head had given me nothing but time to think. "I've been a crap friend, Amelie."

"Grier, no."

"Amelie, yes." I flattened my palms on the granite countertop. "We made all these big plans when we were kids. We had our whole lives planned out from renting our first apartment together, attending the same college, working in the same city so we could do lunch dates every Friday. I was even willing to sacrifice my self-respect and marry your brother so that we could be real sisters."

A snort escaped her. "The way I remember it, you were eager to fall on that particular sword."

"Again—" I had to shake my head "—you are *way* too invested in my nonexistent love life."

"I'm your best friend." She reached over and took my hand. "It's my job to look out for you. I've kind of sucked at that lately."

"I'm not done yet." I stopped her there. "Let me get this out in the open."

Amelie mimed zipping her lips, the action giving me the nerve to continue.

"I got...sent away...and that path dead-ended for me. I lost my shot at having that perfect life, and when I got home and saw you had kept going, accomplishing all our goals without me, I didn't know how to deal." I scratched my nail over a speck of glittering mica. "I was hurting so much, being back here, trying to pick up my life when there wasn't anything left to hold on to, and seeing how well you're doing made me jealous."

"I should have tried harder to understand. It was just easier pretending none of it ever happened. That things were back to the way they used to be. Even when I offered to help you talk it out, I hoped you'd keep turning me down because I didn't really want to know what they did to you in there. My imagination is bad enough. I was sure the reality was worse, and I couldn't deal. I'm not as strong as you."

"You have to know that I'm proud of you. You do know that, right?" I covered her hand with mine until we ended up in a contest to see whose hand came out on top. "You stayed the course. You're living your dreams. You're on your way to achieving all your goals."

"Not half as proud as I am of you." A fat tear rolled down her cheek. "You survived."

"Some days I'm not so sure," I admitted with a sad little laugh. "Mostly I try not to think about, well, anything, really. I live in the moment. But then I come home from work, and it's quiet. There are no crushed herbs perfuming the air, the house doesn't rattle on its foundation when Maud blows something up in the basement, there are no strange guests wandering through the house all hours of the day and night."

"You're lonely."

The lights overhead dimmed in agreement.

"Yeah." I patted the nearest wall. "I guess I am. We both are."

"Pinky promise time." She whipped hers out and waited for me to pony up mine. "We both need to get out more. Starting this Friday night, you and me are going to find trouble to get into at least once a week. Deal?"

"Deal."

"Are y'all done jawing in here?" Boaz stomped around the corner, giving us fair warning. "Our ride is waiting."

I twisted on my stool until I faced him. "*Our* ride?"

A grin twitched in his cheeks. "You didn't think I was letting you go alone, did you?"

"Yes?" I had Mr. Hacohen as an escort after all. "Did the invite specify either way?"

"Don't know," he said, shrugging. "Don't care."

"I have to go. My first tour leaves in an hour." Amelie groaned. "Meet you back here after work?"

"Pick up Mallow on the way, and you've got yourself a deal." I launched myself at Amelie before she could wriggle off her stool, and clung to her like kudzu on a brick wall. "I love you, Ame."

She clung right back. "Love you too, Grier."

"Group hug." The eight-hundred-pound gorilla in the room joined in and squished us until our eyes bulged. "Now that my girls have kissed and made up, let's get this show on the road."

"Eww." Amelie elbowed him in the ribs. "Brother cooties. I'll have to shower after this."

"Too late." He pressed a smacking kiss to her forehead. "You've been colonized, little sis." He got me on the ear when I turned my head to escape, then licked his lips. "That was waxier than I imagined."

"Whatever." I shoved him, and he stumbled into the wall. I jumped up and ran to him, hooking my arms under his. "I'm—"

"—a sucker," he crowed, wrapping me in his arms and rolling across the floor with me until I was laughing so hard I couldn't breathe. "I can't believe you fell for that. This leg is the best thing that's ever happened to me. I get all the sympathy points from hot chicks."

After shoving Boaz off me, I stood and straightened my top. Amelie hiked it back up my shoulder and smoothed down my hair so I would look halfway presentable. Though Boaz stuck out his hand for help up, we both ignored him. *Jerk.*

After walking Amelie out, I stood on the porch and touched on the wards. Holding steady, thank the goddess, but weak, too weak to be any real protection. I had to knuckle down and get them repaired for both our sakes. The next time Volkov... I exhaled a shuddering breath. No. There wouldn't be a next time. I would see to that. Whatever it took, I was going to figure out a way to keep us both safe.

Since Mr. Hacohen was nowhere to be seen, I assumed he had retreated to the air-conditioned comfort of the car to await me. I was taking the steps down when warm fingers encircled my wrist from behind. Panic seeped in before my brain could throw on the brakes, and I snapped my arm up, breaking the hold.

Startled to find me standing a yard away from him, Boaz wrinkled his brow. "What?"

"I can't deal with surprises." I inched back to his side and looped my arm through his instead. "Not yet."

"Let me know your limits." His eyes softened. "For once, I won't push them. I swear."

"Thanks." I leaned my head against his shoulder. "You're not half bad half the time."

He led me down the drive. "And the other half?"

"You're a holy terror, exactly as Amelie described."

The driver greeted me with a nod as he opened the door to reveal Mr. Hacohen on his phone. I wobbled back a step as my vision tunneled on the yawning blackness of the interior. The car was the same model as the service Volkov used. A Lincoln Continental. Not even the deep crimson paint job, which screamed High Society, could keep my heart from rabbiting.

"I can't do this." I broke from Boaz and stumbled back. "I'll get Jolene and meet you there."

"You can't go out alone right now." Boaz kept his hands to himself but inched closer. "Let me drive you."

I focused on my breathing until normal sight and sounds returned. "Okay."

"Wilhelmina is in your garage. Hope you don't mind. I needed somewhere to stash her when I left, and I figured she could use the time to bond with her little sister, Jolene."

Ignoring the fact that he seemed to believe my garage was *our* garage, I had to stop him right there. "You named your new bike Wilhelmina?"

Smiling so wide he displayed every tooth in his head, he wiggled his eyebrows.

"Oh, Boaz. No." I groaned when I got the joke. "You did not name your bike that so you could ask girls to hop on your Willie."

His rolling chuckle only confirmed my suspicion.

"Perv."

He winked down at me. "Never claimed to be otherwise."

NINETEEN

Passing on the ride was one thing, but Mr. Hacohen meant to ensure I didn't give the same treatment to the Grande Dame's summons. The car tailed us straight to city hall, and we left the crimson sedan idling at the curb as we entered the darkened building and rode the elevator down to the Lyceum. Boaz trailed after me through the long, dark hallway leading to the Grande Dame's office where my courage abandoned me.

I held my knuckles poised above the wood for so long that Boaz crowded me, his arms a cage I didn't want to fight, and knocked for me.

"Say the word," he promised, "and I'll take you home."

"The sooner I do this, the sooner she leaves me alone. I want to help find who did this to me." Any vampire with the age and power to unite multiple clans was not going to let this go, let *me* go, not when the abduction had felt so personal. "This won't be fun, but it's necessary."

The door opened, and the Grande Dame rushed forward. "Grier, I was so worried." She shocked me by gathering me against her in a delicate hug. Her slight build left me feeling like I was holding a spun-sugar sculpture. Her air of fragility was camouflage, my head knew that, but my heart... Once again, the similarities between her and Maud formed a hard lump in my throat. I could almost pretend the arms enfolding me were hers. Almost. "I thought we'd lost you."

We broke apart, and she shooed me toward the only open seat while she circled the burled monstrosity she called a desk and sank into her chair.

Following her example, I straightened my back and folded my hands in my lap. "I understand I have you and Boaz to thank for my rescue."

A smile parted her ruby lips. "What is family for?"

Thankfully, she didn't wait for an answer.

"I'm certain you've surmised the reason for my summons. Let's begin, shall we?" Using a manicured nail, the Grande Dame flipped on a recording device and got down to business. "We interviewed your friend, Ms. Amelie Pritchard, when she reported you missing. She told us Heritor Danill Volkov arrived under the guise of friendship and tricked you into stepping outside the wards set on your home. He then used his lure to incapacitate you. His men subdued Ms. Pritchard while he forced you into his vehicle. Once the men released her, you were gone."

Fury simmering in my veins, I fixed Boaz with a glare. "Did they hurt Amelie?"

"A few bruises, but she earned those fighting to escape. She wasn't hurt otherwise."

Relief left me slumped in my chair. "She didn't tell me."

"There was no reason to make you feel worse than you already do."

The Grande Dame cleared her throat, demanding our attention. "What we must determine now is who the conspirators are so that we can round them up and put them someplace where they can't hurt you again. I'm sure you understand where I mean."

Atramentous. She had just sentenced these vampires, admittedly bad ones, to life in prison.

I wanted to vomit.

"The vampires in residence didn't match the name on the deed," she continued. "It's not unheard of. Some clans use the names of human relations to prevent the mortal authorities from looking too closely at property records. What can you tell us about your captors?"

"Not much," I admitted. "Volkov was there. I saw him a few times that I remember, but the maid hinted he was there more often. He was brought in to use his lure when I fought back or..." my fingers curled into my palms, "...when I had panic attacks."

Boaz clamped his hand on my shoulder in quiet support, and I relaxed enough to rediscover my voice.

"The maid, Lena, was the only person who spoke to me." I shied away from the remembered echo of her death screams. "She was kind to me, in her way, but she followed orders to the letter. There were guards, but I didn't catch their names, and they all dressed the same. I had no idea they belonged to different clans. They worked as a unit and seemed familiar with each other."

"What about your accommodations?" She leaned forward. "Where did they keep you?"

"I woke in a little girl's room. It was all pink, and there were dolls and children's books on the shelves." I fingered my collar, remembering the frilly pajamas that matched the decor. "I'm not sure how long I was there or how many times Volkov put me under before I woke the last time."

There was more. Snippets of conversations itched at my brain, things I ought to remember, but scratching my head only tangled my helmet hair.

"What happened then?" she prompted me.

"I tried the door and the window. They were both locked. It reminded me of..." Years of confinement. Latches on all the doors. Bars on all the windows. Endless, hopeless days grinding my will to dust. "I couldn't breathe. I'm not sure if I fainted before Volkov got to me that time. I can't remember. I was in a different suite when I woke. This one had French doors leading out onto a patio in a small, walled-in garden. They left the doors open day and night to keep me calm."

One of her perfect eyebrows arched. "They weren't concerned about escape?"

"They drugged me," I said flatly.

Ignoring my tone, she pressed onward. "How do you know?"

"You don't forget the feeling." Her expectant look forced the symptoms out of me. "Weakness, poor balance, confusion, drowsiness, memory loss." The polite veneer I'd worked so hard to hide behind crumbled a bit. "I assume you drew blood to run a tox screen the night I was recovered." She didn't contradict me. They would have wanted to be certain I hadn't been hexed or otherwise damaged. "It was the same drug they use in the prisons, wasn't it?"

The absence of withdrawal symptoms told me they had flushed my system after they examined me.

"We suspected the vampires had contacts within Atramentous," Boaz answered for her. "The only people who knew you resuscitated the human were in that prison yard when it happened. The inmates' communications are screened, and they're often too sedated to comprehend what's written to them, let alone return the message. That leaves the guards."

"Sentinels work the prisons." I connected the dots. "That means there are necromancers involved too."

"Only a necromancer would understand that your progeny rose... different," the Grande Dame agreed. "Someone realized the value of the information and sold it to the highest bidder. The Elite has hunted down each of the guards on duty that night and interrogated them. Two have failed to report to work since your release, but we hope to have them in custody by the end of the week."

Too much time had passed for it to make any difference. The information would be in circulation now.

"Now," she said, leaning forward, "explain to us how you escaped."

Slowly, tugging the details from crannies in my warped memory,

I outlined my plan, starting with the bunny I'd spotted in the pink room, touching on Dr. Heath's cryptic insistence I tour the front gardens, and ending with the night I got the news the master was to return and made my move.

"It's a pity you couldn't have waited one more night." Her lips pursed. "We could have ended all this."

"Lena was preparing me for my presentation to the master, and to the clan." The sting in my palm told me I'd drawn blood, and I didn't care a whit. "Another maid found an engagement ring in Volkov's room and gossiped with Lena about how he planned to solidify our union once the master returned. Forgive me for not waiting around until I was blood sworn to Volkov before attempting an escape neither he nor his clan would have allowed once we married."

"Ah. I had wondered," she murmured. "This master vampire offered your hand to the Volkov clan to get them to defect the Undead Coalition."

"They defected?" I croaked. "The entire clan?"

Leaving the Coalition meant walking away from the Society's protection and going rogue. History was a favorite subject of mine, and I was witnessing it now. No clan with such ancient bloodlines, and the wealth to support their continuance, had ever made such a drastic choice.

Who was this master that he commanded such absolute loyalty?

"This leaves us with the problem of how best to protect you." The recording ended with an audible *click*. The rest must be off the record, not a comforting thought. "The Society was sympathetic to your plight, this time, but I can only tap communal resources so many times before our members start demanding answers I can't give them without exposing you. They'll start whispering I'm abusing my power or using my position for personal gain."

Those few sentences tied my hands. The only thing more dangerous than Clarice Lawson as Grande Dame was Clarice Lawson fighting and clawing to stay atop her pedestal. I had no doubt if she went down, she would take me tumbling with her.

"The flip side of the coin is I can't use Lawson resources without drawing as much, if not more, attention to you. The Society will expect me, as your closest living relative, to help you get back on your feet. This recent attack ought to extend that window, but soon there will come a time when others notice my efforts to protect you and wonder if that sudden interest after years of estrangement isn't linked to the highly unusual nature of your pardon."

All the buildup, the slathering on of guilt, the vague threats, led to one conclusion. "I assume you have a solution in mind."

"Of course, dear girl." She pressed a button on her desk, and the door to her right swung open. The somber man who entered positioned himself at her right shoulder. "You understand that, given your current circumstances, I must insist on a few precautions to protect my investment."

This was Volkov all over again. The Grande Dame was backing me into a corner, and this time I might not be able to fight my way out.

"Linus will continue your necromantic education until such time he deems you proficient. Lessons will begin tomorrow evening." Pride shone in her eyes when she glanced at the newcomer, the most genuine expression she'd worn tonight. "Do keep me informed of her progress, darling."

Linus examined the room's crown molding with a critical eye, his body language screaming he would rather be anywhere other than here. "Yes, Mother."

Boaz clenched his fingers where they rested on my shoulders in response to the tension thrumming in the air.

The years had honed Linus Andreas Lawson III into a blade, and it was becoming clear that his mother wielded her heir, the Lawson scion, with expert precision.

Gone were his chubby cheeks and black-rimmed glasses. His freckles had paled, but they still splashed across his face in russet flecks. The watery blue eyes he used to weigh the world through before snubbing reality in favor of burying his nose in a mystery novel had darkened, sharpened. Contacts? Either way, the contrast was eerie.

A black suit molded to his body, all six feet and change of it. Dark auburn hair brushed his wide shoulders, a carefree style that contradicted the stick I knew to be clenched firmly between his butt cheeks. Full lips tilted down at their corners, shielding his perfect smile, a masterpiece of orthodontics, and his square jaw flexed until I wondered how many retainers he'd gnawed through since the days when his dental appliance used to spend weekends in Maud's guest bathroom next to mine.

Linus wore a perfect mask of boredom, but his eyes gave away his turmoil, gleaming with bitter emotion I was unable to decipher. I sucked in a shocked breath as wisps of black shadow fanned his pupils, sending a million thoughts tripping through my head.

Son of a biscuit. Linus had bonded with a wraith. There was no other excuse for the darkness in him.

A tendril of curious magic caressed me from shoulder to fingertip, drawing my gaze to his, and it was as though that roiling blackness in him had recognized me and reached out its spectral fingers. Jerking back to attention when Linus turned his head, I replayed the Grande Dame's words. "Lessons?"

"Yes. Lessons." She rose in a fluid motion. "Wide gaps were left in your education. Linus will tutor you until you're up to speed." She straightened his tie. "He's quite brilliant, you'll find. Takes after Maud in so many ways."

Linus watched his mother fuss without blinking, and I flashed back to a dozen half-forgotten memories of the young boy he had been standing with the same stiff back while she cooed over him. He must have worked up an immunity to her hovering by now, much the same as the Pritchards had with their mother.

"Are you packed?" She flattened her palms against his lapels. "Is there anything else you need?"

"Arnaud loaded my bags into the car earlier." He caught her by the wrists and took a half-step back. "Anything I've forgotten can be couriered over later. I'll be across town, Mother, not across the world."

Boaz smothered a laugh and coughed *Momma's boy* into his fist, but I didn't find any of this funny.

"Bags?" I glanced between mother and son. "What bags?"

"Linus will be staying with you," she announced. "He can take up residence in his old room. I assume it's as he left it?"

"No." I pushed to my feet, grateful I could stand without wobbling. "He's not welcome in my home."

Linus wore a masterful poker face, but the wraith had tipped his hand, and I recognized him right back.

"You're hardly in any position to argue." She faced me and anchored one hand on her hip. "Linus will stay with you at your home, or you will stay with us at mine."

Abandoning Woolly wasn't going to happen.

"He broke into my house," I snarled. "He *hurt* her. And he stole my parakeet."

A thin line formed between the Grande Dame's perfect eyebrows. "I fail to see your point."

Boaz tightened his grip on my shoulder, anchoring me before I committed murder for real.

"I would never hurt Woolly." Linus linked his hands behind his back. "The sigil I used was one Maud taught me herself. The house was incapacitated, yes, but there was no permanent damage done."

"You released a wraith in my house." I laughed maniacally. "That hurt her, and it could have hurt me."

The snarl Boaz released from over my shoulder would have intimidated a lesser man, but Linus ignored him.

"The wraith was under my control," he explained slowly, like I should be anything other than terrified to find myself on the wrong side of one. "You were never in any danger." He leaned down and bussed his mother's cheek. "I'll call when I'm settled."

"Be careful," she said softly. "This won't end with Volkov."

"I can take care of myself." Linus dismissed her concern with practiced ease then crossed to me. "More than that, I can teach you to defend yourself. That's what you want, isn't it?"

More than anything. Just not enough to kiss his feet for offering. I had already been kicked in the teeth while I was down plenty, thank you very much.

"Trust me when I say I want to be your guest as much as you want to host me. The harder you work, the sooner I can return to my home and my life, and the sooner you can transition into the next phase of yours." He offered his hand. "Do we have a deal?"

"Fine." I took his hand, and his long fingers wrapped around mine, his skin cool as the grave. "But if you ever violate the sanctity of my home again—"

"You are in no position to issue threats," the Grande Dame murmured silkily. "Goddess-touched or not, if you harm my son, I will break you into tiny pieces and shove those through the grate in your old cell for the mice to feast upon. Do you understand?"

Muscles fluttered in Linus's jaw, the black in his eyes coalescing. "Mother."

"Very well." An indulgent smile spread her lips. "Handle matters how you see fit."

"Thank you," he said to her, but his eyes never left my face. "You have nothing to fear from me."

"I'm not afraid of you." For some reason, that made his lips twitch in what passed for a smile.

Boaz placed his hand on my lower back. "Are you ready to leave?"

I studied Linus for another moment before I nodded. "I thought you'd never ask."

TWENTY

Linus took one look at Wilhelmina as Boaz and I climbed on then slid into the idling sedan with Mr. Hacohen. The driver pulled out behind us and followed us to Woolworth House. No sooner had Boaz turned up the driveway than his phone started going bonkers. He was hitting redial before we parked.

While he talked, I watched the driver carry Linus's bags onto the porch while the man himself stood on the lawn and gazed up at Woolly with fondness that made me feel a skosh better about having him as a house guest.

"That was Heath." Boaz followed my line of sight and grimaced. "We've got a case in Raleigh that needs our attention."

"You're leaving already?" I transferred my frown onto him. "I was hoping to get another day at least."

"Sorry, Squirt." He tugged the ends of my hair. "Duty calls and all that."

"Don't have too much fun with your new partner."

"I won't." He radiated smugness at my snappish tone. "She's married."

"Oh." That absolutely was *not* relief coursing through me. "Guess you'll have to get your jollies elsewhere."

"Guess so." He gazed down at me, paying particular attention to my jeans, like he had an idea about where said jollies might be found. "Are you sure you feel safe being alone with Linus after all he's done?"

I worried my bottom lip between my teeth. "I'm too valuable to the Grande Dame for him to lay a finger on me."

"It's more than that." He tugged on the end of my braid. "He knows a workaround for your wards—"

Linus must have walked over while Boaz and I were saying our goodbyes. As usual, his presence had rendered everyone else invisible. I really had to work on my situational awareness skills.

"I'll show you what I did to Woolly and how tomorrow, Grier. We can work on ways to shore up her wards so that it can't happen again." Ignoring a black look from Boaz, Linus gestured toward her wards. "We also need to discuss your vandalism problem."

Vandalism was a pretty word for the ugly act of disfiguring my home. "Woolly is my top priority."

"I can help you make the necessary repairs," he offered. "She will require new wards."

"Not if you're the architect." To create a new design, you must also understand how to deconstruct it, and I wasn't about to hand him an all-access pass to Woolly's defenses.

"Consider it your first assignment." He rubbed the stubble across his jaw. "We'll start with one of my designs, and you can unravel it until you learn the underpinnings. For a final exam, you can construct your own wards, and I'll launch an offensive to test them."

Homework the fifteen-year-old in me whined. Good thing the twenty-one-year old was tougher.

A cellphone trilled in the conversational lull, and Boaz cursed, ignoring it in favor of addressing me.

"Don't forget my number," he warned. "I'll be back in two weeks. Pencil me in your schedule."

"Will do." An easy promise considering I had no schedule.

Gently, oh so gently, he gathered me against him, palmed my cheek and brushed his lips over mine in a gentle kiss that flushed my skin. "I mean it. Don't forget."

"I won't." I cleared my throat. "And stop kissing me."

He wet his lips like he wanted another taste. "What's a goodbye smooch between old friends?"

"Behave." I waggled my finger at him. "Be safe."

"I will definitely be one of those things," he agreed, backing away. "Later, Squirt."

Boaz paid Linus no mind at all as he hopped on Willie and sped away while Linus acted bored with him.

"Let's see about getting you settled." Linus and I climbed the front porch together, and I sang out, "I'm home."

The porch light blazed in welcome, and the front door opened under my hand as I glanced back at him. "Your old room probably needs a good airing. I haven't cleaned any of the spaces I'm not using daily. I have clean sheets if—"

I jumped a foot in the air when the front door slammed on my heels. On the other side, Linus swore with impressive eloquence. "Woolly, what are you doing?"

The floor registered rattled and hissed, spitting condensation on my ankles.

"Guess you figured out it was Linus who sent the wraith, huh?" I winced as a door slammed somewhere upstairs. "He's very sorry for what he did to you, and he promised to show me how to fix it so no one can hurt you again."

Woolly stayed silent, her decision made.

"I understand." I wouldn't press her on this. "He has to earn you trust. Mine too."

The chandelier in the foyer sparked to life. Good. At least she was listening.

"How about this? I'll settle him in the carriage house for now.

You can make up your mind about him later, and I'll honor whatever you decide."

The locks on the door twisted *click, click, click,* and she opened it a crack.

Linus stood there with a hand covering his face and blood dripping through his fingers.

"*Woolly,*" I squeaked. "You broke his nose."

That was *not* the way to impress his mother into letting us continue our two-woman show.

"She has every right to be angry." His palm muffled his voice. "I'm sorry, Woolly. I was given no choice."

Meaning he was wrapped around his mother's little finger. At least he knew it. At least he owned it.

"Do you remember the way to the carriage house?" It was a stupid question. Of course he did. He knew the property almost as well as I did. "Head that way, and I'll grab some ice and meet you there."

Operating in panic mode, I bumped the door shut with my hip, dashed into the kitchen, and filled a sandwich bag with ice. I veered into the downstairs bathroom and grabbed a washcloth for insulation on my way out the back door into the garden. The carriage house was closer this way, and I almost beat Linus there since he had to juggle the gate and his luggage one-handed.

"The living room is a mess." I held the door for him. "Watch your step."

I trailed after him, passed him the washcloth, and watched as he took in the stacked trunks.

"Are all these...?" He let the sentence trail, muted by the fabric. "It's dangerous to leave anything that belonged to Maud where a thief might luck onto it."

"Boaz packed up all her things after I was sent away. He kept the trunks in his parent's garage for a few years, until the estate was settled and he was sure I got to keep Woolly. He stashed everything out here so I wouldn't have that job waiting for me."

"He expected you to come home?" Linus dropped his bags near the door. "He must have a lot of faith in the system."

I angled my chin in his direction, unable to decide if he was being sarcastic. "He never gave up on me," seemed like the safest answer. "In some ways, it was as much for him as it was for me."

Linus appeared to consider that and nodded then picked up his smallest bag. "Is the bathroom this way?"

We had never played in this house as children. It reminded me too much of a mausoleum, as though Mom was walled up out here like in the ghost story I'd told Volkov.

Shaking off those grim thoughts, I guided him into the small half bath near the spacious laundry room. "Anything I can do to help?"

"It depends." He leaned over the sink to assess the damage in the mirror. "Have you ever reset a broken nose?"

"No." I had a strong stomach, though. Necromancers were born with cast-iron guts. "Can you walk me through it?"

"How steady is your hand?" He retrieved a fountain pen from his jacket and passed it over to me. "A pen feels different than a brush, but magic guides it all the same."

"I've never seen anyone use a pen for sigils." The scent of herbs and the tang of magic wafted to me when I pulled off the cap. I drew a smiley face on my fingertip, and potent magic sparked in the ink, causing my skin to itch. "I was trained with a brush."

"It's an experiment." He shrugged it off like a groundbreaking innovation was no big deal. "I use brushes for resuscitations and complex magics, but I'm convinced a fountain pen and an empty cartridge work just as well."

"That's surprising." I glanced over at him. "I would have pegged you for a traditionalist."

"There's a lot you don't know about me, Grier."

Maybe so, but I knew the most important thing. He had been planted in my life by his mother, and I would soon reap what she had sown.

Twirling the pen through my fingers, I glanced up at him. "What do I do?"

"Listen and follow my directions." He sat on the closed toilet seat. "I'm going to walk you through a quartet of sigils that ought to fix the problem."

"Ought to?" I hesitated. "Is this more of your experimental magic?"

"I test theories out on myself all the time." He tilted his head back, holding the cloth under his nose in anticipation of a fresh bleed. "Can you handle this? I've learned to draw the sigils backwards when I have to use a mirror. I can—"

"Just walk me through it." A thought occurred to me. "My magic is on the puny side. Will it be enough?"

"For this? Yes." Determination honed his features. "We'll address your magic tomorrow in class."

A spark ignited in my chest. The Grande Dame hadn't mentioned my magic in any of her speeches. I'd assumed since she wanted my blood that my education would be practical, in the same way Maud taught me theory for concepts I would never, as an assistant, use. But if she wanted me able to perform resuscitations eventually, then maybe this education would be more hands-on. And if I got my full powers back online...

"Grier?"

I snapped to attention. "I'm ready."

Slowly, he walked me through the four interlocking designs required to create the peculiar healing motif. I cupped his chin in one hand and rested the other against his cheek while I worked. This close to his freckles, I had to admire my childhood self's restraint. How he had survived to adulthood without me connecting all his dots was a minor miracle. One cluster in particular, just under his left eye, reminded me of the petals on a daisy, not that I would ever tell him so.

"Did you get contacts?" I finally had to ask. "Your eyes are so much darker than I remember."

The change from a murky, lake-water blue to rich indigo distinguished him from his mother.

Needless to say, it was an improvement as far as I was concerned.

His brow furrowed. "I'm surprised you remember my eye color at all."

A pulse of embarrassment thrummed through me. We hadn't been close as kids, but it's not like I'd never noticed him. He'd sat across the table from me at dinner, nose stuck in a book, ignoring Maud and me while we chattered, a million times.

His weight seesawed on the seat before a calm descended over him, and he resumed his perfect posture. "It's an unexpected side effect of bonding to a wraith."

Thinking on the shadows that whirled in his eyes when his temper rose, I had to admit it made sense. What other changes, too small or seemingly benign to notice, had the wraith inflicted on him? There must be other costs to wielding such power. I was shocked his mother allowed him to initiate the bond.

Linus studied the blades of grass stuck to the tops of my feet with dew. "Does it bother you?"

"Your eyes?" I glanced between them, weighing memory against reality. "No. I was just curious. My memory isn't..." Trustworthy? Reliable? Accurate? I had no memory of resuscitating a man. What else had I forgotten? "Most of my life from *before* is intact. Or it seems to be as best I can tell. All the rest is a blur. Sometimes it's hard to tell when a memory is true."

"You've only been out for a few months," he said gently. "Don't be so hard on yourself. Recovery takes time."

The kindness did it, snapped some tether reining in the temper his mother had unleashed down in the Lyceum, and I had to fight the sudden urge to stab him in the eye with his own pen, because that would get me a passing grade for sure.

The Grande Dame had twiddled her thumbs while I was sentenced, and she would have kept on twiddling until she received my death announcement and laid claim to the rest of my inheritance if I hadn't proven more valuable to her alive.

This act of Linus's was good, too good. There was no way someone like the Grande Dame had produced a thoughtful, kind heir instead of a raging psychopath. There had to be more he was hiding from me, just like Volkov. And just like Volkov, I was sure the truth about him would sucker-punch me eventually.

Paranoid. Yes. I was. I liked to think I'd earned it the hard way.

One final sweep of the borrowed pen, and the effect was instantaneous. His swollen nose emitted a crunching sound, and his eyes watered as the bridge realigned while I watched.

"I think we're done here." I capped his pen, stuffed the bag of ice in his hands, and walked out. "Night."

"I meant the wraith," came his answer.

The wraith? Oh. That's what he had been asking if I minded, not his eyes.

"It doesn't matter, does it?" I stopped outside the bathroom. "You're here now, it's here now. It's not like I can separate you two, and it's not like I invited either one of you."

I walked out before I said something I would regret. The fact remained that I needed his help, now more than ever if he was serious about returning my magic to me. Huffing out a breath, I made a promise to myself that tomorrow I would behave. I would be polite, gracious, and absorb every crumb of information he was willing to feed me until I was bloated with knowledge, until I could stand on my own and protect what was mine.

Too wound up to go back in the house, I trotted around to the front porch and plopped down in the swing. I toed off the planks, dropped my head back to stare at the ceiling fan whirring overhead, and let the chill in the night air cool my temper.

I was free. I was home. And the Grande Dame had just given me another weapon to add to my arsenal.

Linus was here to educate me, and what I wanted to learn most was what had really happened to Maud the night I was framed for her murder. Still aching from her loss and stunned by my change in circumstances, I hadn't dwelled on the specifics of my good fortune. But that was before I learned Maud had been keeping secrets from me, secrets that might one day cost me the freedom I had just won.

It was time I learned the truth. About her death, Mom's life, my father's identity. All of it.

Let the Grande Dame have her schemes. I was hatching a few of my own.

May the best necromancer win.

ABOUT THE AUTHOR

Hailey Edwards writes about questionable applications of otherwise perfectly good magic, the transformative power of love, the family you choose for yourself, and blowing stuff up. Not necessarily all at once. That could get messy. She lives in Alabama with her husband, their daughter, and a herd of dachshunds.

www.HaileyEdwards.net

Head Above Water #2

Hell or High Water #3

Gemini Series Novellas

Fish Out of Water

Lorimar Pack Series

Promise the Moon #1

Wolf at the Door #2

Over the Moon #3

Araneae Nation

A Heart of Ice #.5

A Hint of Frost #1

A Feast of Souls #2

A Cast of Shadows #2.5

A Time of Dying #3

A Kiss of Venom #3.5

A Breath of Winter #4

A Veil of Secrets #5

Daughters of Askara

Everlong #1

Made in the USA
Middletown, DE
10 August 2018